D1633167

DUFFY AND SON

Damien Owens is the author of five novels – *Dead Cat Bounce, Peter and Mary Have a Row, Married to a Caveman, The Bright Side,* and *Little Black Everything.* The latter two were published under the pen name Alex Coleman. He is also the creator and writer of *Trivia,* a television comedy/drama which ran for two series on RTÉ. He lives in Dublin with his wife, two daughters, and a small animal that is most likely a cat.

Duffy and Son

DAMIEN OWENS

CAVAN COUNTY LIBRARY
ACC No.
CLASS No.
INVOICE NO
PRICE

HarperCollins*Ireland*

CAVAN COUNTY LIBRARY
ACC No. 3498884
CLASS NO. F/IR
INVOICE NO. 12011 IES
PRICE €11.85

Cavan County Library
Withdrawn Stock

HarperCollins*Ireland*
The Watermarque Building
Ringsend Road
Dublin DO4 K7N3
Ireland

a division of
HarperCollinsPublishers
1 London Bridge Street
London SE1 9GF
UK

www.harpercollins.co.uk

First published by HarperCollinsIreland in 2022

1 3 5 7 9 10 8 6 4 2

© Damien Owens 2022

Damien Owens asserts the moral right to be
identified as the author of this work

A catalogue record of this book is available
from the British Library

TPB ISBN 978-0-00-847307-5

Typeset by Palimpsest Book Production Ltd, Falkirk, Stirlingshire

Printed and Bound in the UK using 100% Renewable Electricity
at CPI Group (UK) Ltd

All rights reserved. No part of this publication may be reproduced,
stored in a retrieval system, or transmitted, in any form or by any means,
electronic, mechanical, photocopying, recording or otherwise, without
the prior written permission of the publishers.

MIX
Paper from
responsible sources
FSC
www.fsc.org   FSC™ C007454

This book is produced from independently certified FSC™ paper
to ensure responsible forest management.

For more information visit: www.harpercollins.co.uk/green

To the memory of Michael Bradley

1

It's hard to know where you should start a story. You pick a point in time and then a wee voice in your head pops up saying, *Yeah, but that only happened because this other thing happened* . . . So you back it up a step – and there's the voice again; *Yeah, but* . . . You could drive yourself mad. Sooner or later, you have to draw a line. I'm drawing this one on the Friday night when I asked Jim if he was gay.

The shop stayed open late on Fridays. Always had, even in my time. I usually had my tea at the regular hour, but sometimes I waited for Jim to get home so we could eat together. On this occasion I'd waited, and I was sorry I had. My stomach was growling and shuddering as I sat in the front room, flicking around the channels, taking an odd glance at my watch – 7.20, maybe 7.30, was his normal Friday arrival time. It was almost eight now, and no sign. I was about to say to hell with him and throw the chips in the oven when I was swept away by a vision. Suppose he'd been on the point of closing up when one last customer walked in. A woman. Early thirties, say. Not too hard to look at. Pleasant. Suppose she was trying to put up a shelf

1

or do some other simple thing and was all embarrassed because she didn't know what she needed. Suppose Jim made some wee joke and she smiled. Suppose he showed her what to buy and the two of them fell into a conversation. Suppose there was no awkwardness, no ugly silences, like they'd known each other for years . . .

It was a lot of supposing, granted, but I forgot all about the chips and let the fantasy wash over me. I was just losing the run of myself altogether (naming the grand-children) when I heard a key scratching its way into the front door.

A moment later, Jim stuck his head into the room. 'Da.'

'Well. You got held back?'

'Some eejit dropped a thing of wood stain and the fucker burst open. Had to clean it up.'

'Shite.'

'Did you eat anything yet?'

'No. Waiting on you.'

'I'll throw a few chips on.'

'It's all right, I'll–'

'Sit where you are. Fish fingers?'

'Grand. And a few peas, maybe.'

'Yeah. We'll push the boat out, since it's Friday. Party night.'

He smiled thinly and left. When I was alone again, I stared out the window, not sure if I felt angry or sad. *Party night*. He was joking, of course. Still. What kind of existence was this? About to turn forty and still stuck at home with his old man, who was about to turn seventy. No social life. No hobbies to speak of. No women anywhere. And not only that, as far as I could tell he had no interest in getting any of those things – the last one, least of all. Why? Did he like the idea of dying alone? Was there something wrong with his lad? Did he have one of those unusual mental problems where you're convinced you're brutally ugly even though you're just averagely ugly? Or was it something else? Something more basic? I'd wondered if he might prefer men plenty of times over the years. I always brushed the thought away pretty sharpish, partly because I knew he'd had the odd girlfriend in the past but mostly because I plain old didn't like the idea. It wasn't that I had anything against the gays. Even back in the days when you were more or less encouraged to, I never had anything against the gays. It was their nature, and you can't argue with nature – look at those fish that go about stuck to sharks. It wouldn't appeal to me, but that was the way God made them. Let them get on with it and mind your own business, that was always my attitude (to the gays, not the fish . . . actually, to both). No, the reason I hoped Jim was heterosexual was purely practical. Monaghan was a small town, and while I was sure it had the average percentage of gay men, I doubted it had enough of them to make Jim a shoo-in for finding love. It was a question of mathematics, that was all.

We didn't talk much as we ate. When we were having a cup of tea afterwards, Jim launched into a story about Packie McArdle. Packie was around my age and had been recognized as the town's leading religious nutter for as long as I could remember. We weren't short of religious nutters, mind you, but most of them were harmless. They took things a bit too seriously, that was all. With Packie, you got the impression that he was a nutter in general and just happened to have poured his nuttiness into a bucket called Catholicism. If he hadn't had religion for an outlet, he might have been out setting fire to cats or running naked round Lidl. Anyway, he had been in the shop that morning.

'Is that right?' I said when Jim told me. 'Handing out leaflets or looking to buy?'

He took a long, slow sip of his tea. 'Looking to buy a paintbrush. I was ringing it up for him and you know what he says to me?'

'What?'

'He says every time he's in the shop, he always stops by the nails.'

I shook my head, getting where this was going at once. 'Because of the crucifixion.'

'Because of the crucifixion, aye. He says he stops at the nails and he thinks about our lord and saviour Jesus Christ suffering his final torments so that man could know the light of . . . Ah, I forget, exactly. You get the gist.'

'Indeed and I do.'

'I loved the "every time I'm in the shop". I haven't seen him in there in ten years.'

'No, he was never a regular. Came in once in a blue moon to badger me about putting posters in the window. Abortion or divorce or whatever the referendum of the day was.'

I made a little sound. A squeak.

'Are you all right?'

'I'm grand,' I said. 'Something stuck in my throat.'

I lifted my mug to give my face something to do. The truth was, I'd spotted the perfect opening and I couldn't believe my luck.

'He didn't look well,' Jim said. 'I know he never looked

4

well. But he really didn't look well. Not a pick on him. All stooped over.'

I nodded and managed a 'Was he?'. My mind was racing on ahead. Making plans. Choosing words.

'Didn't smell all that great, either. Not bothering to look after himself at all, would be my bet. You know how people get when they hit your age.'

This was a joke. I almost missed it, then screwed my face up and gave him two fingers. He sat back, satisfied. I did some more planning. Then he pushed his seat back and started to get up.

'I'd say he was in good form during the gay marriage one,' I said quickly. 'The referendum.'

It wasn't enough to stop Jim getting to his feet, but at least he didn't leave the room. 'No doubt,' he said from the sink, where he was doing a poor job of washing his plate.

'I'd say he was raging about it, the oul gay marriage.'

'Equal marriage.'

'What?'

'It's not good form to call it gay marriage. You're supposed to say equal marriage. So I believe.'

I hesitated. On the one hand, he sounded like someone who got his information second hand. On the other, he was setting me straight about gay stuff. I decided to plough on.

'Right. I'd love to have run into him after it was all over. Because it wasn't even close, was it? The vote. People were all for it.'

'Yep.'

'No one cares about that stuff anymore. And they're right not to. It's nobody's business who anybody gets into bed with, is it? I mean, provided everyone involved is a grown adult and not a child or a, y'know . . . sheep.'

Despite this poor choice of example, I had his attention now, I could see. He turned to face me. His left eyebrow had climbed up his head a little, as it did when something on the telly caught his interest or a mouthful of food proved spicier than expected.

'All very different in my day,' I went on. 'If I'd told your grandfather that homosexuals would be getting married in Ireland one day, he'd have dropped down dead, crossing himself the whole way. Didn't cost *me* a thought, mind you. I was always very broad-minded about it, right from–'

'Da.'

He gave me a deadly serious look. My heart did a loop-the-loop. 'Yes?'

'Are you trying to tell me that you're gay?'

For a moment, I thought he was serious. He was always good at holding a straight face. And then he allowed himself to crack up. I held my tongue, waiting for his laughter to fade.

'No,' I said. 'But I sometimes wonder if you are.'

It just popped out, despite my intention to sneak up on it, slowly and surely. Jim rolled his eyes, thinking I'd hit him with a shockingly hopeless comeback. Then the truth landed on him. His entire face puckered up.

'What?'

'Well, I–'

'You think I'm *gay*?'

'I don't "think" you're gay, Jim, I'm asking–'

'I'm not!'

'I–'

'I'm not gay!'

'All right—'

'Why would you even *ask* if I'm gay, out of the fucking blue?'

This was tricky ground. The real answer was, *Because you haven't had a girlfriend since Jesus was a boy and if things don't change, you'll soon be too old to turn the ship around.* I thought that might not go over so well.

'Don't make a big deal out of it,' I said. 'I wondered, I asked, and now I know. Subject closed.'

He fumed at me for a moment, then gently placed his mug on the draining board. I'd braced myself for a slam, so that was a pleasant surprise.

'I know it might be hard to believe,' he said, 'but not all of us can have your fabulous success with women.'

I felt myself slump, as if someone had opened a valve. He had delivered the blow with his chin in the air, like a child, unable to believe his own nerve. Now he looked away, tapped his thigh with his knuckles, and headed for the door, looking ashamed.

As well he might.

Jim stayed in his room for the entire night. That wasn't a particularly rare occurrence, but it didn't do much for my state of mind, the thought of him hiding up there like a teenager who hadn't asked to be born. I tried to read for a while (*Bury My Heart at Wounded Knee*), then fumed in front of the telly, plotting what I would say when he finally showed his face. There was nothing sensible on, of course. I'd watch almost anything about history and literally anything about the Second World War. There were no such options tonight. Not so much as a Nazi treasure hunter shining a torch round a basement. The choice was so bad I wound up watching one of those shows about a bunch of young ones getting locked up in a house together so they can have arguments. It was atrocious, but I stuck with it, getting perverse satisfaction out of hating everyone involved. Two of the inmates, or whatever they call them, were almost coming to blows over the whereabouts of some cheese when my mobile rang. I hit mute on the remote and answered the call.

'Hello?'

'Daddy.'

'Eleanor, how are you?'

'Well, I've been better.'

I gathered from her tone that this was about something I'd done. Had I missed a birthday?

'I'm after getting a text from Jim,' she went on. 'You told him you think he's gay?'

I spluttered and choked for a few seconds before actual words came out. 'Jesus Christ. I didn't tell him I *think* he's gay, I *asked* him–'

'Daddy, for the love of–'

'Did he tell you what *he* said to *me*?'

She sighed. 'What?'

'He said not everyone could have my fabulous success with women. So you needn't be giving me the *poor Jim* routine. I'm the one who should be getting an apology here.'

There was a pause. 'Well,' she said then, 'I'm sure he's sorry he said that.'

'Are you, now? Do you think there's any danger of him coming down here and saying so? Because he's been hiding in his room ever since.'

'Tell you the truth, I think he's waiting for you to say sorry first.'

'Ha!'

'He's very upset.'

'So am I.'

'You started it with the gay thing.'

'There's nothing wrong with being gay, Eleanor.'

'I know that.'

'Does Jim?'

'Of course.'

'Then what have I to apologize for? It was only a question.'

'Because he's *upset*. It's not the question, it's the implication. He thinks you're sitting around every day wondering why the hell he hasn't found someone and moved out.'

'I am!'

'Daddy!'

The 'Daddy' thing had bothered me for years. It made her sound like a six-year-old. I almost said something, like a drunk gambler saying to hell with it and pushing all his chips into play. But I didn't. One fight at a time.

'Eleanor, he's turning forty soon. It's getting to be a now-or-never kind of thing. And I don't want rid of him. I want him to be happy, that's all. Before it's too late.'

She sighed. I knew from long experience that the best move I could make was to shut up and let her talk herself around. So I started counting to ten in my head. I made it as far as six.

'I worry about him too.'

Progress. I allowed another few seconds of silence to let it bed in. Then I said, 'Does he ever say anything to you about it?'

'Being single? God, no. Sure I hardly hear from him.'

'I could understand it if he was doing his best and things were never working out or whatever. It's the showing no interest whatsoever I can't get my head around.'

'What do you mean, no interest?'

'I mean, he doesn't . . . put himself about.'

She considered this for a moment. 'He still goes out with the boys, doesn't he?'

'Now and then, I suppose, but the boys aren't really *the boys* any more, not the way you remember them, anyway. They're all married and raising children. Even when they do go out, I'd say they spend their whole time comparing lawnmowers and complaining about the price of school uniforms. It wouldn't exactly be lock-up-your-daughters time. Even Smokey's married, for God's sake.'

Smokey was one of Jim's oldest pals. He was a desperately unattractive man. When I first heard he had a steady girlfriend, I assumed it was the start of a joke.

'And he's not in any, I don't know, clubs or anything?'

'Eleanor, he works and he watches a bit of telly and he sleeps. That's it. I have more chance of meeting a single woman than he has. At least I go to the odd funeral.'

'Well, that's step one then, isn't it?' she said. 'Get him out there.'

'Who? Me? It's my job now, is it?'

'He needs help, doesn't he? And I'm in Dublin. So, yeah. You.'

'What the hell do I know about this kind of thing? Do you think I know where all the cool pick-up joints are but I've been keeping them to myself?'

'I'm not saying you have to go out on the pull with him, am I? I'm saying encourage him to be a bit more . . . social.'

'I don't know, Eleanor. After tonight, I'm inclined to stay the hell away from this whole business.'

'Fine. Fine. Do that if you want. So long as you're happy with the idea of him living with you forever.'

I chewed it over for a moment. 'What would I do, exactly? Squirt him with aftershave and push him out the front door every night?'

'Just get him to, I don't know, do stuff. Join stuff. Be a bit more active. What about a book club or something like that?'

'A *book* club? Are you joking? I've never seen Jim with a book in his life. I'm not even sure he can read.'

'Is that the sort of joke you crack to his face? Because that wouldn't exactly help, would it? That's another thing you could be doing, building up his confidence.'

I spluttered and flapped. 'So, if I'm following you correctly, it's suddenly up to me to tell him he's brilliant at everything and then make him join a book club. Is that right?'

There was another pause. A long one. Then another sigh. A long one. 'Fine. Be like that. I'm trying to give you advice here and all you're interested in is stupid jokes. Typical.'

Eleanor had a lot of good qualities. A wonderful sense of humour was not among them. I should have known better. There was a real possibility that I was going to end the day with both of my children pissed off at me. So I took the simplest way out and changed the subject.

'We'll talk about it some other time,' I said. 'How are you, anyway? How's the family? Having a good summer?'

As usual, she said nothing about herself and far more about her husband and son than I was comfortable knowing. Adrian was getting over a minor illness. Everything that wasn't nailed down had come out one end or the other, sometimes simultaneously. He had made a poor patient – this, I could believe – and she was glad that he was on the mend. He was heading off to Galway the next morning with a pal. A golfing weekend. I imagined him having a sudden relapse on the thirteenth green, preferably in the middle of one of his boring work stories, and had to stifle a chuckle. Miles, meanwhile, had fared much better in his first year of primary school than he had at preschool. There had been no more attempted arson, at least. The biting seemed to be a thing of the past too.

We talked for another ten or fifteen minutes (or rather, she did) and any bad feeling between us evaporated. When the call ended, I tried to get back into the terrible television show, but it was no good. My mind kept wandering to Jim. The simple truth of the thing was this: if he was capable of making progress on his own, he would have done it by now. It wasn't about to start getting much easier for him, either. If he was anything like his old man, he was going to wake up one of these days to find himself home to even less hair and even more belly. I sighed and slapped a cushion into shape. Maybe Eleanor wasn't talking complete rubbish. There might be some small way I could help. It wouldn't kill me to give it some thought, at least.

So that's what I did. I gave it some thought.

2

I was born in the little village of Emyvale, County Monaghan, in August 1948. My parents ran a pub and never showed the tiniest bit of interest in anything that happened outside its walls. They talked about Glaslough, the next village over, as if it was Shanghai. They weren't bad people. There were lots of things about them that I admired. They were honest. They were kind. They worked like dogs. But their world was tiny, and that was how they wanted it. That was something I couldn't understand, let alone admire. I vowed that, whatever else I became when I grew up, I would for certain sure be curious. *My* world would be enormous and I would never get tired of learning about it.

Anyway, I left school at fourteen and wound up running a small hardware shop a few miles away in Monaghan town. The main thing about the universe, I've always found, is that it likes a joke.

I don't know if my father drank before my mother died. Maybe he'd never had a problem and circumstances led him to discover an amazing natural talent. But, gun to my head, I'd guess he'd been ramping up for years and her sudden death – she suffered a stroke while brushing her hair when I was thirteen – gave him the excuse he needed to really let rip. Either way, within weeks of her funeral he was more often drunk than sober. A couple of months later, he was barely functioning. Small as Emyvale was, it had more than one pub. Punters had a choice and most preferred not to drink in a place where the landlord had trouble pouring a pint by eight and was basically uncon-scious by ten. Still, he never went out of business. No matter how bad things got, he always held on to a few customers. Some stayed out of loyalty. Some stayed out of stubbornness. Some stayed because they could more or less help themselves behind the bar. As for me, I was dragged out of school at the first available opportunity and put to work, or rather, to full-time work. I'd always helped out in the evenings and at weekends, sweeping this, wiping that. I never minded because I assumed that better days were ahead. It was clear to me now that those *were* the better days. I lay awake at night in my damp little hutch of a room, wondering which would be worse – for the drink to kill my father quickly, making me an orphan with nowhere to go, or for it to kill him slowly, leaving me with the pub and its dozen customers. In the end, neither scenario came to pass.

On 14 November 1964, I yawned and scratched my way through a typical day and when the last customer had shuffled away into the cold, I helped my father to bed. Although there were nights when he couldn't put one foot in front of the other, this was not one of them. He was able to climb the stairs alone; all I had to do was follow closely behind and gently shove him forward when he leaned too far back and threatened to topple. Upstairs, I helped him out of his shoes and made him promise that he would remove at least some of his clothes before he got into bed (or, more likely, collapsed across it). I had long since given up on the prospect of getting him into his pyjamas or the bathroom, where his ancient toothbrush was gathering dust in a grimy glass. A couple of hours later, I woke up abruptly, feeling panicked and sick. I lay there coughing and trying to remember the nightmare that had upset me so badly.

For years afterwards, I tortured myself with the notion that I wasted a precious hour or more, but it was probably no more than a few minutes before I realized what was going on. Stories about fires are usually full of phrases like 'tried bravely' and 'beaten back by the inferno'. Mine isn't. When I opened my bedroom door a crack, I saw orange and immediately slammed it closed again. My window let out on to the roof of our coal bunker and I lost no time taking advantage of that fact. The rest is a blur. I remember knocking on doors and shouting in the street and I remember a rough-looking fireman giving me a clap on the back, as if I'd just scored a goal – 'Good man, Eugene.' That's all. My father died, of course. Later, I overheard three separate people joking that he would have gone up in seconds, given his alcohol content.

Problem number one, obviously, was where to put me. I was sixteen years old and felt perfectly able to look after myself, but the pub was simply gone. There were no obvious answers. My father had one sibling, a brother, who'd died in infancy. My mother had two sisters, who lived together in Canada and, depending on who you asked, had always been either 'eccentric' or 'out of their fucking minds'. I spent the period immediately after the fire with my neighbours, the McEntees. How this was arranged, I have no idea. I've always assumed that Father Devlin had something to do with it. Priests had a hand in everything in those days and I can easily imagine the old goat (something of a boozer himself, it was whispered) taking the easiest possible way out. Boy lost his father and his home? No aunts or uncles around? Stick him with the physically nearest family until some class of a relative, however distant, can be dug up and told they'll have one more mouth to feed.

There were four McEntees in that tiny house, Mr and Mrs, and twin boys of about ten. Mrs McEntee couldn't have been more than thirty-five. She always looked frail and exhausted, as if she was recovering from some terrible illness and had tried to do too much, too soon. The boys, Patrick and Anthony, were sullen and humourless. The only time they showed any enthusiasm for anything was when they were knocking the shite out of each other, which was at least once a day. They could fight about anything. I once saw them come to blows over a cloud (Patrick said it looked like a lion; Anthony saw a horse). Mr McEntee was older than his wife, maybe mid-forties. He was a short, barrel-chested man whose features all seemed to have subsided to the lower half of his face. Even though he rarely spoke and communicated mostly by pointing and grunting, menace wafted off him like a bad smell. When he walked into a room, everyone stopped talking and clenched. No one ever caught his eye on purpose. That could lead to trouble. I learned to dread his arrival home from the furniture factory every day. It didn't occur to me until years later that maybe the reason why his kids were so withdrawn and his wife so withered was that they'd been beaten into it. Maybe not. The alternative is that he'd ground them into the dirt using his personality alone, and that seems almost worse.

The days ran into one another in those first few weeks, making one long blur of sadness and loneliness and fear. It did occur to me that I could just leave, run away in the middle of the night and never look back. I stayed put. While the McEntees didn't have an awful lot going for them as hosts, there was no denying they had a roof and walls. Then, one Saturday afternoon, with no warning and no ceremony, my life was transformed. I was in the little back yard with Patrick and Anthony. They were throwing stones at a tin can and I was doing what I was usually doing in those days, which was staring at my feet and trying not to throw up. Mrs McEntee appeared at the back door and said I had a visitor. Something about her tone told me that she didn't know this person herself. I had no idea who it could be, but I certainly didn't envisage anyone who looked like Tommy Moore. Then again, I'd never *seen* anyone who looked like Tommy. The man was a giant, not only absurdly tall but absurdly thick, wide, and deep. It was as if someone had taken a normal human and blown him up in every dimension by twenty-five per cent.

When I first laid eyes on him in that sticky little kitchen, I felt something stronger than curiosity or surprise. Awe, maybe. He was like something out of a circus. Mrs McEntee made the introductions and said she'd leave us alone. I'd no sooner registered that this seemed odd before she slipped out of the room and up the stairs. Tommy hadn't said a word yet. I imagined that when he did, the windows would shake and my hair would blow back. Yet when he held out his dinner plate of a hand and said it was nice to meet me, I found that his voice was not unlike my father's. Same heavy Monaghan accent. Same slow delivery. Tommy's had a gentle rattle to it. I was reminded of a cat's purr. We sat down at the kitchen table and he said the usual: he had known my father and was sorry to hear of his death. With my mother not long gone, it must have been, etc., etc.

I thanked him and waited for him to run through the rest of his piece, to say whatever it was that would make him feel his duty was done and he could leave. For what seemed like an age, he was silent. Having ebbed away, my interest was renewed. He didn't look like a man who couldn't think of what to say. He looked like a man who had something very specific to say and wanted to make sure he got it right. Finally, he noted that it was good of the McEntees to take me in. I agreed that it was and he nodded. Then he said that I couldn't stay there forever, of course. I agreed again. He nodded again. I'd be needing a more permanent arrangement, wouldn't I? I would. And there were no close relatives around who could step in? There were not.

And then, having slowly tiptoed his way around these few thoughts, he suddenly launched into a sprint. His proposal came tumbling out of him in what felt like one enormous sentence. He was a builder. He and his wife, Rose, lived in Monaghan town. They had no kids and a bit of spare room. It wasn't a palace, but it was comfortable. I could, if I wanted, come and live with them. On top of that, I could go out to work with him, learn a trade. When he made it to the end, he was out of breath. He took a moment to get himself together and then, before I could get a word in, started explaining the many good things about life as a builder. Although he was less frantic now, it was still a long way from a normal conversation. It was like he had tried to get me to work for him before and I'd turned him down, so he was back with fresh arguments. I let him talk for a little while, mostly out of amazement, and then finally interrupted to ask the one question I wanted answered above all, which was, 'Who *are* you?'

He blinked at me and then started into it all over again. He was a builder, he lived in Monaghan with his wife, Rose . . . I shook my head and asked my question again. This time he gave his answer some thought. He gave it so much thought, in fact, that I wondered if I'd offended him somehow. Was I supposed to know this guy? There was a moment when I was sure he was about to tell me that he was my real father. Instead, he entwined his fingers, each one like a prize-winning carrot, and said that it was very simple. My father had done him a favour once, a long time ago. A serious favour. The sort of favour that you think you'll never get a chance to repay. This was his chance and he hoped I'd let him take it. I asked a second question, the obvious one. He smiled and shook his head. The nature of the favour wasn't important, he said. I never asked again.

The Moores lived in a decent-sized bungalow that Tommy had built himself, off a road off a road off a road on the southern edge of Monaghan. After my lifetime over a pub and a few weeks in the terrace with the McEntees, it felt like a cathedral to me. At first, everything was as awkward as you might expect. Although I believed Tommy when he said he had his reasons for taking me in, nothing on earth could convince me that his wife was happy about it. Rose was what my mother would have called a 'stout' woman. Not fat, barely even overweight, but . . . robust. Sturdy. Her hair was a vivid ginger and impressively curly. I tiptoed around her at first, barely speaking for fear of saying the wrong thing, certain that she would snap one day and kick me out on my arse, roaring that she'd never wanted me there in the first place. After a while, Tommy took me aside and told me he wanted a word. In my head, I was already packing, wondering if they'd let me stay in the shed for a while before I moved on. Rose was worried, he said. She thought I didn't like her and wanted to know what she could do to make me more comfortable. I burst into tears.

Tommy took me out to work with him almost straight away. Although I was too small and clueless to be of any real help, he never made me feel like I was a burden. He employed a loose gang of other men, some of them more or less permanent fixtures and some of them picked up only occasionally, like specialist tools. None of them were unkind. Slowly and surely I learned, and slowly and surely I grew. Eventually, I was just one of the lads. The only difference was that I arrived at the site in the same van as the boss. No one ever wondered how come Tommy and Rose had taken me in. Kids moved around all the time in those days, for all sorts of reasons. You didn't ask.

Rose had a thing about little porcelain figurines. She had a couple of dozen of them scattered around the house, on windowsills, on bedside lockers, on random shelves. Some of them were dogs, some were cats, some were little girls holding an umbrella and looking sad, some were little boys holding a ball and looking happy. Different manufacturers, different styles. Although there was no pattern that I could see, I always assumed they meant a lot to her.

One Saturday morning she broke one of them dusting, and took the pieces to the kitchen table to glue back together. I was there already, working hard on a six-inch-high plate of toast. After a few minutes, she sat back and shrugged, saying nothing could be done. The thing was only fit for the bin. I was surprised by how casual she was about it. Weren't the figurines her pride and joy? She scoffed at the idea. They were pretty knick-knacks, that was all. It was amazing she'd never broken one before, really. And they'd all have been smashed to pieces a long time ago if she and Tommy had been blessed with kids. I caught her eye over my mug of tea. She looked away. I was young; I wasn't stupid. I saw it all clearly. They weren't childless by choice. They'd wanted to be parents and for some reason or another, it hadn't happened. I wasn't a cute wee baby, I was a spotty lump of a teenager, but I was better than nothing. A consolation prize. That was fine by me.

That Saturday morning at the kitchen table was a real turning point. I'd grown comfortable with Tommy and Rose, and was extremely grateful to them both, of course. Now I started to think of them, really and truly, as my second parents. In one regard, they were actually an improvement on my real parents. I'm sure my mother and father loved each other, but that's something I'd worked out from subtle clues, like a detective. Once in a blue moon, my father would pat my mother on the shoulder as he squeezed past or she'd give him a wink as she straightened his tie. I never saw them embrace, let alone kiss, and I could no more imagine them in bed together than I could imagine them playing for Arsenal. Tommy and Rose were like a pair of teenagers. They never parted for any length of time without a hug. I mean, Tommy would be going out to cut the grass and they'd say goodbye like he was off to war. When I was alone with him, he'd tell me something she'd said that made him chuckle. When I was alone with her, she'd worry that he was too kind-hearted for business. They held hands on the sofa watching old movies. It sounds corny, verging on nauseating. But it was a lovely thing to be around.

I lived with the Moores for eight years, right up until the day I got married, and by the end, I loved them as much as I've ever loved anyone. Before I left the house on my wedding morning, I stood in the front room with Tommy, just me and him, and we knocked back a couple of whiskeys. Everything was changing for me, again. In a matter of hours, I'd have a new wife. We'd arranged to rent a little flat in the town. I'd been to the bank and plans were underway for me to open a small business of my own, a hardware shop. I was already feeling emotional and the bright burn of the alcohol loosened my tongue even more. All I wanted from life, I told Tommy, was to have even a fraction of what he had in his relationship with Rose. It was soppy talk for any time. For Ireland in the early 1970s, it was the sort of thing that could get you sectioned. Tommy didn't laugh at me. He looked down at me from his great height and said he wished me the same. Then he told me why he had come for me, all those years ago. About the favour he was paying back. I think I gasped. I certainly braced myself. For some reason, the word 'murder' popped into my head. Tommy had done someone in and my father had helped him dispose of the body? Tommy had made an enemy and my father had bumped him off? No. My father was the one who introduced them. Tommy and Rose. That was it, and that was all. My father introduced them and Tommy was so unspeakably grateful he upended his entire life when he heard about the fire. It was a beautiful send-off for a young man on his way to meet his bride at the altar. I stepped out of the house, tingling at the prospect of married life.

Like a fucking eejit.

3

Frank Clarke was my best pal and had been for decades. His name wasn't Frank, his name was Larry. The nickname was an old one, which he'd earned through a lifetime of gravely insulting people with what he called 'simple honesty' and everyone else called 'shocking rudeness'. We went for pints once or twice a week, whenever the mood struck us. A few days after the unfortunate incident with Jim, we met in McDaid's, our usual haunt. Frank was a widower and spent far too much of his time interfering in the lives of his daughter and her husband, who lived in the town and ran a bakery. Tonight, he was in high dudgeon because they'd called round for dinner and not brought anything.

'Nothing,' he gasped, mortally offended, 'not so much as a fucking cheesecake.'

I shook my head in sympathetic disbelief. 'Poor form.'

'And them with a bakery!'

'There's no excuse.'

'Not that it's a *good* bakery.'

'Ah, now. I don't think–'

'It's shite. I'd never get a thing out of it if I didn't have to. As it is, I only get the odd bun.'

I knew from long experience that there was no point in arguing. One night recently, Frank had raised the subject of his son-in-law's new car. I thought a three-year-old Volkswagen Golf was a solid choice. He thought it was proof that Simon 'had no taste in anything except women who should know better' and, of course, he had 'told him as much'. We went back and forth on the subject of Golfs for a solid twenty minutes and I might as well have been singing sea shanties. Didn't budge an inch. On this occasion, I gave Frank another few minutes to complain about the bakery's flaws, and the many times he had 'helped' by pointing them out. Then I made a bid for a change of subject.

'C'mere,' I said, interrupting him in mid-flow, 'can you remember turning forty?'

'Turning forty what?'

'The *age*.'

'Christ, Eugene, I can hardly remember what I had for breakfast. Why?'

'Ah, nothing, really. Our Jim'll be forty this year. I was reading a thing the other day that said a lot of people get depressed. I don't think I did.'

Frank swirled his pint. 'People can get depressed about any old bollocks these days. Why, has he said something?'

'Nah. I worry about him, that's all. In general.'

I put a bit of weight on the last couple of words, hoping he would pick up on it. And fair play to him, he did. That was Frank – liable to march up and tell you your new jumper made you look like a paedophile, but a surprisingly sensitive listener.

'What do you mean, in general?'

'Well, for one thing, I wish he, y'know . . . had someone. In his life.'

'A woman?'

'That sort of thing, yeah.'

'You reckon he's lonely?'

'I don't know. I don't see how he could be anything else. When he's not in the shop, he just rattles around the house with me. I know I'm great craic and all, but that's not right.'

Frank shrugged. 'Maybe he likes being a bachelor.'

I frowned at the b-word. 'Maybe.'

'You want him out, is that it? Bit of extra room?'

'No! I mean, I do want him out, but for his sake. He's turning into *me*. It's not healthy.'

'Huh? Sure what's wrong with being you?'

'I dunno, I just . . .' I pouted and shrugged, let a few seconds pass.

'Go again?'

He pointed a finger at my glass. I nodded and he hauled himself upright. 'One more won't kill us,' he said, a standard line, and shuffled off. This was another of Frank's quirks. You could be halfway through telling him you'd grown an extra set of balls, but if it was time to go to the bar, it was time to go to the bar. Your balls thing would have to wait.

McDaid's wasn't a young person's kind of place. Tonight there were only two people under the age of fifty, a couple, sitting a few tables away on our right. I took a guess at their situation. Married ten years or so. A couple of kids. Having a rare night out on their own. Probably talked through all sorts of exciting options before realizing they only had enough energy for the pub. They looked like they were enjoying each other's company well enough. The husband was about Jim's age and sort of similar, physically. Not bald, but probably starting to worry. Not fat, but not getting a lot of work modelling Speedos either. He had nothing going for him, as far as I could see, that Jim didn't have. And that was taking nothing but looks into account. Jim had his own business. Granted, it was a business that was long past its meagre prime and could be sent under for good if things went wrong for more than a couple of months on the trot. Still. When Frank returned with the pints, I pointed out the chap I'd been looking at, and why. Frank agreed with the gist of my assessment.

'Oh, aye. Look at the cut of him. That's a shitty pair of glasses, for a start. They're far too big on him. He looks like a fucking owl. And I'd say he did that haircut himself.'

'I–'

'That's some nose too. Wee fishy lips. Your Jim's a Greek god next to this lad.'

'I–'

'Horrible shirt.'

'Jesus Christ, I'm not talking about your man there in particular. I'm saying *generally*. I don't see anything especially wrong with Jim that should make it hard for him to find someone.'

Frank supped at his pint for a moment. 'Well . . . maybe he's not into women. Maybe he's a gay.'

'He isn't.'

'Come on, Eugene. It's not like it was in our day. Sure the Taoiseach's one! I wouldn't vote for him, now, but it wouldn't be because of that. His voice gets on my nerves. You have to–'

'I already asked him, all right? I already asked him and he isn't.'

Frank gawped at me. 'You *asked* him?'

'Yes.'

'You flat out *asked* him?'

'Yes! As opposed to what? How else was I going to find out?'

'I don't know, search his room for pictures of nudie men?'

'You think that'd be a better bet than asking him?'

'Well, he probably wasn't all that pleased to be asked, was he?'

I hid behind my pint for a moment. 'Not really, no.'

'And why would he be? You're basically saying, "I was wondering if you might be gay because I can't think of any other reason why you'd be such a disaster with women." Jesus Christ, Eugene, have you no cop on?'

The couple I'd been watching chose that moment to head for home. We stared as they passed and the husband seemed to feel it. He looked down at us, puzzled. I looked away, embarrassed. Frank raised his glass and noted that it was 'a chilly enough evening', which it wasn't.

'You don't have to give me the whole speech,' I told Frank then. 'I already had it from Eleanor.'

'Eleanor? What the fuck did you tell her for?'

'Jim told her. He was raging. He's *still* raging. Hardly speaking to me.'

'That's shite.'

'It is.'

'Shite altogether.'

'Wait'll you hear this: Eleanor reckons I should help

him get a woman. Or point him in their general direction, at least.'

Frank shook his head in what I foolishly mistook for sympathy. 'Sure what do you know about getting women?'

'Thank you.'

'You know what I mean. You wouldn't be one of the world's leading experts, that's all I'm saying.'

'She's not suggesting I give him the benefit of my expertise–'

'Just as well.'

'–she's suggesting I give him a bit of a push to be more social.'

'Right. Well, sure, what harm? You can do that much. Tango.'

'Excuse me?'

'Tango. Dancing. Or salsa or rumba or whatever. There was a thing in the paper. It's all the rage now. Supposed to be a good way to meet people because everyone lets on they're not there to meet people.'

I gave it some thought, but not much. 'I can't think of many activities our Jim is less likely to be up for. He's not exactly light on his feet.'

'That's the whole point, isn't it?' Frank said. 'You show up hopeless, and the next thing you know, you're foxtrotting the hole off it. Have you never seen *Strictly Come Dancing* on the telly?'

'I have, and I never once thought, *That's the very thing our Jim should get into.*'

'Well, start thinking it. Sure it's perfect. Women love men who can dance. Or who give it a go, at least. You get a lot of points for even trying. Plus he'd be getting up close and personal with a lot of women. Even if he never got anywhere, romantically speaking, it might whet the old appetite. Remind him what he's missing.'

'I know he hasn't had a lot of girlfriends lately, Frank. I don't think he's forgotten what women *are*.'

Frank pointed a bony finger at me. 'I'm never wrong, Eugene. Dancing.'

He was frequently wrong. One time he convinced me that a teenage Eleanor only *thought* she wanted a clothes voucher for Christmas; what she really wanted was a high-quality microscope. I did some research and spent a fortune. She threw it at me and cried until mid-January. But as he moved on to other subjects that night – why rats make the best pets, how Manchester United could return to glory, the trouble with the French – I found myself thinking that this time at least, he could well be on to something.

Back at home, I checked out the paper and, sure enough, there were two different dancing evenings in the town. One of them looked like it was for people my age – and up, to be honest. The other more or less advertised itself as a meat market. Now all I had to do was convince the meat to show up.

4

My marriage to Una got off to such a happy and carefree start, it made me double up to think about it later. I couldn't believe she'd wanted to go with me in the first place and the idea that she was now my wife was almost more than I could stand. I'd had a few girlfriends before her but (to put it kindly) they were all in my league. Una was a seriously good-looking woman. Everyone said so, usually before they cracked some joke about what the hell she could possibly be doing with the likes of me. I always laughed along. They could have their wisecracks; I had Una.

Duffy Hardware was not what you would call an immediate success. There were two other similar shops in the town. Nobody had a good word to say about either of them and I assumed it would be easy to steal their customers away. For a start, I wouldn't spit on my own floor every two minutes (Colm McManus) or call you a bollocks if you didn't buy anything (Tony Lawlor). Habits are hard to break, though, and the sudden rush of customers, delighted to have somewhere to buy a hammer without slipping on gob or being insulted to their faces, did not materialize. I probably would have run out of road within six months if it hadn't been for Tommy sending people my way. He knew every tradesman in the county, it seemed, and not a day went by without at least one of them coming through my door, mentioning his name and buying something he probably didn't need. Between them and the few regulars I managed to snag on my own account, I was able to keep the lights on. Things picked up after a year or so when Tony Lawlor got up early one Sunday morning, told his wife he was off to get the papers, and walked into a lake. No one took over his business and, harsh as it sounds, that was good for mine. The ground under my feet started to feel a lot more solid. And it stayed solid. Although Duffy Hardware was never a roaring success, it never got into trouble either. I made a living, that was all. As far as I was concerned, the main thing was I went home every night to Una.

At first, she was every bit as happy as I was. I'm sure of it. She showed a breathtaking talent for lying later on, granted, but no one's that good an actress. I loved her, she loved me, and we both loved our little flat. It wasn't much, just a pokey kitchen-cum-living room and a bedroom that was barely bigger than the bed. When Una's folks or Tommy and Rose came to visit, I had to stand and pretend that I preferred it that way. Despite its tiny size, the place was impossible to heat. Every inch of carpet was permanently gummy. Drawers stuck shut and doors swung open. The curtains were fire-damaged. The sofa was lumpy. The table was wonky. It smelled of mildew. We didn't even have a bathroom of our own; we shared one with another tenant, Mr Hughes, a mysterious fifty-something bachelor who came and went at such odd hours we decided he was most likely a burglar by profession, or possibly a sex-maniac axe-murderer. Despite all of this – the cold and damp, the lack of space, the constant fear of sex-maniac axe murder – we were blissfully content. It was our little nest. Every night we'd curl up together and listen to records, taking turns to make the selections – Elvis, The Beatles, Loretta Lynn, The Dubliners. She'd tell me what she'd been up to that day as I played with her hair or stroked her neck. At some point, a record would stop and neither of us would move to replace it. Then one of us stood, the other followed suit, and off we went to the bedroom. It was a kind of heaven, and not just for a while. We made it last for a couple of years. Then we started talking about finding somewhere better to live.

House-hunting went like this: Una would pick a place we couldn't afford. I'd walk round it with her, then tell her it was impossible. I'd pick a place we could afford. She'd walk round it with me, then tell me she wouldn't be seen dead. This went on for months. There were no real arguments, no major fallings-out. Every so often, one of us would dramatically roll our eyes or put a little extra mustard on a comment – that was about the height of it. Still, I felt a kind of panic. The little flat seemed to be getting littler by the day. The damp was more noticeable. The table felt wobblier. The records didn't sound as good, and we went to bed at different times. Something was slipping through my fingers.

The house we ended up buying had three bedrooms, a decent back garden, a little driveway where you could park the car. It didn't take in a lot of natural light and none of the rooms were huge, but you can't have everything. There were plenty of worse options in town and compared to the flat, it was the Palace of Versailles. We had to view it five times before Una agreed that we should make an offer. Despite her reluctance, I was relieved. At last, I thought, we can start over, get that old feeling back. Just the two of us, nesting. We couldn't, of course. And after a while, we stopped trying. The truth of the thing came to me slowly. Una had been genuinely content in the flat, but only because she thought it was the humble beginning that we would one day look back on with a smile. It was my fault, I suppose. Long before we were ever married I'd told her that the plan was to start small with the shop, slowly build a reputation, and then move on to bigger premises. Somewhere along the way, I'd open a second outlet, then a third, and before you could say 'self-made millionaire', I'd have a chain all over the country. I wasn't lying when I talked this way. I believed it completely, and must have convinced Una too. Every passing day made it more obvious that none of it was going to happen. When I looked at our new house I saw a major step up. Una saw a slightly bigger box, one that she would most likely never leave. It wasn't about money, not really. It was about me. She'd thought she was getting a fancy businessman, an entrepreneur, and wound up with a nobody who ran a little hardware shop. I was a disappointment. She didn't say any of this out loud. She didn't have to.

We waited a while to start a family (Una's idea). Eleanor came along in 1977 and Jim in 1979. The shop puttered on in its unremarkable way. There were new clothes when we needed them and plenty of presents under the Christmas tree. It wasn't awful. We weren't miserable. Still, there was a sense of promise unfulfilled. And then, one day in July 1981, Una put the children to bed, made tea, and told me she had something to say. I don't know what I was expecting. I know what I wasn't expecting, and that was, 'I've been having an affair, but it's over now, and I thought you should hear it from me.' She said it firmly and slowly, like a doctor giving bad news. If I hadn't been sitting, I would have fallen. It was a while before I could speak. While I gasped and shuddered like a landed fish, Una waited patiently. At one point, she took a sip of tea, a detail that immediately turned to stone and lodged itself in a corner of my mind, where it has remained ever since. So many questions occurred to me at once, I felt dizzy. The first that made it out through my mouth wasn't the more obvious 'Who is he?' but 'What do you mean, hear it from me?'

It turned out to be the only question I needed to ask. She gave me the whole story. His name was Brendan. He owned a restaurant in Dundalk. She'd been introduced while visiting her sister there. They'd 'met' a dozen times or so and then she'd decided to end it. He wasn't taking it well, was drinking a lot, and had threatened to spill the beans. She didn't think he meant it but had decided to come clean anyway. It was a mistake, she regretted it, and now she wanted to put it behind her. That would be easier, she reckoned, if I knew the truth, provided it came from her. With the basic facts laid out, my emotions caught up with me. I cried like a baby. Una made no effort to comfort me. When I sniffed my last sniff, I told her that she had to promise this would never happen again. She did, immediately and confidently. And that was more or less that. I made some noises about 'needing time to process it' – a line I'd stolen from the telly, I think. That was bullshit. There might be processing, but the outcome was already obvious. I would forgive her and we would go on.

I stayed on the sofa that night – a token gesture. Amid all the anger and hurt and confusion, one thought above all kept me staring at the ceiling until close to dawn. She hadn't cried. Not a single tear. She hadn't cried, and she hadn't said sorry. A wiser man than me would have read something into that.

5

When Jim took over the shop, I made a solemn promise that I wouldn't be constantly popping in to check on him. I thought it was what he wanted to hear and was pretty chuffed with myself for thinking of it. I kept my word too. For the first few months of his reign, I went weeks at a time without putting my nose inside the door. It wasn't hard. At that point, he had been my co-manager in all but name for years. I had no concerns about how he would cope. Then, one evening when we were parked on the sofa in front of a Bond movie, he turned his head halfway towards me and said he could tell how much I missed the shop. It would be fine with him, he said, if I wanted to come in a bit more often. I almost laughed and told him I was grand staying out of it – but I caught myself on. Jim had been by my side since he was old enough to see over the counter. He may well have been perfectly capable of running the place, but that didn't mean all this was easy for him. He *missed* me. I didn't take my eyes off Roger Moore, who was creeping about it a safari suit, gun drawn. That'd be nice, I said. I think I even threw in a thank you.

It could have made for yet another story of high-quality parenting (if I say so myself), if I hadn't cocked it up by wildly oversteering. I started showing my face in the shop almost every day, making small talk, offering an occasional opinion and generally hanging around. After a few weeks, Jim had another word. There was nothing subtle about it this time. He dragged me to one side in the shop, stuck his finger in my face and told me he was going to lose his fucking mind if I didn't give him a bit of space. I wish I'd been big enough to say that I understood and would back off. Unfortunately, I told him I'd been perfectly happy leaving him to it and wouldn't have bothered my hole going near him if he hadn't begged. That was a poor choice of word, 'begged'. He didn't take it well and things went very sour between us for a while. I stayed away from the shop and we avoided each other at home, which wasn't easy. Eventually, though, relations improved and we fell into a more natural rhythm, shop-wise. I didn't shun the place. I wasn't a permanent fixture either. Once in a while, I'd drop by, if I happened to be passing.

So there was nothing unusual about me calling in that morning. I had no cause to be nervous or to put on any kind of act. Still, I had to take a moment outside the shop door to remind myself of that. I'd been feeling jittery since breakfast and was half-convinced I'd walk in and loudly declare, 'DON'T MIND ME, I'M HERE FOR NO SPECIFIC REASON, AS USUAL.' It was about half ten, which was always a busy time of day – the hour when stranded tradesmen and amateurs of various stripes realized they weren't as fully equipped for the day ahead as they'd hoped. There were four or five customers in the shop on this occasion, all men, all dressed in multi-pocketed workwear, all splattered with paint or plaster or sealant. I didn't recognize any of them. There was no sign of Jim. Behind the counter, and leaning over it like a man not unhappy to be getting his prostate checked, was Noel Quinn. The shop had seen quite a few assistants come and go over the decades. Some had been godsends. Some had been hopeless. Noel was in the lower half of the table. I'd hired him myself, about a year before I retired, and had never been convinced it was one of my better moves. Not long after I plucked him from the dole queue, he apologized for being a bit late one morning. He'd forgotten he had a job now.

'Eugene,' he said. 'It's yourself.'

'Hello!' I cried with a lot more enthusiasm than I'd meant to put into it. Nerves.

'Grand morning. We'll get a summer out of it yet.'

'Not bad, no.'

'Supposed to rain later, mind you.'

'It wouldn't surprise me.'

'Looking up again for the weekend, though. So they say.'

'Glad to hear it.'

We went through some version of this same conversation every single time I visited. Aliens could have landed in the town the night before, rounded up the women and children and laser-beamed them to nothingness. Noel would still open with a comment on the weather. I was brought up in a pub and spent my whole adult life in a shop. Harmless small talk was second nature to me. Still, there were days when I wanted to scream in his face that he lived in Ireland so of course it was going to rain later. It was always going to rain later. You didn't have to *say* it, even in June.

'Where's the Big Boss Man?'

'He's in the bog.'

'Right.'

'Must be a shite, I'd say. He's been a while.'

'I see.'

'Whatcha got there?' Noel said, nodding at my right hand. What I had there was a dozen or more flyers for Sunny Salsa Dancing Lessons.

'Flyers,' I said. 'Dancing lessons or something. I bumped into the guy on his way in, said I'd leave a few by the till for him.'

This was a lie, of course. I hadn't bumped into anyone. I'd taken a flyer from a chipper round the corner and run up the copies myself. They featured a poor-quality drawing of a young couple locked together, heads thrown back, apparently having simultaneous orgasms under something that I assumed was supposed to be a spotlight, even though it looked more like a bucket of water being tipped out. The man in the drawing had a square jaw and arms like tree trunks. The woman had a tiny waist and breasts the size of her head. There were contact details and information about location and kick-off time. Across the bottom were two stars containing the words *SPICY FUN!* and *MEET NEW PEOPLE!* The impression I had was that they'd only given the couple clothes at the last minute. It was all a bit grim, I thought. Cheap-looking. Still, if it turned out to be what they were strongly hinting it was – one step down from a full-on orgy – I had faith that our Jim wouldn't find himself holding the coats.

'Dancing?' Noel said. 'Show us.'

I peeled off a flyer and handed it over. 'Salsa,' I pointed out, in case the word 'lap' had popped into his head.

He looked the document over and whistled. 'Some pair of tits on your one there.'

'She's a drawing, Noel.'

'I know, I know. But still.'

'She wouldn't *be* there. She doesn't *exist.*'

He kept staring, lost in his filthy thoughts. 'Supposed to be a good way to meet new people.'

'Oh? Where did you hear that?'

He didn't get the joke. More staring. I had a sudden premonition of trouble and grabbed the flyer back. Too late.

'Might be something to think about,' he sniffed, snapping out of it.

I did my best to smile. 'Ah, I doubt it'd be your sort of thing, Noel. Wall-to-wall eejits.'

'You reckon?'

'God, yeah. I'd steer clear if I were you.'

He pulled a *maybe so* face and in that moment of relief, I realized I was going about this arseways. This wasn't a setback. Just the opposite. It was a better way in.

'Then again,' I said quickly, 'it could be wall-to-wall eejits and still have that special someone in there some-where. You never know, isn't that it? Faint heart never won fair lady and what have you.'

Noel's face brightened. 'Exactly, Eugene. Exactly. You have to think positive.'

I nodded slowly, letting on I was thinking this strange new idea through. 'Would you go on your own?'

'As opposed to what?'

'Might be good to take a pal with you.'

'Would it?'

'I'd say so, yeah. If you went on your own, you might look a bit desperate. Or obvious, anyway. If there was a

41

couple of you, you'd be nothing more than a game pair of lads, giving something new a–'

The door behind the counter swung open, and Jim appeared. He gave me a nod, looking neither pleased nor displeased to see me. Things were still a bit tense.

'There he is,' I said.

'Da.'

I jumped right in. 'Guess where Noel's going.'

Jim sniffed. 'Out to the back to tidy up, like I asked him to an hour ago?'

'I'll give you a clue. He's taking up a new hobby.'

'Deep sea diving.'

'What?'

'Hot-air ballooning.'

'No, for f–'

'Salsa dancing,' Noel put in. He snatched the flyer back and held it up like a lawyer showing off Exhibit A. 'It'll be rotten with women. Look at the cans on this one.'

Jim frowned. 'You do understand that she's a drawing? I mean, she's not going to *be* there.'

'Like father, like son,' Noel muttered. 'I know what a drawing is, for fuck's sake. I'm saying, they wouldn't be allowed to draw a woman like that if it was full of old biddies. Advertising standards and what have you.'

This wasn't brilliant, logic-wise, but I wasn't about to say so.

'Christ,' Jim sighed. 'This is worse than the time you said you fancied the cow in that yoghurt ad.'

'She had nice eyes,' Noel said, hurt.

'You don't think it might be a bit of a laugh?' I said, too suddenly, too loudly. 'I mean, I'm not saying he's going to bump into Raquel Welch–'

'Raquel Welch, holy shit.'

He was forever telling me that my references were out of date. *The Rolling Stones are not the latest thing, Da.* 'Or whoever,' I said. 'I think it sounds . . . fun.'

'Yeah? Why don't you go with him then? Worst came to worst, you could dance with each other.'

Any grumpiness was gone now. He leaned back against the wall, tucked one hand behind him, enjoying himself. I'd put a lot of thought into my patter, but it all went out the window. I decided to plough on.

'Hilarious as ever,' I said feebly. 'In all seriousness, what about you?'

'What about me?'

'Noel was saying a minute ago he'd rather not go on his own. You could tag along. Put a couple of pints in you first, I'd say you'd have great craic.'

It had occurred to me during the planning phase that this would be the most dangerous moment. I wasn't worried that he would say no. I mean, I was ninety per cent certain he would say no, but the thought didn't *bother* me. The truly bad outcome was that he'd put this ruse together with the gay incident and things would turn nasty.

'Absolutely not,' Jim said. He kept smiling, though. No pennies dropped.

'Suit yourself,' I shrugged. The trick now was not to push it. Maybe I'd work on him again later, maybe not. 'So, did your man ever come back in with the drill?'

'Not yet,' Jim said. 'I told him on the phone, there's no–'

'We could all go,' Noel said. 'The three of us. Work night out.'

Jim groaned. 'Give it up, Noel. You'll be making a solo run on this one.'

'I don't even work here any more,' I reminded him. It was just something to say. The script was in the toilet at this point and I needed a moment to think.

'I know you don't,' Noel said, 'but you're hardly a stranger to the place, are you? Go on. It'll be brilliant.'

'Think of his health,' Jim said. 'An oul lad like this would wind up in hospital if he tried so much as a waltz.'

I faced him full on. 'I'm as supple as a reed and I could dance rings around you, you big fucking lunk.'

He snorted. 'Da, you can't get out of a chair without making a noise like a tennis player serving. Twice a week you tell me you can't turn your head because you "slept funny".'

'All right, maybe there's a few creaky bits here and there, but we're not talking about climbing a mountain here. It's dancing! I have more rhythm in my big toe than you have in–'

Noel held up his hands. 'Lads! Listen. Listen. There's only one way we're going to solve this and that's if we all go along on . . .' he inspected the flyer again, 'Thursday night. Right?'

Jim rolled his eyes and I rolled mine. Nothing was said for a few seconds. I held my breath, certain that this was suddenly going my way and that I'd ruin it if I said a single word.

'You mentioned pints,' Jim said to me then.

'I don't think a pint or two would hurt, no.'

He scratched the tip of his nose, popped his shoulders up and down. 'Could be a laugh, I suppose.'

I mirrored his shrug. 'Yeah. Could be.'

Noel clapped his hands together and rubbed vigorously. 'It's all settled, so. Right, Jim? The three of us? Thursday night?'

A long pause. And then, 'Maybe. All right – yeah.'

Noel swivelled to me. 'Eugene?'

I made a big deal of rolling my eyes again. 'Go on, so. If that's what you want. Grand.' And that was that. Twenty minutes later I was on my way home again, feeling pretty good, for once, about having hired Noel.

6

Una had her second affair – second that I knew about, at least – in 1985. I wouldn't have found out if I hadn't been in the grip of a health kick at the time. I'd noticed a steady tightening of my clothes over the previous couple of years and had finally decided to do something about it. My new lifestyle, as I insisted on calling it, basically amounted to eating a bit more fruit and talking loudly about how everyone else should eat a bit more fruit too. Although it wasn't much, I was deadly serious about it. Every day at about noon, I'd walk up to the little supermarket at the top of Glaslough Street and buy a banana or an apple. (It was a journey of about forty seconds each way, but I counted it as having taken up exercise on top of transforming my diet.)

I was performing this little ritual one bitter December day when I saw an old man go on his arse right in front of me. It was the sort of fall that Buster Keaton would have been proud of. He didn't so much slip as launch both feet into the air, waist-high. If he'd been a young lad, I'm sure I would have laughed. But he must have been seventy-odd and I thought he had surely done himself a serious injury. I shuffled over to him, taking care not to suffer the same fate, and got down by his side, asked if he was all right. He didn't answer my question. Instead, he did a lot of swearing and slapped the icy pavement, like a toddler disgusted to have been betrayed by the physical world. I took that to mean that he wasn't in agony, at least, and helped him get to his feet. He wiggled his hips experimentally, still clinging to my arm, and then rotated his ankles. Everything seemed to be working, but when he thanked me for helping, I detected a tremor in his voice. The embarrassment was fading now and the shock was catching up with him. He needed a sit-down and a sugary cup of tea, I told him, and invited him back to the shop. He declined. There was a bus leaving for Clones in twenty minutes, and he had to be on it. That was where he lived. He'd been in Monaghan visiting an aunt, whom he described as 'elderly'. I could only imagine what kind of nick she must have been in. Well, what could I do? Tell an old man who'd had a fright and would probably soon find himself in pain that he'd better hurry up because the bus wasn't going to catch itself? No. I told him there'd be no argument about it. He was coming back to the shop for tea and a biccie, then I was driving him home. He made some half-hearted swipes in the direction of protest, but he could see the sense of what I was saying. So that's what we did. We had the tea and a bit of a chat, did one more tour of his bones to make sure, and headed off to Clones. The man's name was Andy. He was a retired schoolteacher, a bachelor, and not much of a conversationalist. After we'd said everything there was to say about his slip – which was before we'd left the shop – there was an awful lot of smiling and nodding. In the car I turned on the radio, hoping the news would give us something to talk about. Andy wasn't having it. He was content to stare straight ahead and issue an occasional sigh or burp (he'd told me Custard Creams didn't agree with him but I had foolishly insisted). Clones was only a dozen miles away, but it seemed to take us several hours to get there. By the time I walked him up to his door and said goodbye, any warm glow I felt about being such a decent human being had long since passed. I couldn't wait to get back to the shop. At least people there didn't just stare at you when you asked them a direct question.

Andy lived on the far side of Clones. There had been no delays on the way through – Clones wasn't what you'd call a notorious congestion hotspot – but I found myself creeping along on the way back. The source of the trouble was obvious. A truck driver up ahead was making deliveries to a pub and rather than find a sensible parking spot had decided there was nothing wrong with stopping in the middle of the street and putting on his magic hazard lights. I'd almost reached the truck and was preparing to take my turn scooting around it in the oncoming traffic when a silver BMW came along and slid slowly past. I glanced at the driver, a middle-aged man, and then at his passenger, who was my wife, Una. She was in the middle of saying something. We locked eyes. Her hand flew to her mouth. Later on, I thought she might have been able to lie her way out of it if it hadn't been for that gesture. Suppose she'd spotted me and waved enthusiastically, maybe even nudged her companion and pointed me out. *Look, it's my husband. Hello!* It might not have worked in the long run, but at least she would have given herself a chance.

I didn't react very dramatically. I didn't react at all. I sat there until I had my chance to go around the truck. It felt as if someone had turned on a hairdryer inside my head. There were no specific thoughts in there, just a lot of indistinct noise. A few minutes later, back on the road to Monaghan, my heart started to go nuts. I'd never felt anything like it and was convinced I was about to die. I pulled in at a farmer's gate and tried to get my breathing under control. It took a while. And then I burst into tears. I don't know how long the crying fit lasted. It might have been five minutes, it might have been forty-five. When it passed, I rolled down my window to get some air and finally put my brain into gear. I wasted no time on the 'hilarious misunderstanding' theory. The hand-to-mouth thing had killed that stone dead. Plus, there was the simple fact that she had no reason to be in Clones that I knew of, least of all in a car with a strange man. If she'd had one, she would have surely mentioned it that morning before I left for work. No. There was nothing to ponder, no angles to work out. She'd done it before and, by all accounts, she was doing it again. The only question I had to consider was this: what was I going to do about it?

I went back to work for the rest of the day. I couldn't think of any reason not to. My assistant in those days, and for many years after, was a man called Bobby Brennan. Bobby had a drink problem – it killed him in the end, when he was only fifty-two – but you would never have guessed it if you encountered him in the shop, where he was relentlessly upbeat and professional. He was also a skilled reader of people. When we were locking up at the end of the day, I caught him staring at the side of my face. He asked me if everything was all right and when I said of course it was, sure why wouldn't it be, he asked again. I got out of there as quickly as I could. It had been a hell of a day already. If I'd cried all over Bobby on top of everything else, I think it might have been the end of me. So I cried in the car again instead. And then I drove home.

Eleanor was eight years old at the time, Jim six. When I arrived home and opened the front door, I found senior sitting on junior in the hall, beating him over the head with a cushion. He was doing that hysterical laugh kids do when they're right on the point of deciding this is no fun after all and screaming bloody murder. I separated them and kissed them hello. They started babbling at the same time, as was their habit, filling me in on their day's adventures in a string of two-sentence anecdotes. I usually nodded my way through this little ritual, paying no real attention. Today I needed the pause, so I took a seat on the bottom stair and gathered them close. They were delighted by this unusual turn of events and continued talking, then shouting, over each other. Eleanor had done badly on a maths test, but it wasn't her fault. Jim had found a Lego spaceman on his way home, but it was missing its legs. Eleanor's friend Mary had lost a tooth overnight. Jim had seen the smallest dog in the world. Eleanor's teacher had said a bad word, then said another one when she realized. Jim's class had a new boy and he smelled funny. When I could put it off no longer, I hauled myself upright and forced my legs to carry me down the hall. The kids followed right on my heels. I tried to remind myself that Una was the one who should be feeling nervous. It did no good. I was shaking.

In the kitchen, I found her upending a bag of frozen peas into a pot. She looked over quickly and performed a small nod. I nodded back and sat at the table. Jim and Eleanor joined me, instantly resuming their chatter. After a few minutes, Una deposited our plates and joined us. On the drive home, I'd wondered if she would have the nerve to try a blanket denial. *Clones? Why would I be in Clones? It must have been some woman who looks like me.* It was clear from the eerie silence between us that she wasn't going to go that route. She didn't so much as look up from her food while we ate, even when Jim knocked over his milk. Eleanor, being much more sensitive than her brother, seemed to notice that something was up – I could see it in her sideways glances – but she was more interested in talking about roller skates (her current obsession) than in making enquiries.

Our custom when tea was over was for me to head into the living room while Una tidied up and the kids resumed trying to kill each other. I wondered if I should stay put on this occasion, so we'd be alone when the other two ran off. But I decided there was no point. What was the use in grabbing a few minutes? Whatever we were going to say would have to wait until after they went to bed, when we'd have plenty of time. So I stuck with the routine and wandered off to my usual spot on the sofa. From there, I heard Jim and Eleanor thumping up the stairs, already screaming at each other about the whereabouts of a blue pencil. I wasn't surprised when Una didn't follow me. She'd come to the same conclusion I had, no doubt, on the futility of getting into it now. Eventually, the kids got tired of fighting on the landing and came down to watch telly. I'd been sitting in silence, which they found hilarious. They switched the box on and soon settled on a holiday programme. A few minutes into it, as the mahogany-skinned presenter was saying that Spain is a land of contrasts, I heard Una going upstairs. She didn't come back down.

We watched telly for a while – or the kids did, at least – and then it was bedtime. I trooped them upstairs and did the necessary. When I kissed Eleanor good night she asked if it was really true that Mammy had a headache and needed a lie-down. This was the excuse I'd given when they'd asked after her earlier. Of course it was true, I told her, doing my best to smile. Why would I lie? I got out of there quickly in case she had her own clever answer to go along with her clever question. Downstairs again, I began to wonder if Una was going to stay away, forcing me to make the first move. I hoped not. Although I had no idea what I was supposed to say to her, I wanted the big scene over with. I'd just rooted out an ancient bottle of whiskey and sat down with a foolishly large glass of it when she walked through the living-room door. We looked at each other for a long time in silence. Then she sat down and started talking. She wasted no time pretending that I hadn't seen what I had seen or that there was a reasonable explanation for it. He was a businessman from Cavan. Something to do with animal feed, she wasn't sure, exactly. Fergal. It had been going on for a couple of months. Not a serious thing. There were no feelings involved. And it was over now, as of today.

The first time she'd admitted to an affair, she was so casual about it, as if she'd accidentally broken a mug I liked. This time felt a little different, I thought. While she still wasn't anything like as upset as you might expect, I did detect a note of regret in her voice. I listened without interruption, waiting for her to break down properly. Hoping for it. She never did. Instead, she provided a long list of Fergal's many flaws. He told dirty jokes, apparently, and they were never even funny. He was vain. He was a bad tipper. He was a little bit racist. I thought maybe she was telling me this because she thought it would make me feel better – as in, he may have been screwing your wife but, to tell you the truth, he was an awful gobshite. It was confusing because how was *that* supposed to help? As she went on and on, however, never once pausing to check how I was feeling or ask for a reaction, it slowly dawned on me that none of this was for my benefit. It was for hers. She'd been bottling up a lot of complaints about her boyfriend and was glad of this chance to air them all. Then she sighed and said she was furious with herself because she'd intended to finish with him soon and I would never have been any the wiser. So there it was. It wasn't regret I'd noticed in her voice. It was self-pity. She'd almost been home and dry and – typical! – her crappy luck had run out. In that instant, I felt like I knew absolutely nothing about her or what she might be capable of. Was it possible she was dangerous? Were the children safe? My thoughts crashed together. The room began to spin. I felt dizzy and sick. She was still talking, but I got up and left.

Upstairs, I stood over the sink, splashing water on my face and trying not to throw up. After a while, the nausea passed. And so did the panic. She wasn't a maniac. She wasn't a threat to anyone's safety. She was just a terrible, terrible human being. My marriage was over, clearly. This was Ireland in 1985, so there was no such thing as divorce. Would we separate or stay together for the sake of the kids? I had no idea. Suddenly, all I wanted was to sleep. It was only when I was lying in bed, facing the wall, wondering if she would have the nerve to join me, that I realized I hadn't spoken a single word to her since I got home.

7

I was fully prepared for Jim to talk his way out of salsa dancing. As the day drew closer, I braced myself every time he cleared his throat, convinced that the next words out of his mouth would be, 'Listen, about this dancing shite . . .' They never came. He never mentioned it at all, in fact. It wasn't until the evening before the event that I finally copped on. He wasn't looking forward to it; he'd completely forgotten we were going. When I reminded him, he slumped in his chair at the kitchen table and made a noise like a cat going through a difficult birth. The objections I'd been expecting came pouring out in one long unbroken wail. I didn't interrupt, just let him exhaust himself. It took a while. Then I shrugged and said, 'You never know, it might be all right.' It was all I had.

He rolled his eyes. There was an awful lot in that eye-roll. I got some weariness, quite a lot of doubt, and a big dose of irritation. I took it as agreement.

We'd agreed to meet in the Widow McKenna's, for reasons of geography. It was not a pub I frequented regularly. For decades, it had been a rough sort of joint, the kind of place where large men broke each other's faces over some tasteless remark a second cousin had made to a sister-in-law's nephew. In the 1980s, it suddenly gained a reputation as an IRA stronghold. Whether that was deserved or not, I don't know, but it was whispered that more than one bombing plot had been hatched on its gummy seats. More recently, for reasons I couldn't pretend to understand, it had become hugely popular with the young people. They spilled out on the street on Friday and Saturday nights, shrieking and cheering and freezing in their wildly unseasonable outfits. More recently still, the youngsters had drifted away, leaving the place strangely lost. It no longer seemed to know what it was.

Noel, Jim informed me, had gone there straight from work. I winced when I heard that. It could mean that he'd decided to eat there, nursing a solitary pint, or it could mean that he was skipping food entirely. He had been known to overdo it on the alcohol front. As soon as we walked in the door, it was obvious which of these scenarios we were dealing with. Noel was sitting at the bar, waving his arms over his head in the service of some anecdote while a barman stared at him, pretending to be amused.

'For fuck's sake,' Jim sighed, obviously drawing the same conclusion I had. 'Take that wee booth, Da. I'll get the pints.'

I did as I was told. He joined me after a couple of minutes, with Noel in tow.

'Noel's pissed,' he announced solemnly.

'Oh, I am not,' Noel said, dropping in heavily beside me. 'I'm pleasantly merry.'

'It's only half seven,' I hissed at him. 'You can't have

even been here in that long. How many pints have you in you?'

'Only three, Eugene! And a few whiskeys. Sure you know yourself.'

He tried to wink and failed, blinking stupidly first at me, then at Jim. I knew for a fact that he couldn't wink even when he was sober, but that wasn't much comfort. Even by his standards, this was a particularly poor effort.

'So!' Noel went on, rubbing his hands together. 'What's the plan?'

'Not to make complete tools of ourselves,' Jim said. 'There's already a big hole in it.'

'What's that?'

'*You*, ye tit,' I said. 'We were supposed to meet up for a quiet pint or two before we headed over to the—'

'Will you give over,' Noel said. 'Jesus Christ, it's like being out with your ma. Lookit, if it makes you feel any better, I'll make this one my last pint. All right?'

He sounded properly angry. There was no point in making a fuss, I decided. 'Fair enough,' I said. 'Let's say no more about it.'

Before we left, about forty minutes later, Noel had three more pints, not including that one.

The lessons were held in the wee hall attached to St Joseph's church, a two-minute walk from the Widow McKenna's. It was the sort of facility that local people used for everything from meetings of Gamblers Anonymous to, well, salsa dancing. I hadn't set foot in it in a long time. My last visit, as far as I could remember, was something to do with a charity of some kind. A cake sale, maybe? The details were gone. Still, when I walked through the door with Jim and Noel, the place felt instantly familiar. It took me a moment to realize that I wasn't remembering this room in particular. The creaky floorboards, the weird echo, the cheap plastic chairs stacked along the walls – I was thinking of all the school gyms where once upon a time I'd attend PTA meetings, Christmas plays and the like.

'Ugh,' Noel said as the door closed behind us, 'it stinks in here.'

He was exaggerating, but only a bit. The air was dusty and stale with a strong undercurrent, for reasons probably best left uninvestigated, of boiled cabbage. Although we were a few minutes early, there was already a decent crowd, gathered together in the middle of the floor. Maybe twenty people, I reckoned, more or less evenly split between male and female. A few of them glanced in our direction as we approached. One man waved enthusiastically. The others went straight back to their conversations. There was a small table off to one side with a battered-looking stereo on it. Beside it, frowning at a piece of paper, was a tallish woman with long grey hair tied up in a ponytail. Mid-fifties was my guess. She was dressed head to toe in black, including some class of a poncho or shawl. Our instructor, I assumed.

I surveyed the group as we blended in, nodding and smiling. The first thing that struck me was that I was not the oldest person there. I wasn't even in the top two. That honour went to Seamus and Lilian Doherty, who were both well over eighty. Long-retired, the Dohertys had run a sweet shop in the town for decades, despite their obvious loathing for people in general and children in particular.

They were both tiny and stooped over. Nothing to do with their advanced age – they'd always been that way, as far as I could remember. Generations of Monaghan kids had known them only as two walnut-like heads, peering suspiciously over the top of a glass counter. I didn't know them well personally but, as a fellow retired retailer, I thought I should say hello. When I took my first step towards them, however, Lilian gave me such a withering look I not only stayed put, I almost went home. I fell back on smiling and nodding, taking the opportunity to focus on the reason why I was there in the first place.

Not counting Lilian and the lady by the stereo, there were nine women present. Five were in their twenties and too young for Jim. One of the remaining four was married, I knew, and another was clearly there with her boyfriend. That left two possibilities, at most. One was about Jim's age, I guessed, and one looked younger, early thirties or so. The younger one was seriously good-looking. Long red hair, perfect skin, cheekbones you could cut yourself on. He was my son and I loved him unconditionally, but I had to be realistic. There was as much chance of this woman fancying a go on Jim as there was of me winning the Oscar for Best Cinematography. So, we'd been inside the building for sixty seconds and I'd already concluded there was only one woman there who could conceivably become my daughter-in-law. If you'd told me that in advance, I would have been crushed. Instead, I felt a growing sense of excitement. When I thought about the sort of partner I wanted for Jim, all sorts of qualities sprang to mind, from the obvious (she should be faithful, ha ha) to the more fanciful (she should think George was the best Beatle). Number one, though, head and shoulders above all the others was this: she should be kind. This woman looked kind. She was standing a little outside the main group, chatting to one of the twenty-somethings. The younger one seemed upset. She was staring at the floor and fidgeting like she was getting paid for it. Jim's future wife was leaning in close, whispering, smiling gently, and performing regular arm pats. I walked around the throng to join them.

'Hello there!' I said brightly, trying to sound like a man with an attractive son. 'Eugene. This is my first time here.'

'Ruth,' she said. 'Nice to meet you, Eugene. This is Louise. It's our first time too.' Louise briefly threw her eyes up to the level of my knees then returned them to the floor.

'Oh, that's nice,' I said. 'Good that we're not the only new blood. I'm here with my son and–'

'I didn't want to come,' Louise said angrily. 'She made me.'

Ruth's smile didn't waver. 'It's good to try new things, I think. And meet new people.'

'Absolutely,' I said. I was a bit confused about the nature of their relationship. There was more than a hint of mother-daughter about it, but their ages didn't allow for that. They had different accents too. Louise was from somewhere in the midlands, I guessed. Ruth sounded local.

'Have you done much dancing before, Eugene?' Ruth asked.

'Oh God, no. Complete beginner. Yourself?'

'I think I tapped my toes one time. That's about it.'

I turned to Louise for her story and she finally looked up. 'Beginner,' she said and immediately followed up with, 'I'm going to the toilet.' She brushed past me and away.

'Don't mind her,' Ruth said. 'She wasn't joking, she really doesn't want to be here.'

'And you . . . made her?'

She leaned in my direction. 'Bad break-up. Not coping well. He was her first real boyfriend. We work together and she confides in me a bit.'

'So you're doing the old plenty-more-fish-in-the-sea bit?'

'It's not even that, it's just to get her out of the house. I tried to disguise it as a work outing, with a whole gang of us? They all pulled out at the last minute. Bastards.'

'You came anyway. Good for you.'

She shrugged, deflecting the compliment. I knew it. *Kind.* 'What about yourself?' she said. 'Took a notion?'

'Ah, it's kind of a work thing too. I used to run a hardware shop. My son has it now. We sort of dared each other to come and no one backed down, so here we are, with another lad. We're all clueless, but sure it might be a laugh. My son says it'll broaden our horizons. Jim. His name's Jim. That's what he's like, our Jim, forever trying to broaden his–'

I was interrupted by a tap on the shoulder. The instructor.

'Hello,' she said. 'Thought I should introduce myself. I'm Annie, I'm the one who's supposed to know what she's doing.'

Her voice was soft and gentle. It sounded like it belonged to a much younger woman. A Belfast accent, I wondered? More northern than mine, at any rate.

'I normally have a partner in crime,' she went on. 'Philip. He can't make it tonight. Man flu.'

This raised a chuckle from Ruth. I supposed Philip was Annie's husband. A family business, then, like my own.

'Nice to meet you, Annie,' I said. 'Uh, Eugene.'

'From the town here?'

'I am.'

'Good man. Listen, I only have one piece of advice for you: don't take it too seriously. Sure it's only a bit of craic.'

'Right. Thanks. Thank you.'

She smiled and turned to find another newcomer to welcome. I tried to get back on to the subject of Jim and his availability, but Ruth went off on a long speech about how welcoming Annie was. By the time I got a word in, Annie had walked to the front of the group and issued a brisk trio of claps.

'Good evening, everyone,' she said. 'Will we get started? You're all very welcome, especially the new blood. Before we get into the fun stuff, there is, as ever, the unfortunate matter of money. It's ten euro each, please. There's a wee biscuit tin on the table there. I'll avert my gaze and if you wouldn't mind . . .'

She made a big show of turning away in horror from the unpleasantness, her right arm wrapped around her middle, her left hand shielding her eyes. I wasn't sure what I thought about that. If she felt all that bad about taking our money, she could have given lessons for free. I fell in beside Jim as we dropped our tenners in the biscuit tin.

'So far, so good?' I said.

'It hasn't even started yet, Da.'

He had me there. When everyone had paid up, Annie got us underway. There was a lot of counting and clapping and a bit of stepping back and forward. It wasn't what you would call dancing, not yet, and I felt I was keeping up. I looked across at Jim and he too seemed pleasantly surprised. Then Annie announced that she would need a partner for the proper demo. There was a chilling moment when I thought she might pick a man at random – I prepared myself to fake a pulmonary embolism – but she asked for volunteers. Only one was forthcoming, a skinny man with greasy, coal-black hair. He actually danced his way forward to join her, making little noises that he (mistakenly) thought sounded like a salsa beat. His name was Rob and I decided I hated him. Annie restarted the music and the two of them began to demonstrate the basic steps. They went nice and slowly and she described everything they were doing in a smooth, calming tone that made it seem like the easiest thing in the world. My growing confidence grew a little more. And then it was our turn. There was a system for picking who danced with whom, it turned out. The women gathered in a circle, facing out. The men formed a wider circle around them, facing in. We were to practise the simple back and forth we'd been shown with the person opposite. Every so often, we'd pause and the men's circle would rotate a little, giving everyone a new partner. It was a clever system. I could imagine it appealing to Tommy, who was a sucker for good engineering.

The first woman unfortunate enough to get me was one of the twenty-somethings. Having started out reasonably well, I was genuinely amazed at how bad I was. It didn't seem possible. Pure chance alone, I marvelled, should have seen me making the right move once in a while. Nope. There wasn't a single second of the few minutes we spent together when I was doing what I was supposed to be doing. The twenty-something wasn't upset by my incompetence, I was relieved to find. We were all beginners, she reminded me when I apologized for the fifth time. She did take some of the good out of it, mind you, when she asked me in all sincerity if I was absolutely sure I knew which one was right and which one was left. I kept an eye on Jim, of course, as I made an eejit of myself. He was dancing with Christina McClave, the woman I knew to be married, and seemed not to be miserable, at least. His feet were under his direct control too, as far as I could tell, which was more than could be said for his old man.

My second partner was Louise. There was no improvement in my dancing ability, but it didn't particularly matter. If anything, she was worse than I was. At least I was doing everything wrong. She was barely doing anything at all. It was like dancing with a tailor's dummy. Must have been some break-up, I thought. When we switched again, I got Lilian, from the sweet shop. Jim got Ruth! They greeted each other with the same embarrassed smiles that everyone was employing at changeover time. That was good, I supposed. Normal. Love at first sight was a bit much to hope for. I tried to keep watching them, but it wasn't easy, given the angles and the number of couples between us.

'Are you still at the paint?' Lilian barked. She was staring at me, beetle-browed, like I was something hairy she'd found floating in her soup.

'Hardware,' I said. 'I had a hardware shop, not just paint.'

'All I ever got in there was paint.'

That doesn't mean it was a paint shop, you miserable old harpy, is what I wanted to say. 'My son runs it now I've retired,' is what I actually said. 'He's here tonight too.'

'I hope he's a better dancer than you are.'

'It's my first time!'

'It's only my third time. Can you not count, man?'

'Of course I can—'

'Or if that's too hard for you, is quick-quick-slow too much to remember?'

'Listen, I'm doing my best here. If you're–'

There was another loud clap. Only one this time. Annie again, I thought, getting our attention to make some point. I turned and saw that, actually, no, some commotion was afoot. There were gasps all round and hands covering mouths. I guessed it was some sort of medical emergency – specifically, that Lilian's husband, Seamus, had finally fallen off the perch – but then I saw that all eyes were on Noel and the good-looking redhead. I knew. I knew straight away. He'd done something terrible and she had slapped his stupid face.

'What's going on?' Annie said, making her way across to them. 'Cathy? Is everything all right?'

Cathy – the redhead – folded her arms and stepped back, then angrily forward again. 'No,' she said. 'Everything is not fucking all right. I want this prick gone.'

She pointed at Noel, who pulled an unconvincing *who-me?* face.

'He grabbed my ass! It's the fucking salsa! He has no business anywhere near my ass!'

All the blood ran out of my head. Before I had time to process the information, Jim came tearing across and pushed Noel, hard, on the shoulder. He half-spun and for a moment, it didn't seem likely that he'd stay on his feet.

'What's wrong with you?' Jim growled at him.

'I didn't do anything,' Noel protested. He sounded neither truthful nor sober. Then, apparently having decided that if he really put the effort in he stood a good chance of making this worse, he said, 'All right, I may have brushed a hand against her ass, just for half a second, but it was an accident.'

'It wasn't an accident,' Cathy said firmly, 'it wasn't a brush, it wasn't half a second, and it wasn't one hand.'

Noel opened his gob to say something else stupid. Jim stopped him with a poke in the chest. 'You're leaving,' he said. 'But not before you apologize.'

There was a pause. You could have heard a pin drop. At least you could have if not for the salsa music that was still going full volume. Noel rubbed the end of his nose and shrugged.

'I'm willing to say I'm sorry,' he said, not looking at anyone in particular. 'I'm not willing to say it was an on-purpose thing. Lookit, I haven't a notion what I'm doing, I had a few jars before I arrived, you know yourself' – he tried to wink and failed, as usual – 'and I might have had some kind of flashback to a slow set. Back in the oul disco days. My hands, maybe, might have possibly wandered off of their own accord.'

Although it wasn't perfect by any stretch of the imagination, this struck me as a reasonable effort, given the material we were working with. The main thing, as far as I was concerned, was to get Jim back dancing with Ruth as quickly as possible.

'Lookit,' I said, 'let's not overreact. Couldn't we–'

'Spoken like a true dinosaur,' Cathy snapped.

A lot of eyes swivelled in my direction. Annie put a hand to her forehead. She looked pained. I swallowed hard. 'Well, I don't mean to suggest–'

'Oh, I know exactly what you meant to suggest,' Cathy said. '*He only grabbed your ass, what's the big deal? No reason we should have to stop fucking DANCING.*'

'I really–'

'*Women got their asses grabbed every half hour in my day and no one seemed to mind.* Well, guess what, grandpa? Those days have gone and they're not coming back.'

Every woman in the room – even Lilian – burst into applause. It was mortifying. My instinct was to run away, or at least walk away very quickly. But that wouldn't help, I knew. Might as well hold my hands up and say, *You got me, I'm a real scumbag.* I scrambled for some form of words that wouldn't amount to digging myself an even deeper hole. Nothing came to me.

'I didn't mean any offence,' I said meekly.

This drew a few tuts and some eye-rolling. It seemed so unfair. Noel was the one with the wandering hands and at that exact moment, he could have snuck away without anyone noticing. I was grateful when Jim spoke up again.

'I think the best thing is if we leave you to it,' he said. 'With apologies. Right?' He looked at Noel, who (eventually) performed a sort of half-nod, half-shrug. Then he looked at me. So did everyone else.

'I'm sorry,' I managed to say. It came out like a question – *I'm sorry?* I sounded like a sulky teenager.

'Come on, Da,' Jim said, stepping towards me. He pointed at Noel. 'You too.'

We gathered into a sad little triangle. As we turned for the door, I felt Jim shove me in the back to hurry me along. We walked away. The salsa music played on.

8

1990 was a big news year. The two Germanys reunited. Nelson Mandela was released from prison. Iraq invaded Kuwait. In Ireland, these and other major events were overshadowed by the madness of Italia '90. It was the first World Cup we'd ever qualified for and we wound up getting to the quarter-finals. The entire country completely and utterly lost its mind. I was never a big fan of sport myself. I'd have a fiver on the Grand National, maybe, and once in a while I'd leave the golf on in the background (I found Peter Alliss soothing). I certainly never gave a damn about football. It made no difference. That summer I fell in beside the rest of the population as we sang ourselves hoarse and drank ourselves blind in honour of the Boys in Green, as you were legally obliged to call them, with a tear in your eye.

Four years later, we qualified again. USA '94. I thought things might be a bit calmer second time round, but no. It was like we'd just been practising with Italia '90 and now it was time to show off what we'd learned. Long before the tournament began, the shops filled with all manner of ridiculous, overpriced tat. You could sell anything, it seemed, so long as it was green or had a picture of a football on it. I didn't go anything like as crazy as some people and only made two purchases. One was a poor-quality replica shirt. The other was an emerald afro wig. The shirt was itchy and started stinking of sweat before you'd finished pulling it over your head. The wig was massive and constantly shed little fibres. Walking behind me when I was wearing it must have been like driving behind a trailer-load of hay.

Our first match of the tournament was against Italy, the team that had knocked us out of Italia '90. I met Frank and a few others to watch it in McDaid's. We arrived good and early in the hope of securing a decent vantage point, but that turned out to be pointless. By kick-off time, there were so many bodies squeezed into the place – sitting, standing, balanced on this, hanging off that – that there was no such thing as a decent vantage point. As soon as you congratulated yourself on being in a good position, some upheaval in the crowd would relocate you against your will. Shifted a mere two feet away from your perfect spot, you'd now find yourself looking at a pillar or the back of some lad's head, awaiting the next upheaval and hoping for better things. I don't remember much about the game itself, other than the obvious fact that we won – a beauty from Ray Houghton, very early on. I have more memories of the aftermath, weirdly enough, despite the fact that I was an awful lot drunker then. I remember Frank telling me that he loved me and then immediately denying he'd said anything at all. I remember swapping wigs with a man who came into the shop once in a while, and then spending half an hour trying to find him again because I got all emotional about my original. I remember spilling a young woman's drink, buying her another, and then over-explaining that I wasn't trying to pick her up. I remember singing until my throat hurt. I remember smoking my first cigar. I remember going outside because I was suddenly gasping for air, and then deciding that was a sign I should go home. I remember backing away, bowing to the pub and its patrons and the match and the team like they had combined somehow to form a god.

I remember turning and heading for home.

Eleanor was seventeen in 1994. Jim was fifteen. They'd got themselves into the odd scrape in recent years – sneaking cigarettes in the bathroom, coming home with a few beers in them, nothing dramatic. No face tattoos, no pregnancies, no drugs, no run-ins with the law. Eleanor was doing her Leaving Cert the following summer and, all being well, would be going to university. Although Jim wasn't as academic, he was a decent human being with his head screwed on, and that was the main thing as far as I was concerned. They knew their parents weren't as close as some – they must have done – but they were emerging from childhood in good shape. I was prouder of that than I'd been of anything in my life. I'd stayed with their mother for their sakes and it had paid off. The question now was, what next? Una and I were civil enough to each other, usually, but there was no relationship to speak of. We lived like office colleagues who had been thrown together to work on a tricky project even though they didn't get along. I couldn't see the point of continuing the farce once the kids had flown the nest. I also couldn't see how we'd end things. It was like a blurred picture on the edge of my vision that vanished when I turned to see it properly.

As I meandered home on the night of the Italy game, plastered, still singing when I was sure there was no one around, I wasn't thinking about the humiliating shambles that was my marriage. I was thinking about the next match: against Mexico, in Orlando, Florida. It would kick off in the late afternoon, our time. Lots of businesses would be closing early. I saw no reason why mine couldn't be one of them. I'd shut up shop, change into my shirt and wig – they'd need a wash before then – and head to McDaid's again. There were no lights on at home, which wasn't a surprise. It was late. I tiptoed in and made straight for the downstairs loo. While I was in there, I checked myself out in the mirror I'd done a poor job of installing over the sink. Beer-stained, sweaty, clearly pissed – I wasn't a pretty sight. Worse still, my wig had ridden up my head a little on the walk home and looked more ridiculous than ever, which was some achievement. I got the giggles and shushed myself as I closed the door behind me. A pint of water, I told myself. And bed. That was what I needed now. I opened the kitchen door – and shrieked like a little girl. Eleanor and Jim were at the kitchen table, sitting stiffly upright with their hands clasped in front of them, faces like stone. I started to laugh at my own shock. The sound died in my throat. They were unnaturally still and quiet. My first thought was that Una had died, somehow, but that made no sense. There would be people. Activity. Someone would have come to find me in the pub. I asked what was wrong. They stared at me, neither of them apparently able to speak. I asked again. They kept staring. I stared back. Then Eleanor got the words out. Their mother was gone. For good. With a man. Not long after I went out, she'd sat the two of them down and explained that she had met someone she loved and didn't want to be with me any more. She was leaving the country and would be in touch again when she was settled. They weren't to worry about her. She would be fine. The doorbell had rung while she was speaking. At that point, she went upstairs and returned a minute later with a suitcase. Then she hugged them and walked out.

I made Eleanor tell it twice and then asked Jim for his version. They were both in floods of tears by the end of it, and furious at me for my stupid questions. *Yes*, that was all there was to it. *No*, she didn't say where she was going. *No*, they didn't see the man. *Yes*, it took the five minutes it sounded like it took. When they had finally convinced me that it was true – or, more to the point, when I had finally convinced myself – I spent a long time standing there, saying nothing, as they cried. I almost passed out, but I didn't. I almost threw up, but I didn't. I almost screamed in fury, but I didn't. I just stood there. And then I finally did what I should have done immediately. I moved around the table and bent between them, hugging them so close I almost muffled their sobs. My only task at that moment, it seemed, was to let them know that it wasn't their fault. This wasn't the first time she'd been unfaithful, I told them. It had been happening since they weren't much more than babies. So they mustn't think it was anything to do with them. It was me she had a problem with.

When I finished my little speech, Eleanor pulled my wig off and let it fall to the floor. It wasn't helping.

9

I was miserable after the salsa disaster, which was not like me. Normally, I was the buoyant type. I shrugged things off. I bounced back. Something about that night got me down and kept me there. I moped around the house, mulling it all over, and got nowhere. The only conclusion I reached was that it had nothing to do with the failure of my laughable plan. That was disappointing, to be sure, but in the giant mess we'd made, Jim still being single was only a small smudge. There was something else going on, something I couldn't put my finger on.

Jim was barely speaking to me. From the few words he threw in my direction, I gathered things were even worse with Noel at the shop. While I had no idea how we'd all get back to normal, I supposed it would happen eventually. And then Eleanor called. Her mother-in-law was dead. A heart attack, by all accounts. I'd only met Adrian's mum a handful of times – Theresa, she was called – and had found her decent enough. A small woman, forever on the go, she was given to tapping her hands together in a way that always put me in mind of a field mouse working on a nut. One thing I knew for sure, she was a hell of a lot more pleasant than her son, who must have inherited his awfulness from his long-dead father. I offered my condolences and asked Eleanor to let me know when the funeral arrangements were finalized.

Two days later, Jim and I got up early and pointed the car at Dublin. He still wasn't wasting any actual words on me when he thought he could get away with a grunt, and I settled in for what I assumed would be a more or less silent journey. And that was how it went, at first. Jim put the radio on and we listened to a panel of weirdos discussing whether or not it's a good idea to walk around naked in front of your children. In more normal times, this was the sort of thing that would have had us both cracking jokes every thirty seconds (mine better than his). On this occasion, we listened in solemn silence, even when one of the contributors, a man with a thick Cork accent – I could hear his beard through the speakers – used the phrase 'architectural coherence' in relation to willies. We'd been on the road for half an hour or more before Jim said a full sentence to me. But it was a pretty good one.

'I'm going back to the dancing this week,' he said.

My eyebrows shot up. 'What? Why?'

'I want to apologize,' he said. 'For the way things went.'

I stared ahead, confused. 'You already apologized.'

'No, I didn't. I made you and that other fuckwit apologize.'

'Well, we're the ones . . .' I paused and chose my words carefully. 'The ones that people were mad at.'

He shook his head. 'That doesn't matter. No one's going to remember who said what when. They're going to put the three of us together. I can't have that.'

'Right. Thanks a million.'

He looked right at me for a long moment, which wasn't ideal, given that he was driving. 'What do you expect? He's the ass-grabber and you're the horrible old bastard who can't see the harm in a bit of ass-grabbing now and again.'

'Why are you bringing this up now? You've hardly said two words to me since but now we're stuck together in the car, suddenly you're all chat.'

He shrugged. 'I wasn't going to bother bringing it up. Changed my mind. Well?'

'Well what?'

'Why did you stick up for him?'

'I didn't stick up–'

'You said she was overreacting!'

'I didn't, I said something about us *all* overreacting and–'

'What's the fucking difference?'

He'd raised his voice. A lot. I couldn't tell him the truth – that I wasn't thinking straight at the time because all I wanted was for him to keep dancing with Ruth.

We drove on in silence. I could tell that he was still expecting an answer. He somehow communicated drumming impatiently on the steering wheel with his fingertips without actually doing so. As I struggled to come up with a response, I started to cross-examine myself. What would I have done, I wondered, if Noel had ripped that girl's shirt open? Never mind whether or not that was ever a possibility. Would I still have thought that the main thing was to keep Jim dancing with Ruth? No. Of course not. But didn't that mean that I had a line in mind, a line that couldn't be crossed? It seemed so. Then didn't it follow that I considered Noel's grab, however awful, to be on the safe side of that line? I sat with it for a moment, hoping the logic would break. It didn't. *This* was why I'd been feeling so down. I was exactly what they all thought I was. A creepy old dinosaur who didn't think that Noel had crossed the line.

'What are you thinking about?' Jim asked eventually.

I mulled it over for a little while and decided that I could do worse than tell him the truth. 'There was a series on the telly in the seventies, or maybe the early eighties, called *Mind Your Language*. You'd hardly remember it.'

'Nope.'

'It was a British thing about a lad teaching English to foreigners. In London. A night class, I think. The Italian student was a greasy Romeo. There was a scary German woman who was all cold and efficient. A sexy Swedish au pair. A Japanese lad who said, *"Ah so"* . . .'

'Jesus Christ.'

'You get the idea.'

'I sure do.'

'I loved it. Thought it was hilarious altogether. And it never occurred to me in all the time since that it might not have been particularly, uh, sensitive. It hadn't entered my head in years, but there was a thing on about racism one night a while back and they showed old programmes that were examples of, y'know, how bad things used to be. *Mind Your Language* was Exhibit A. The young people on the programme couldn't get over it. How awful it was. They talked about it like it was . . . a crime. I felt like they were calling me a racist through the telly – me personally – because I'd liked it. I went to bed in a foul mood, and then I lay there for ages, wide awake, fuming. Just raging. I calmed down after a while. I thought it through and I decided that I wasn't mad at the people on the telly. I wasn't even mad at myself. I was mad at *time*. It was making an eejit out of me.'

Jim sighed. 'I know you're not a racist, Da.'

'I'm not. And I'm not a sexist prick who thinks there's nothing wrong with grabbing women either. But I'm knocking on, Jim, and I'm not . . . calibrated the way younger people are. I shouldn't have said anything about overreacting. It was stupid. I'm sorry.'

He did some thinking of his own. 'Seventy's not that old, Da.'

'It's not that young either. And you're only saying that so you'll feel better about forty.'

He did me the courtesy of smirking. I settled back in my seat, feeling at ease for the first time in days. We drove on.

Theresa's funeral mass was in Malahide, on the north side of the city. We found the church with no trouble and congratulated ourselves on our timing, which was spot on. The service was due to start in ten minutes. We parked around the corner and shuffled over, spotting Eleanor straight away. She was standing near the church entrance with her son Miles, looking around her like she'd lost something. Her hair was different, I noticed. Shorter and kind of . . . swishy. It wasn't quite as blonde as had been, either. Despite the circumstances, she looked good. Eleanor always looked good. We raised our hands as we crossed the church grounds, but she didn't respond. We were practically on top of her, in fact, before she noticed us.

'I can't find Aidan,' she said, instead of hello. 'We were inside and he said he needed air. He's not out here. So where the hell is he?' She genuinely seemed to think that we might know.

'I'm sure he hasn't gone far,' I said. 'Probably doing a lap, stretching his pins.' I embraced her then, and that seemed to snap her out of it.

'Thanks for coming,' she said, then gave Jim a quick hug too.

'And how is the big man?' I said, moving on to Miles. I fully expected him to give me a dirty look and turn away – that was his usual reaction, but he raised his arms and even briefly caught my eye. I guessed that he'd been getting a lot of hugs in the last few days and had given up struggling.

'Look at the height of him!' I said to his mother, faking astonishment. I always said something along these lines, as if there was something unusual about a child not staying the same size and I thought that at least one if not both of them deserved special credit. I hugged him and then pushed him out to arm's length, my hands resting on his bony shoulders. 'What are you now, nineteen? Twenty?'

'I'm six.'

'Well, you could have fooled me. I thought–'

'Daddy!' he suddenly squealed, pointing.

He wasn't wrong. Aidan was walking towards us, hands in his pockets, head down. Even for a man attending his mother's funeral, he looked brutal, like he was having trouble putting one foot in front of the other. I'd always thought he looked a bit like Art Garfunkel. Now he looked like Art Garfunkel with gastric flu.

'Aidan,' I said when he arrived. 'I'm so sorry about your mum.' I extended my hand, then had a rush of blood to the head and went in for a hug. That was a first.

'Thanks, Eugene,' he muttered into my ear.

Jim offered his condolences too but limited himself to a handshake.

'You can't just go wandering off like that!' Eleanor hissed. 'People were asking about you.'

Her tone made me cringe. The man had lost his mother.

'I went for a walk,' Aidan said flatly.

No one spoke for a moment. Then Jim jabbed a thumb in the direction of the church door. 'Will we, eh . . .?'

'Yep,' Aidan sighed. 'Let's get it done.'

We went inside.

Tommy died of stomach cancer in 1996. Rose had a heart attack three years later. If you included them – and I did – I'd attended a parent's funeral four times. None of them affected me the way Theresa's did. The service had been underway for only a few minutes before I felt it for the first time, a sort of awful heaviness that settled around me like a blanket. I worried I was taking a turn of some kind and mentally scanned my body up and down, looking for a sign that something was about to burst or collapse or otherwise go badly wrong. Everything seemed to be fine. Jim nudged me in the ribs.

'Are you all right there?' he whispered. 'You're breathing awful heavy.'

'Sorry,' I whispered back. 'I'm grand.'

The priest's name was Father Boyce. He was about three hundred years old. Every part of him – limbs, digits, facial features – seemed to be in motion at all times and none of it looked voluntary. I focused on him hard and tried to imagine the story of his life, to distract myself. After a few minutes, the desolate feeling passed. When he got to the homily, I abandoned the biography I was giving him in my head (enthusiastic but terrible poet, addicted to chocolate, secretly in love with his housekeeper of forty years) and started paying attention to his actual words. I'd be spending a good part of the day talking about Theresa. This was my chance to learn a bit more about her. Father Boyce spoke in the sort of raspy hiss they give snakes in cartoons. He ran through the basics – place of birth, education, frequency of mass attendance (high) – and then he coughed for what felt like ten full minutes.

'Theresa,' he said, looking down at his notes and wiping a bit of spittle from the corner of his mouth, 'was a quiet woman. She kept to herself. Never drank. Never smoked. Didn't bother anyone. She liked crosswords and listening to plays on the radio. Her house, just up the road from us here today, was always kept immaculate. She was, of course, devoted to her children, Aidan and Fiona, and to her three grandchildren, Nichola, Katie, and Miles. They were regular visitors to that immaculate house and we think of them today, in the depths of their grief, and urge them to take comfort, as we all must, in the certainty of God's love and the promise of the resurrection.'

That was it. That was the whole thing. As the old goat moved on to the next part of the service, I looked left and right. No one else seemed bothered, not even Aidan or his sister. I checked behind me. It wasn't a big church. Anything north of a few dozen people could have made it look reasonably full. We'd taken up less than three rows. I got another nudge from Jim.

'Who are you looking for?'

'I'm not looking for anyone.'

'Just exercising your neck, is that it?'

I leaned closer still. 'It's awful empty, isn't it?'

He shrugged. 'Sure, what do you expect? She was a wee old woman, not Princess Diana.'

I wanted to tell him that there was surely a happy medium between wee old woman and Princess Diana, but I stopped myself. There was an unwritten rule about talking during a mass. You could get away with a quick back and forth once in a while; you couldn't take the piss. I returned my attention to Father Boyce and tried to ignore the gloom that had overrun me once again. It'll be over soon enough, I told myself. You'll be outside again, breathing fresh air. There'll be plenty of time then to get to the bottom of whatever the fuck this is.

Not everyone who attended the funeral Mass made the short trip to the cemetery at the rear of the church. Some, I noticed, pretended they were walking that direction but then slowed down and peeled away. By the time we settled into position around the grave, the circle of mourners was only two people deep. Theresa was being buried with her parents who, according to the mossy headstone, had died in 1974 (him) and 1988 (her). I thought about those dates and they felt like yesterday. My mood did not improve.

When the short ceremony came to a close, Aidan and three other men, none of whom I recognized, lifted the ends of two long straps that had been run underneath the coffin. They leaned back a little and took the strain as the under-taker – a great wall of a man, who put me in mind of Tommy – manoeuvred the cargo into position. Then, when the wall gave them a solemn nod, they slowly let the coffin slip down. Duty done, Aidan bent low and gently placed the strap on the ground, as if it were a sacred and delicate relic rather than a grubby length of cloth. He had seemed to be on the verge of tears throughout and now the dam burst. His sister, Fiona, was standing next to him. She leaned her head on his shoulder, gripping his arm tight, but the sobs kept coming, loud and prolonged. He sounded like a terrible actor in a cheap sitcom. Eleanor, who was on his other side, patted him briefly on the back. She looked embarrassed by him, I thought. Next thing I knew, I too was crying.

'What the fuck?' Jim whispered.

'Poor Aidan,' I croaked.

'What the fuck . . .' he said again. This time, it was more of a statement than a question.

His confusion was understandable. He'd probably never heard me say a single good word about his brother-in-law. Just the opposite, in fact. Over the years, I'd regularly declared that Aidan was a braggart, a bore, a snob, and a miser. If truth be told, I hadn't even made much of an effort to hide my opinion from Eleanor. I looked over at her now and saw her staring at me, slack-jawed. She moved her lips in silence. The unspoken words, I would have bet the house, were, *What the fuck?*

I looked away and put everything I had into getting myself under control. Throughout the couple of minutes it took me, I could feel Eleanor's gaze from across the grave and Jim's from my immediate right. I kept my eyes down and waited for matters to conclude. When they did, I walked away immediately, and at a fair clip.

I thought Jim would be on me like a rash as soon as we were alone, but he kept to small talk all the way to the hotel where we planned to gather for lunch. He thought the Mass had been 'nice' and made no mention of the small crowd or the piss-poor homily. I said next to nothing.

The hotel wasn't far away. I presumed Aidan and Fiona had chosen it for that reason because it wasn't particularly pleasant. The word that occurred to me as we walked through its pokey lobby, with its vending machine and dusty plastic flowers, was 'grubby'. Once again, our feeble numbers had been whittled down by the change of scene. All told, there were fourteen of us. To seat every last person who wanted to raise a glass and say farewell to Theresa Mary Kennedy, née Ryan, took two tables. Jim and I were seated at what I couldn't help but think of as the 'good' table – that is, with the principal mourners, Aidan and Fiona. The other one was for elderly cousins – Theresa had been an only child – and a handful of neighbours.

I'd only met Fiona and her husband, Owen, once before, at Aidan and Eleanor's wedding. I'd formed no strong impressions of them then but warmed to them quickly now. She was quite a bit older than Aidan, short and slender, with bright blue eyes and a shy smile. He was short too (although definitely not slender), with limp salt-and-pepper hair. They were friendly, warm people and had a habit of finishing each other's sentences, which I found sweet. Their twin daughters, Nichola and Katie, were about eleven or twelve, I guessed. We were receiving our soup starters when Nichola suddenly started to cry.

'I've just realized,' she wheezed as her mother pulled her close. 'I'll never see granny again.'

A hum of sympathy went around the table. Consoling phrases ran into each other. Some of the adults made eye contact and tilted their heads to the side, touched by the girl's innocence. I wanted to scream. We could flutter and coo all we wanted about living on in our hearts or, worse, meeting again in heaven one day, but the girl was right. No one would ever see Theresa again. That was the whole point of death, wasn't it? You were *gone*. How come no one ever said anything about it beyond useless guff like, 'She's in a happier place' or 'He was a big age'? How were we ever able to talk about anything else? By the time I had thought these thoughts, Nichola had recovered and everyone had gone back to their soup.

Eleanor and Aidan were sitting with Miles between them, which limited their interactions. Still, I kept an eye on them. I was sure I'd detected hints of frostiness earlier and wanted to know if I'd imagined it. I got my answer soon enough when Aidan rose to his feet and, for a second, I saw Eleanor pulling a *here-he-goes* face. Something was definitely up. Money troubles, maybe. She'd worked in advertising once upon a time and had dropped it like a hot spud when Miles came along. I sometimes got the impression that they'd never adjusted their spending accordingly.

'Hello, everyone, if I could . . . Yeah. Hello. This won't be a big speech or anything, I just wanted to thank you all for coming.' He paused and made an attempt at a smile. I'd never seen him be anything other than annoyingly confident. He was clearly nervous now. 'I know people usually do this sort of thing at the end of the meal. I wanted to get it . . . I was going to say I wanted to get it out of the way, but that sounds . . . Does that sound bad?' We all shook our heads and murmured our 'no's. 'Anyway, no big speech, like I say. Let's just raise a glass to Mum.'

He hoisted his wine and we did likewise. Only Fiona could rightfully join him in the 'Mum' business. Most of the rest of us said, 'To Theresa', but I did hear one or two of the elderly cousins getting it wrong and then looking confused. Aidan sat down again once the toast was complete, as waiters began arriving with the main course.

'Well done,' I said across the table.

He glanced up suspiciously. I had been known to direct an occasional sarcastic remark his way. He saw that I was sincere. 'Thanks, Eugene.'

We turned our attention to our plates. There were conversations going on, but they were all appropriately muted and solemn. It was like eating in a library. Then Miles suddenly threw his fork against his glass, causing me and I presumed everyone else to clear their seats in shock.

'This chicken is horrible and I hate it and I won't eat it,' he declared. It had been a strange day and I was almost relieved to see some familiar and predictable behaviour.

'You haven't tasted it yet,' his mother said.

'IT'S THE WRONG COLOUR,' the boy roared, silencing the room. 'DISGUSTING.'

One of my many complaints about Aidan was that he was a hopeless disciplinarian and, worse, had dragged my daughter down to his level. Left to her own devices, she would surely have taken no nonsense. Instead, she let Miles get away with anything short of a bombing campaign. I watched her now, waiting for her to give him a cuddle and tell him she'd get him something more to his liking. When she stood up, dragged him off his chair and marched him out of the dining room, I gasped aloud.

Jim leaned towards me. 'Not herself,' he said quietly. 'Stress.'

'Did you get any kind of a decent conversation with her yet?' I asked Jim. 'How did she seem?'

'Wasn't really talking to her properly, but what do you expect? A death's hard on everyone.'

Eleanor returned a few minutes later with a sheepish-looking Miles in tow. Everyone pretended to be fascinated by their lunch until they had taken their seats. When I thought it safe, I looked up and saw my grandson tucking into his chicken with industry, if not enthusiasm. It was only then that I noticed his mother had barely touched her own. Something was most definitely up.

When the meal was over, a few people drifted away to the bar and others swapped tables to chat with fresh faces. I spotted my chance and relocated to sit beside Eleanor.

'Well, Miles,' I said, peeking around her, 'did you like your dessert?'

He glanced at his mother. 'It was very nice,' he said in the tone of a hostage assuring loved ones they're being treated well.

'The whole thing was very nice,' I said to Eleanor. It certainly wasn't, but I had to start somewhere.

'Aidan picked the hotel because it's near,' she said, singing her husband's name. 'I think it's a hole.'

I'd been planning to sneak up on her slowly. This, however, was an open goal. I lowered my voice. 'Is everything all right with you two? You seem a bit . . . y'know.'

She looked away, embarrassed. 'We're fine. Everyone's all over the place since Theresa died.'

'If you ever need to talk about–'

'Daddy. I'm fine. We're fine. Okay?'

'All right, all right. If you say so.'

'I do.'

I didn't believe her, but there was no point in pushing

it. 'C'mere,' I said, 'remember that other thing we talked about? With your brother? And the . . . socializing?'

We both looked across the room to where Jim was standing with Aidan. 'Yeah?'

'We went to a salsa dancing lesson the other night.'

Her eyes bulged. 'Salsa dan– . . . Wait, *we*?'

'Keep your voice down, Jesus Christ. Yes, and yes.'

'I'm in shock here. How did you manage that?'

'It wasn't even hard. Maybe he's realized on his own that he's turning into me.'

She ignored that. I wasn't sure if I was relieved. 'And? How did it go?'

'He's engaged. Carla. An Italian lingerie model. Twenty-four.'

That won me an eye-roll. 'Not great, then?'

I wasn't about to get into the actual details. 'No, it was pretty, uh . . . I mean, it wasn't . . . It was grand.'

'Are you going again?'

'I'm not. He says he might.'

'That's great. I'm still having awful trouble picturing *him* salsa dancing, never mind you.'

'There you go. Life's full of surprises.'

Miles tugged at her sleeve. 'Mammy. I have to . . . go. Y'know, *go*.'

'Excuse us,' she said and got up to lead him to the facilities.

I sat alone for a minute then got up to join Jim and Aidan. They had pints. 'There he is,' Jim said, raising his. 'Will I get you one?'

'Sure I might as well, thanks.'

When Jim had gone, Aidan and I looked at the carpet for a moment. 'A sad day,' I said, uselessly.

'It is,' he agreed. 'And a long one. Feels like nine o'clock at night and it's only lunchtime.'

'I can imagine.'

Back to the carpet-staring. We had no history of easy-going chats. Why the hell I thought we'd have our first at his mother's funeral do was a question I couldn't answer. I wished I'd gone to get my own pint. Over the course of lunch, the strange weight I'd been feeling had started to lift. Standing there with Aidan, feeling awkward and wishing I was somewhere else, I felt more and more like my normal self. I managed to squeeze out some lies about the hotel being a nice one and Aidan made some noises about other venues he had considered. That got us through to Jim's return with my pint. I took a sip and asked Aidan if he was taking much time off work due to his mother's death. Jim added that he probably needed it. Apart from all the stress and emotional mayhem involved, there were practical matters to take care of, no doubt. It was the last input either of us got to make for five solid minutes.

I'd never quite managed to get my head around what it was that Aidan did for a living. It was something to do with telling other people how to run their business. He used the word 'restructuring' a lot. Sometimes his job sounded legal in nature. Sometimes it sounded financial. Once or twice, I'd thought it sounded just short of showing up in a balaclava and swinging a baseball bat around. In any event, his firm was having a reshuffle of its own. If all went well, he would be taking the step up that he so richly deserved. It wasn't a done deal, of course. Certain conversations had to happen. Certain wheels had to be greased. Certain truths had to be underlined. Certain myths put to bed. It was vintage Aidan. He bragged about how valuable he was to the company, heaped ridicule on those he saw as his rivals for promotion, and reminded us that even if he didn't get moved up, his life was already a huge success. It was as if someone had thrown a switch. The vulnerable, bereaved son was gone. The pain in the hole was back. I couldn't tell where the switch had been thrown. Was it in his head or mine?

We hung around in the hotel for a surprisingly long time. Jim grumpily switched to Coke because he was driving. I had another few pints. Two of the elderly cousins, Oliver and Rory, turned out to be both good company and alarmingly accomplished whiskey-drinkers. I was amazed to learn, right before we left, that Rory wasn't the not-far-from-eighty I'd imagined him to be but ninety-frigging-six. He was an excellent advertisement for drinking and telling dirty jokes. When it was time to go, Eleanor, Aidan, and Miles walked us to the front door. As we said our goodbyes, Aidan marvelled that Jim was still driving the same old car and Miles solemnly picked his nose. I gave Eleanor an extra-long hug and whispered in her ear that she could call me any time, day or night. She still had that look about her, some combination of distraction and irritation. I decided to forget about it. If it was something serious, she would surely tell me soon enough. No point worrying in the meantime.

On the drive south, Jim had bided his time before surprising me about the dancing incident. The trip home was different. We hadn't even left the hotel car park before he slapped me on the thigh with the back of his hand. 'What the hell was going on with you today?'

I played dumb. 'What are you on about?'

'You! With the blubbing and the *poor Aidan.* You couldn't have picked Theresa out of a line-up and you can't stand Aidan.'

'Two serious exaggerations there,' I noted sourly. 'And thank you for your touching sympathy. Any other son seeing his old man in distress would be–'

'Da, don't even start. If you must know, I *was* concerned. What was getting to you?'

I made no reply. We eased out into the city traffic and started creeping along with it.

'Well?' Jim said. 'Are you going to–'

'If you must know,' I said, 'I thought it was all very sad. Nothing to do with Theresa herself, or Aidan. Just . . . very sad.'

'It was a funeral.'

'Correction: it was a poorly attended funeral.'

'And? Not everyone has a big social circle. Especially when they're older. No sisters or brothers either, so no extended family.'

'I know all that. I'm not saying there's people who should have been there but didn't bother their holes showing up. I'm saying, isn't it sad that a human being lives a whole life and when they get to the end of it, there aren't even three fucking rows' worth of people around to say goodbye?'

'Well . . .'

'And then there was the priest. Did you hear him?'

'He was a bit brief, I suppose. Sure maybe he didn't know the woman and–'

'Who cares if he knew her or not? And before you say it, who cares how quiet a life she'd had? That's what you get? A few sentences? Jesus Christ.'

I was getting worked up again, I could feel it. There was no air in the car all of a sudden. I cracked the window open and told myself to say no more on the subject.

'Well, you don't have to be a genius to work this one out, do you?' Jim said after a moment.

'Oh, you've got a theory, is that it?'

'I do.'

'Go on, so.'

'This is about getting old.'

The traffic stopped us entirely. I wound my window up again.

'Maybe,' I said. In fact, the same notion had occurred to me somewhere around my third pint. It also explained why I'd been so upset by the salsa dinosaur thing. You could also argue, I understood now with a barely contained gasp, that it accounted for my sudden interest in sorting out Jim's love life. More than one clock was ticking.

'There's no maybe about it. You're wondering what the priest will say at your funeral and what kind of a crowd you'll get. So it's not even about getting old, is it, really, it's about, y'know . . . death.'

'For fuck's sake, Jim.'

'What? You know I'm right.'

'It doesn't matter if you're *right*,' I told him. 'You don't have to say it *out loud*.'

He found that hilarious. I hadn't meant it to be.

10

'Eugene Duffy?' the receptionist barked, looking up from her keyboard. She sounded put-upon, almost angry, as if working in this doctor's surgery might be a decent enough gig if it wasn't for all the bloody patients.

'That's me,' I said, rising to my feet and, for some reason, waving.

She produced a small smile, or at least stopped frowning as hard. 'Dr McSharry's ready for you now.'

I thanked her and moved off down the little hallway that led from the waiting room to the doctor's office. When I heard 'Dr McSharry' I still thought of the old man, Donal. He'd been my doctor for decades. He was a tall, straight-backed man, always cheerful, always beautifully dressed. Impressive. Trustworthy. He'd been retired for years now. His son, Ciarán, had taken over in much the same way, I supposed, that Jim had taken over from me. I had nothing in particular against Ciarán. He was all right. But he wasn't Donal.

'Mr Duffy,' he said brightly when I tapped on the door and entered. 'Not a bad day out there, thank God.'

Even though every single time I'd seen him I'd told him to call me Eugene, as his father had always done, he insisted on the formality. My theory was that first-name terms are best in a job where you might have to rummage around in someone's ballsack.

'Not bad, no. Hello.'

'Please, sit, sit. What can I help you with?'

I sat. Dr McSharry – this one – was a round-shouldered blob of a man, like something you'd blow up with a foot-pump. He looked at me expectantly.

'I think I've got cancer,' I said and exhaled so hard the papers on his desk moved. 'I mean, I don't really think I've got cancer. But I have a thing, a skin thing, and it occurred to me that it *could* be cancer and even though I'm ninety-nine per cent sure it isn't, I keep thinking . . . it is.'

He nodded and smiled, as if this was exactly what he'd expected me to say. 'A skin thing, you say?'

'On my back. Well, my side. My side-back.'

'Could be worse. Could be on your backside.'

He was trying to keep it light, I knew. Talk me down from what was almost certainly an overreaction. Still, I didn't appreciate it. What if the worst turned out to be true? I'd spend the last few months of my life knowing it all started with an arse joke. I stared at him, stony-faced.

'Will we take a wee look?' he said, getting up and coming around the desk.

I leaned to my left and pulled up my shirt. 'Somewhere around there,' I said, waving my hand in the general vicinity of the problem.

He pulled on some rubber gloves and bent down to me. Poked around for a few seconds. 'Ah, yeah. Nothing to worry about there, Mr Duffy. That's called a seborrheic keratosis. Very common and completely harmless. I have three or four of them myself.'

'Right.'

'Is it causing you any discomfort? Sometimes they catch on clothing and what have you.'

'No.'

'You get them removed, you know, if–'

'It's fine. I noticed it and wondered, that's all.'

He snapped off the gloves and retreated to his own side of the desk. 'Anything else I can help you with?'

I hesitated. 'Um . . .'

'Mr Duffy?'

'Well . . . do you think I look . . . all right?'

He tilted his head. 'In what way, now?'

'Just . . . generally. You see me regularly enough. No . . . changes or anything?'

'You look fine to me.'

'Because, y'know, you bump into people and they say, *Have you seen so-and-so lately, he's shocking-looking.* And I always wonder if so-and-so himself knew he was shocking-looking or did he think he was plodding along as normal and–'

'Mr Duffy. Would you like me to give you a quick once-over?'

'Yes. Please.'

He did so. Took my blood pressure, listened to my chest, checked my weight, asked about my diet, my sleeping patterns. I could tell his heart wasn't in it. That was okay. My heart wasn't really in it either.

'You're as healthy as a horse,' he said when he was done.

'Right.'

'But sure you knew that, didn't you?'

'I suppose so.'

'Because you don't feel any different than normal.'

'Not really, no.'

I felt like a child caught out in a lie. He looked at me, tapping his pen against his notebook. 'Any idea what's behind this?'

I shrugged. 'Feeling old, I suppose.'

'Ah, now. You're in good shape. Very good shape, I would say. We could be having this same conversation twenty years from now.'

'And there's the problem.'

He squinted at me, puzzled. 'Where?'

'You're doing your best to cheer me up. You're imagining the best possible future, where I live way beyond the average. And even then, making every possible effort, you can only give me twenty years. You're a lot younger than me so maybe that sounds like a lot to you. Take it from me, twenty years is nothing. I remember what I was doing twenty years ago and it feels like last week.'

His hands came together, separated. Came together again. 'I'm not sure what I can do to make you feel better. You're not a young man any more, no. And death comes to us all in the end.'

'Yep.'

We looked at each other. I could tell that he was frustrated. He really wanted to help. I told him to give my regards to his father, and I left.

Half an hour later, I was sitting in a coffee shop, staring at an uneaten bun and feeling like a right gobshite. I could have thrown the guy a bone, I thought. I could have smiled and said, *Oh well, I'm sure I'll feel like myself again any day now.* It was plain rude, is what it was. Showing up in a doctor's surgery and leaving in a huff because there was nothing he could do about human mortality. I vowed to apologize next time I saw him.

It was a couple of days after Theresa's funeral. That morning, flailing around with a towel after my shower, I'd suddenly convinced myself that the bit of bumpy grey-brown skin I'd been living with for years was in fact skin cancer. This was it. I was on my way out.

'There is a problem?' said a concerned voice by my shoulder.

A waitress. She was pointing at the bun. I'd taken one tiny nibble. Hadn't even removed its casing. It looked as if a mouse had been at it.

'No. Not a thing.'

'Is fresh? Tastes okay?' She was Eastern European, I guessed.

'Honestly, it's fine. Changed my mind.'

'If you are sure?'

'I am.'

She smiled and left me to it. I watched her for a little while, gliding and twirling between tables. She was beautiful, I only now noticed. Twenty-two? Twenty-four, maybe? No more than that. There were men her own age, no doubt, who thought about her day and night. Night, especially. Groaning and rolling around in their sweaty beds. Choosing costumes. Imagining scenarios. It had been a long time since I'd lusted after anyone like her. Eyeing up young women was something that felt tacky after a certain point. In middle age, it became increasingly inappropriate, then shameful. Finally, mercifully, it became ridiculous and . . . stopped. Was that something that happened to all older men, I wondered, or was it just me? I sipped my tea and rephrased the question: was that something that happened to all older men or was there something wrong with me?

Once and once only, around the time when she got married, Eleanor asked me how come I'd never had a girlfriend in all the years since her mother left. We were alone in the kitchen. I was washing, she was drying. At first, I tried to laugh it off: why, did she have someone in mind? She didn't smile. She really wanted to know. What could I do? My only option was to tell the truth. I said I had no idea. She never asked again.

I covered my uneaten bun with a napkin, faintly embarrassed by my failure to eat it, and got up to leave.

It had been a strange day and walking home from the coffee shop, it got even stranger. As that old song had it, I stopped into a church I passed along the way. This wasn't a rarity for me – it was unprecedented. For one thing, I didn't believe in God. Smarter people than me had all sorts of carefully considered reasons for having no faith, I knew. I just thought it sounded like a load of bollocks – the story. The questions that plagued me were the same ones children had. If God made the universe, who made God? And if the answer to that was He didn't have to have a maker, then why did the universe? Either things needed makers or they didn't. You couldn't have it both ways. Also: God loves us like a parent loves his children but He'll burn us for eternity in a lake of fire if we don't suck up to Him enough? He narrowed down everything you need to know about morality to ten simple commandments, and half of them are reminders about how great He is? And so on. There were two ways to look at it. One was that these were silly questions. The other was that religion was so obviously a pile of old shite, even kids could see through it. I took the second view. I'd gone to Mass when Jim and Eleanor were small, of course. Everyone did in those days. But funerals, weddings and the like aside, I hadn't set foot in a church in thirty years.

St Joseph's was not the main attraction for Monaghan Catholics. That honour went to the grand cathedral that overlooked the town from the south. The cathedral was a jeroboam of fine champagne. St Joseph's was the house white. It was a small church, pleasant enough to look at, not at all fancy. Not showy. By its side, crouched like a pet dog, was the little hall where Annie gave her salsa lessons. I passed it regularly, never giving it much thought – never giving it *any* thought. Today, something gripped me as I went by. I didn't stop for a little ponder first. I didn't even slow down. I marched right in, as if this was where I'd always been going. The door swung behind me, paused, then shut tight with that rubbery sucking sound. I wondered if a priest would appear out of nowhere like an assistant in a shoe shop, asking what he could help me with today. For a minute or more, I stood there barely breathing, not daring to take a step, feeling like a trespasser. No one emerged. I had the place to myself.

Back in my mandatory Mass-going days, my favourite part of any church was the little bank of votive candles. It had nothing to do with their purpose. I liked the way they looked, all those delicate flames dancing when something disturbed the air. My heart sank when I saw that

St Joseph's had done away with the real thing at some point and replaced them with little battery-operated lights. Grim. No romance about them, no mystery. I started up the aisle towards the altar but the clicking of my shoes made me so self-conscious that I ducked into the third row and sat down, feeling large and awkward. The entrance to St Joseph's was right on the street, so the silence wasn't perfect. I could hear an occasional muffled laugh or shout, the muted hum of passing traffic. I found it pleasant and started to relax. Maybe this was the whole appeal, I thought. It wasn't about Mass or confession or communion or any of the other crap. It was about having access to a nice building where you could sit and think without anybody bugging you. But that made no sense. *I* was currently enjoying the peaceful atmosphere and I wasn't exactly Padre Pio. You didn't have to sign up for the whole thing to get that. No. The appeal was what I'd always thought it was: nobody wanted to be erased by death. They wanted to keep going. They wanted a sequel.

I'd been sitting there for ten minutes or so, still not sure what I was up to but not in any hurry to move, when I heard the door swish open behind me. I didn't turn around. It felt like the wrong thing to do – rude, somehow. When no one went by, I assumed the new arrival had taken a seat behind me. Then, from the corner of my eye, I saw a bent old woman creeping along at about the same rate fingernails grow. She was as silent as a ninja. When she drew level, she turned her head in my direction and nodded. I nodded back. About half an hour later – at least that was how it felt – she took a seat a few rows from the altar. There was no sitting in silent contemplation for this one. She (eventually) manoeuvred herself down on to her knees, clasped her hands together and got to work. It was possible, I supposed, that she was praying about something minor. A lost set of keys. A grandson doing his driving test. I doubted it. She was here for the main event. The please-let-me-live-forever thing.

After a few minutes, the door opened again. This time I did turn around, because I forgot you weren't supposed to. I recognized the new arrival, although I wasn't sure of his name. Michael something, maybe? An old man, naturally. He was much more sprightly than the old woman and fairly raced up the aisle, before sidling into the second row and getting to his knees. Whatever enjoyment I'd been getting from the experience was gone now. Having company, however far away, had ruined it. I went back to feeling like a trespasser and wondering what the hell had made me come in here in the first place. I'd no sooner decided to take my leave than the door opened a third time. There was a ruckus. I turned to see a schoolboy, maybe twelve years old, standing half inside and half out. Other youthful voices shrieked behind him. There was laughter, jostling.

'*Tiocfaidh ár lá!*' the boy roared, ducking outside again before he'd even finished the phrase. A child's dare. I assumed my companions would be outraged by this intervention. It wasn't easy to picture the old woman leaping into action but I could imagine Michael chasing the boys – or at least following them – down Park Street so he could give them a clip on the ear. Neither of them moved a muscle. Why? Was this sort of nonsense par for the course? Were they used to it? Or were they so deep in prayer that nothing could disturb them, like that Asian monk who set himself on fire for some reason? I had no idea. I also had no idea how shouting crap in a church could be fun for a kid, no matter how bored they were. Little shits. Laughing themselves sick on a corner somewhere now, I supposed. We were the 'three old people', no doubt, in their retelling. Not the two old people and the man who wasn't getting any younger. The three old people, sucking up to God every chance they got because they were going to be dead soon. I still didn't know what I'd gone looking for in there, but I knew I hadn't found it.

I got up and left.

11

'I always hated these fucking things,' Frank said. 'Too small, stupid colour. Weird smell off them, even now, never mind when we got them.'

He was talking about a pair of bedside lockers. I was carrying one, he had its partner. We were on the stairs of his house, heading for the skip out front.

'Stupid colour?' I said. 'They're brown. What's stupid about brown?'

'Stupid,' he insisted.

There was usually at least a glimmer of logic behind Frank's grievances. This was the third occasion today when I'd been unable to spot it. The first two had to do with a standard lamp ('sinister') and a weekend suitcase ('too suitcasey'). I'd queried both of those descriptions too but decided now that I'd keep my mouth shut in future. Frank was in a strange mood of his own. He'd sounded like his usual self when he called that morning, all bluster about having hired a 'big fucker of a skip' because the house was 'full of shite' before realizing the clear-out was a 'two-bastard job'. I said I had no problem being the second bastard and made some remark about not picturing him as the tidy-up type, let alone the clear-out type. He didn't even insult me back, which was troubling.

The lockers were heavier than they looked. I took no chances, working mine on to the lip of the skip and letting it drop in. Frank tried to show off. As soon as I was out of the way, he swung his back and launched it. He got the height and distance he was after but not the direction. The locker crashed on to the driveway, narrowly missing the neighbour's cat, who'd been hanging around all morning, despite Frank regularly advising it that it should piss off. Any other day, this would have been a gift. I would have got a good hour's worth of material out of it. Today I let it go. We picked the locker up together in silence and threw it over the high side of the skip to show it who was boss.

'Is your kettle broken or what?' I said then.

'Oh, right,' Frank nodded, taking the hint. 'Cuppa.'

'What's your criteria here, Frank?' I said when we were on our second cups. 'What stays and what goes, like. I'm not seeing much rhyme or reason to it.'

He shrugged. 'Just getting rid of a few things, that's all.'

'That armchair was in bits, fair enough. I didn't see much wrong with the standard lamp.'

'Never cared for it.'

'No?'

'Nah. One of Bernie's ideas. You know what she was like. A hard woman to talk out of things.'

A thought occurred to me. 'Anniversary must be coming up soon.'

'Last week. Ten years, if you can believe it.'

'Ah, Jesus. I'm sorry, Frank, I forgot.'

'Don't–'

'Did I miss the Mass and everything?'

'It was on Friday. Don't worry about it.'

'Fuckit anyway. I feel like a right prick.'

'It was only an anniversary Mass. A mention of her name, that was all.'

'Ten years, though.'

He tapped the table with a fingernail, looked away. Sat back. Sat forward again. 'Ten years. Yep.'

Another thought occurred to me. 'Is that what the clearout's about?'

He smiled sadly. 'I suppose it is.'

'Yeah. Round numbers get people thinking, don't they?'

'Not that I, y'know . . . not that I *decided*, right, that's ten years, time to dump a load of crap I never liked in the first place. I took a notion. That's all.'

He seemed embarrassed, which embarrassed me. 'I get it, Frank. It's not that you wanted to get rid of stuff. It's more like you realized you were hanging on to it for no good reason.'

'Yes! Yes. That's exactly it. I'm not doing something, I'm stopping doing something.'

'Nothing wrong with that. Not a damn thing.'

We nodded simultaneously. I slurped some tea. He looked out the window. 'The charity thing, though,' he said, turning back to me.

'I'm not following you.'

'When Bernie died, I gave her clothes away. Or her sisters did, at least. I couldn't bring myself to go through her wardrobe. And that was fine. Never cost me a thought. This time, I don't know, I feel different. I hated that standard lamp from the day she landed home with it and I'm delighted to see the back of it. But I don't want anyone else to have it. I want it gone *entirely*; out of use, smashed up in a dump somewhere. It and all the rest of the stuff. I can't explain it. Maybe that makes me a selfish prick. Anyway, that's how I feel.'

'It's your lamp, Frank. You can do whatever you like with it.'

'What do you think Bernie would have said?'

I pictured his late wife. She was a quiet wee woman, not good in large groups, not good at eye contact. Fairly religious by modern standards. Only fifty-four when she went. Cancer, as usual.

'I think she would have said it does no harm to give the place a bit of a freshen-up now and again.'

'You don't think she would have said it was a terrible waste to throw things in a skip when they could be doing someone some good?'

He wanted a no, obviously. I thought it better to take a leaf out of his own book and go with brutal honesty. 'All right, she probably would have, Frank. Yeah. I can hear her saying it, to tell you the truth, in those exact words. So what? You have to do what's right for you, now.'

'Maybe so,' he said and did the fingernail tap again. I didn't get the impression I'd helped even a little bit.

It was absolutely inevitable that we'd wind up in the pub. A quick one for the working men, we told ourselves.

'Christ, no,' Frank said when we were five pints in. 'I wouldn't do that. Jesus. No way.'

I'd been telling him about the salsa incident and Jim's

plan to go back again to apologize. I said I was thinking of joining him, both in the going and in the apologizing. 'Why not?'

'What the hell would you get out of it?'

'Well, I might feel better for one thing.'

'Nah. Forget about it. They probably can't even remember what you look like. Why would you remind them?'

'It was a horrible feeling, Frank, all those people looking at me and thinking I was a complete arsehole.'

'You'd think you'd be used to that sort of thing by now. A lifetime's experience and all.' He was feeling more like his normal self by now.

'The lady who ran it seemed very nice,' I said. 'Welcoming and that. She gave me this look at the end. All . . . disappointed. Like I'd really let her down.'

'So? You're not convincing me here, Eugene. You're not even getting close. I'm telling you, drop it. Let Jim go if he wants to. D'ye reckon he really cares about the apologizing?'

'As opposed to what?'

'You said he was dancing with the woman you picked out for him?'

I looked around nervously. 'Christ, don't say "picked out". I didn't pick her out. I just thought she was pleasant and . . . so on.'

'Well, maybe Jim did too. Maybe that's why he wants to go back.'

'Nah. Sure he was only dancing with her for thirty seconds. He's hardly in love or anything.'

'How do you know? You can't have been talking to her for all that long and you had the pair of them halfway down the aisle.'

106

I pulled on my pint, thinking. I'd been so caught up with my own guilt, I hadn't really thought about how strange it was that Jim wanted to go back and apologize for something he hadn't even done. It was downright weird. The idea that he might have decided he fancied Ruth in the seconds they spent together was at the very least no weirder.

'It's not impossible,' I allowed. I burped then and realized that I wasn't feeling fantastically steady. Frank seemed to notice that I was entertaining regrets.

'One more,' he put in quickly, 'for the road.'

'That was five,' I pointed out. 'Five's my limit these days.'

'We'll make it an even six,' Frank insisted. 'A solid half dozen.'

There was a wildness in his eyes. If we'd been on six, I knew, he would have said something about the seven days of the week or the seven deadly sins. If we'd been on seven, it would have been spiders or octaves. But I didn't argue. It wasn't often we went overboard like this. I got up and went to the bar.

'We'll go again, Pat,' I said to the barman with a sigh.

'You don't have to, you know,' he said, spotting my reluctance. 'I mean, we'll still be pals and all.'

I liked Pat. McDaid's ran through a lot of bar staff, most of whom seemed to be barely out of school. Tubby, middle-aged, monobrowed Pat was the one constant. He'd been there forever and didn't seem to have any intention of ever leaving.

'I should be delighted to have two more of your delicious pints of Guinness,' I said, trying again in – for some reason – an upper-class British accent.

He got to work on the drinks. While they settled, he returned to me and leaned closer. 'C'mere, Eugene,' he said.

'I wouldn't have you down as a particularly vain man. Would I be wrong?'

I was immediately suspicious. 'What's this about?'

Pat pretended to be offended. 'I'm only making conversation. There's no need to take a tone.'

'Pat . . .'

'Fair enough. We're doing a charity night for the Irish Cancer Society. Shave or Dye, if you ever heard of it?'

'Can't say I have.'

'Basically, you get people to sponsor you to shave your head bald or dye your hair a weird colour. It's a good laugh, good cause. We'll be shaving a few heads in here on the night and–'

'No way,' I said. 'Sorry. I've little enough hair as it is.'

'All the more reason to take part!'

'I'm not doing it, Pat. I'll sponsor all round me and I'll show up on the night and I'll cheer as loud as anyone, but no. No bloody way.'

He raised both hands. 'Grand, so. Asked and answered. If you think of anyone who might be up for it, send them my way, will you?'

'I will of course.'

'Good man.'

He went to top off the pints. I got the guilts. It wasn't vanity. I didn't give a damn about my appearance. It was the hassling people for sponsorship bit that made me cringe. I'd be hopeless at it, I knew I would. Although it pained me to admit it, I'd never been a good salesman in my own shop, always letting people feel perfectly comfortable with the cheapest options. I'd tried to tell myself that I was admirably honest, but that was bullshit. It was a sort of cowardice, and not something I was proud of. Jim was definitely an improvement on his old man in that regard. He had no problem telling people to spend a bit extra when it was warranted and no one thought any less of him for it. Two notions hit me more or less simultaneously. The first was that Jim would be a good lead for Pat. The second was that taking part in a charity event would be a great way to meet women.

'Are you expecting a big crowd for this head yoke?' I asked Pat as I exchanged cash for unnecessary alcohol.

'Haven't had one here before, Eugene. I know they did it in O'Gorman's last time and I believe the place was packed. Why, is that what's putting you off?'

'No, no. Just wondering.'

I grabbed the pints and my change. Back at our table, I gave Frank the gist of it.

'Won't work,' he said emphatically.

'Why not?'

'You have to be kind of a show-off to do that sort of thing. Your Jim's not a show-off.'

'It's for charity, though. He might not be a show-off, but he does enjoy a bit of martyrdom when the chance arises.'

Frank supped his pint, thinking. Then he shook his head. 'No. Still no. Shaving himself bald? Or dyeing his hair some mad colour? No way. Not Jim. I can't see it.'

'But—'

'And besides, even if he was up for it, what makes you think he'd be any more attractive to women with no hair or blue hair? Isn't he having enough trouble as it is?'

'It's not about looks,' I said primly, 'it's about image.'

Frank raised an eyebrow. 'You're very pleased with that line, aren't you?'

'I am, yes. And it's true. A man who's willing to make a tit of himself like that for charity is obviously a kind soul. Puts others first. Good sense of humour, too. Doesn't take himself seriously. Pat says there'll be a big crowd at this thing. Some of that crowd will be women. Some of those women will be single. Is it all that far-fetched to think that some of them might see the big picture here?'

'I know what you're getting at,' Frank said. 'It's still a shitty plan. Because he won't do it. He absolutely will not do it.'

He was almost certainly correct, I thought, but I didn't want to argue. I was tired and, surprisingly enough, the sixth pint wasn't making my head any clearer. 'Maybe it won't be necessary anyway,' I said. 'Maybe you're right and he's doing the dancing again so he can see your woman. Maybe they'll hit it off. Maybe they'll start going out.'

'Exactly,' Frank said.

'Although, that is an awful lot of maybes. I'll keep this charity thing in my back pocket.'

He looked at his pint, which was three-quarters gone. I gathered that his interest in the subject was at an end. 'Yeah, yeah, play it by ear. So, listen: will we make it a magnificent sev–'

'We will in our holes.'

12

On the morning of the Thursday when Jim was due to do his big scene at the salsa class, I decided to throw caution to the wind and tackle the big weekly shop. I normally did it on Fridays, but we were out of everyday basics – I'd had a harrowing experience with the last of the toilet roll – and I thought I might as well.

I almost turned back before I was halfway there. When I reversed out of the drive, a cyclist came out of nowhere and missed me by a coat of paint. Even though I'd only been inching out, I stood on the brakes like a man approaching a cliff downhill in a bus. Approximately four minutes later, I completely misjudged the speed of another car coming round a roundabout and crept forward when I had no business doing so. There was never any real danger of a collision, but the other driver, a young woman, flashed her lights and blared her horn and gave me a look that I will still be seeing on my deathbed. I drove the rest of the way to Tesco like I had a stack of plates on the roof. In a few years' time, I realized, near misses like these would have me wondering if I was getting too old to drive.

Even now, I could imagine how the cyclist and the young woman would tell the stories. *This oul lad in a Fiat Punto nearly killed me today. No business being on the road.*

My approach to the big shop was casual, to say the least. There was no list, no standard path through the store. I just wandered around, throwing things into the trolley if they took my fancy. Jim had come with me once or twice and was disgusted by this lack of strategy. My feeling was, shopping was boring enough without turning it into work. Besides, if you weren't tied to some rigid plan, who knew what strange new biscuits might come into your life? That morning, I took off in a random direction as usual, not heading to any particular aisle, not looking for any particular product. Twenty minutes later, I was standing by the shower gels, wondering why anyone would want to smell like a grapefruit, when I got the feeling that someone's eyes were on me. I glanced to my left and saw Annie, the salsa teacher. She flinched a wee bit, but didn't pretend that she hadn't been looking at me.

'I thought that was you,' she said, stepping closer. 'Annie, from salsa?'

'I remember,' I said. 'Believe me.'

'Was it . . . Eugene?'

'It was. Is.'

'Hi.'

'Hi.'

Once again she was dressed head to toe in black – trousers, jumper, wee short jacket – and was wearing huge silver earrings. Her hair wasn't as grey as I remembered it. More grey-streaked than anything. She seemed perfectly calm. I didn't get the impression that she planned to go for my throat.

'I hope everything was all right last week after the, eh, y'know . . . after we left.'

'We survived,' she said.

I put the grapefruit shower gel down. It wasn't helping. 'Listen, I would like to apologize again. Most sincerely.'

It came out a bit more formal than I'd meant it to, but I was sure I saw her posture soften.

'You weren't the one getting handsy,' she said carefully.

Further encouragement. I went all in. 'I wasn't, no. Still, I did try to smooth the thing over. Minimize it, like. I shouldn't have. I should have done what my son did, which was act mortified and push the stupid gobshite out the door.'

'Your son was . . . acting?'

My balls shot up into my abdomen. 'No! Christ, no! I didn't mean *act*, I meant—'

'It's all right.'

'—that, y'know, that sort of behaviour—'

'Eugene! I get it. I was pulling your leg.'

'Oh. Right.'

She studied my face. 'You're properly upset about this.'

'I have been, yeah. I don't like the idea of all those people thinking I'm some awful old git from the dark ages.'

This was a good opportunity for her to say they thought no such thing. She didn't take it.

'You're not so old,' she said after a pause.

'Turning seventy soon,' I mumbled. For a moment, I hoped she might faint in surprise or at least gasp and say I didn't look it. Once again, I was disappointed.

'Seventy's not so ancient,' she said. 'I'm not getting any younger meself. I choose not to think about it.'

'How . . . how do you manage that?' I'd been about to ask her how old she was. Caught myself at the last second.

'I drink a lot of gin.'

'Was that—'

'It was a joke, yes. Well, sort of. I do like the odd gin. So, are you going to give salsa dancing another go?'

This surprised me. 'Would you have me back?'

She bounced a finger on her chin, pretending to think it over. 'You'd have to wear a hair shirt for a while, but I think we could give you another chance, yeah.'

'Thank you. I do believe I'll stay away all the same.'

'Oh? Were you not enjoying it before the . . . incident happened?'

I considered my options. Was there any benefit to be had in telling her the real reason why I'd gone along in the first place? Maybe she'd lend a hand, try to steer Ruth, or any single woman for that matter, in Jim's direction? I decided against it. Apart from anything else, I thought I'd done a reasonable job on the apology front. If I told her I'd been there in my capacity as a pimp for my middle-aged son, I'd be back to square one.

'It's not that I wasn't enjoying it,' I said. 'I got the impression it's really more of a young people's thing. I should have known by the flyers.'

She rolled her eyes. 'Those bloody flyers. They weren't my idea. Philip came up with those. "We have to sex it up," he said. "Get the horny young ones in."'

I felt myself blush. 'That's your husband, is it?' I squeaked.

She giggled. 'No, no, I'm not married. Philip's the other instructor. My business partner, I suppose you'd call him. He's unbelievably gay.'

I lowered my voice. 'Are you allowed to say that? "Unbelievably gay"?'

'It's how he introduces himself a lot of the time! Or he'll shake someone's hand and say, "Hi, I'm Philip, I'm a giant homo." Just to shock people, you know.'

'Maybe I'll bump into him someday and give him the chance to shock me. But it won't be at salsa lessons, sorry.'

'Fair enough.'

'My son's going back, though. Tonight. To do more apologizing. I think he feels worse about it than I do.'

She squinted at me. 'Why? He was the only one who . . .' She paused and chose her words carefully. 'He has nothing to apologize for. Tell you the truth, people spoke very highly of him after you all left. The women especially.'

I almost levitated. 'Is that right?'

'Yeah . . .'

She still looked hesitant. I had no trouble guessing why. 'If you're worried about comparing him to me, don't be. I still want to hear it.'

'There was a bit of that, all right, to be honest. Talk about different generations, that sort of thing.'

'Go on. I can take it.'

'Well, the general consensus was that your son, uh . . .'

'Jim.'

'The general consensus was that Jim had played a blinder and that you . . . hadn't. The other lad, what was his name again?'

'Noel.'

'He barely got a mention.'

'Really?'

'Everyone was just glad he was gone. Anyway, Jim came

out of the whole thing smelling of roses. If he wants to come along tonight, he'd be very welcome.'

'I was about to say I'll tell him, but I won't. Don't want him getting a swelled head.'

'Okay. Well, I'd better get going. I'm glad I bumped into you, Eugene.'

She stuck her hand out. I shook it gingerly. Soft. Warm. 'Me too,' I said.

She turned and walked away in the direction of the detergents. I watched her go, feeling weirdly chuffed that she'd remembered my name but not Jim's or Noel's. So this Philip lad wasn't her husband, I mused. Nobody was. I thought about that, then thought about the fact that I'd thought about that. The marital status of casual acquaintances wasn't the sort of thing I usually pondered.

Pringles had been on the market for years before I so much as tried one. It was a point of principle with me. Someone somewhere had decided that if you made crisps all the same shape and stuck them in a tube, the world's extensive moron population would be more than happy to pay way over the odds for them. I found that offensive and kept faith with my Tayto Cheese & Onion, thank you very much. The first time I tried one was at Miles's second birthday party in Dublin. They'd been de-tubed into a bowl and caught me off guard. I grabbed, without thinking. Two seconds later, the boycott was over and my addiction had begun. By the time I got help, I was on three tubes a day. I say 'got help' – what actually happened was Jim told me to 'quit it with the fucking crumbs everywhere'. Although it wasn't the most sensitive of interventions, it snapped me out of it. I stayed away from the things entirely for years. In the past few months, however, I'd started dropping a tube – just one – into the big shop. I always told myself that it'd last me the full week and I always finished it within twenty-four hours. Or, sometimes, within one hour. I was playing with fire, but I told myself I'd be able to stop again any time I felt like it. That got harder to believe with every passing week and harder still on that Thursday night.

I told Jim about bumping into Annie as soon as he got in from work. He was glad I was feeling better about the whole business now but otherwise didn't seem to think it was worth discussing. I was disappointed by the conversational dead end, even though I had no idea what I wanted him to say. He disappeared upstairs after we ate and didn't reappear until it was time to leave, wearing the big-collared lemon-coloured shirt that he had more than once described as 'daring'. It was good that he was making an effort, I supposed. Still, there was no getting away from the fact that he looked like a presenter from children's telly in 1975. I wished him good luck with the apology and off he went.

Once alone, I found a documentary about the Aztecs on the telly but soon abandoned it in disgust. It was one of those ones with dramatic re-enactments. I'd always hated that shite. History, to me, was experts telling you what happened and showing whatever there was to be shown – a document here, a pot there. I had no interest in actors and scripts. Telly off, I looked around for something to read and settled on the Argos catalogue. I was out a fortune on razor blades and had been thinking of switching to electric. A simple enough prospect, you would think. There were fourteen pages of the things! Some of them cost a couple of hundred euros. All of them looked complicated. I came up in a world where a man chose between a normal razor and an electric one. The choice now was between normal razors that cost more to run than a car and fifty different types of electric, some of which had *screens*. I gave up and threw the catalogue aside, feeling itchy and irritated. Pringles time, I thought. Just a few, to take the edge off. I skipped off into the kitchen and plucked the tube from its hiding place under the sink. It lasted less than ten minutes, which was alarming, even by my standards. Nerves, I told myself, as I brushed the delicious dust from my lap. It was a stressful business, trying to marry your son off to the first woman who so much as looked at him. I buried the empty tube at the bottom of the kitchen bin, then returned to the sofa, where I planned to rest my eyes for a moment. Next thing I knew, Jim was leaning over me, shaking me by the shoulder.

'Da. Wake up. I'm back.'

'Fuck. What? Fuck.'

'It's eleven o'clock. You'll cock your back up, sleeping on the sofa.'

I rubbed my face and worked myself up into a sitting position. I'd drooled down my chin in my sleep, I noticed.

'How did it go?' I asked, disguising drool clearance as a chin scratch.

'Grand. It was grand. I'm knackered, going to hit the sack.'

'Wait, wait . . . What did you say? What did *they* say?'

'I didn't make a big speech or anything. Spoke to Cathy, the girl Noel grabbed, and Annie. Said I was sorry again and that I'd given Noel a very hard time since and that I think he's learned his lesson now.'

'Has he?'

'Has he fuck. I have given him a very hard time, though. That bit was true. He's half-afraid to come into work.'

'Right. Apology accepted I take it?'

'They couldn't have been nicer about it.'

'Did anyone, uh, mention me?'

'Yeah. Cathy said you made her feel physically sick. She's been having nightmares about you every night since. Can't understand how a fine man like me could have a—'

'All right, all right.'

'No. No one mentioned you.'

'Not even Annie?'

A shrug. 'She said she'd bumped into you. I said I'd heard.'

'Right.'

'All done with the questions now, Columbo?'

'Yeah. No, hang on a minute, you said it's *eleven*? Did you . . . stay?'

'I did, yeah.'

'For the lesson?'

'*Yes*, for Christ's sake.'

I squinted at him. 'I thought you were only going there to apologize.'

'Well, I stayed.'

'And? What did you think? Fun?'

'I enjoyed it, yeah. I'm going to go every week.'

A shot of adrenalin coursed through me. I felt like clapping. Cheering, even. 'Good for you,' I said in as bored a tone as I was able to fake.

He nodded firmly. 'Right. Bed. Goodnight.'

'See you tomorrow.'

He left. As soon as he did, I let in the grin that had

119

been knocking on the door of my face. There was no way in hell he had gone from being dragged to salsa lessons to having a terrible first experience to going every week all on his own. Something had happened. No doubt about it. My money was on Ruth.

Ruth had happened.

13

I kept a close eye on Jim over the next while and saw nothing to put me off my theory. Just the opposite. He was in great form practically all the time, cracking jokes and telling stories, not all of which had much of a point. It got to the stage where his chirpy rambling was almost as annoying as his more usual sarcastic arseholery. Things had improved at the shop, he mentioned over a cup of tea one night, because he'd told Noel he'd forgiven him, in the interests of harmony. I almost choked on a Penguin. 'Forgiven' and 'harmony' were not the sort of words Jim regularly reached for. The main thing, though, was the nights out. There weren't all that many of them, but there were more than the usual amount, which was none. When I asked him where he was going, he said he was meeting 'the boys'. That was clearly bullshit. There was no way their getting-togethers had gone from once in a blue moon to twice a week.

I didn't want to get ahead of myself, so I didn't call Eleanor right away. When his good mood stretched past the two-week mark, though, I decided to pick up the phone.

We ran through some basic chit-chat – she still sounded a bit flat, I thought – and then I hit her with the big news.

'C'mere,' I said casually, 'are you not going to congratulate me?'

'On what?'

'You haven't been talking to Jim?'

'No, why?'

I allowed a dramatic pause. 'Seems he has a girlfriend on the go. And where did he meet her? Salsa lessons. And who got him to go there? Your old dad, that's who.'

'Oh,' she said. 'Good.'

My smile froze. 'That's it? "Good"?'

'Well, what do you want me to say?'

'I thought you'd be a bit more excited, that's all.'

'No, no, that's great. Who is she?'

'I don't know. I have an idea. He hasn't actually said anything, as such. But it's obvious he's met–'

'Wait, he hasn't said who she is or he hasn't said he has a girlfriend?'

'He hasn't said . . . anything at all. You haven't seen him, though. He's going on nights out! He's buying new clothes! He keeps *smiling*, Eleanor.'

She made a noise. 'That doesn't sound like Jim, granted. But I wouldn't be picking out your wedding suit just yet. You could be imagining the whole thing.'

I could feel myself getting irritated. 'I could be imagining that he's not here some nights? Fine, then. I'll ask him.'

'Suit yourself.'

She couldn't wait to get off the phone. It was obvious. My irritation gave way to concern. 'Eleanor, is everything all right? You don't sound like yourself.'

'I'm fine. Bit tired is all.'

'Are you sure?'

'Sure.'

'All right then.'

We said our goodbyes and hung up. As phone calls went, it wasn't much of a success. I'd expected whooping and cheering, not to mention congratulations. All I got out of it was vague anxiety.

We watched a movie that night, Jim and me. Liam Neeson was in it. His daughter got kidnapped and he went buck mad over it. Killed all round him.

'That was complete rubbish, wasn't it?' Jim said when it was over. 'Brilliant all the same.'

'Load of old shite,' I agreed, stretching. 'Loved every minute.'

We smiled, saying nothing more for a minute, savouring Liam's terrible fury. 'Might have another cup of tea,' Jim said then. 'Do you want one?'

'Go on, so.'

He hauled himself upright and limped off, stiff-legged, to the kitchen. I hopped around the channels while he was gone, paying no attention at all to the talking heads, explosions, and cereal packets as they flickered by. This was as good a time as any, I told myself. Nice and casual. No need to make a big song and dance.

'Good man,' I said when he returned with the tea. 'So, listen. I have my suspicions about you.'

'Suspicions?'

I twinkled at him. 'Oh yes.'

'What kind of suspicions?'

'I think you know.'

He chuckled. 'I really don't.'

'I'll spit it out, so.'

'I think you should.'

'Have you got a girlfriend?'

The smile dropped off his face. He stared at me like I'd shot him. 'Is this the gay thing again?'

'What? No! I just, well, you seem pretty taken with the dancing, you're out and about more nights–'

'No.'

'No what?'

'No, I haven't got a girlfriend.'

'You haven't?'

'No. I don't know how else to say it. *No.*'

I looked away, at the telly, mortified. 'My mistake.'

'Sorry to disappoint you.'

'I'm not disappointed, I'm embarrassed. I put my foot in it again.' I braced myself. Whatever was coming, I deserved it.

'Don't worry about it. Already forgotten. Give us the thing there,' he said. I knew he meant the remote control and handed it over.

Almost immediately he settled on an old episode of *Star Trek*. Not Captain Kirk, the other lad. 'I used to love these,' he said.

I couldn't concentrate on the story (something about aliens with pipes sticking out of them who live in big square spaceships). How had I got this so wrong? Hope, I supposed. I'd hoped it was true so I'd believed it was true. By all accounts, he'd been in a good mood for no fucking reason. And was still in one, even now. He hadn't thrown any nasty comebacks at me. Wasn't even giving me the silent treatment. Chatting away about the spacemen.

'The special effects look brutal now,' he said at one point. 'But they had really good stories.'

'Hmm,' I said, not wanting to get into it on the grounds that I had no idea what was going on.

'Patrick Stewart, though. Some actor. Pure class.'

'That's him, is it?' I said, nodding at the screen where a bald man was explaining to someone his plan to outwit the pipe aliens.

'Jesus Christ, you don't know who Patrick Stewart is?'

'The name rings a bell. I don't know *exactly* who he is.'

'Fuck me. Captain Picard's one of the most famous characters in television history.'

'If you say so.'

We watched in silence for a while. And as we did so, a window opened in my mind. If I played my cards right, I could bounce back right away.

'Suits the baldy look, doesn't he?' I said a moment later. 'Fair play to him.'

'I don't think he had a choice in the matter, Da.'

'Probably not. Y'know, I was talking to Pat in McDaid's a while back. They're doing some sort of charity event where fellas shave their heads or dye their hair a funny–'

'Shave or Dye.'

'That was it.'

'That's a big thing. They do it all over the country. Cancer research, I think.'

'Pat thought I might be up for it. Imagine that.'

Jim gave it real thought for a moment. 'You never know. Might look good on you. Not the dye option now, the shaving.'

I waited for his mocking laughter. It didn't come. 'I don't think so,' I said uncertainly.

'Why not? Sure you've hardly any hair on top as it is. No big loss.'

'I don't—'

'Not that I can talk. I'm afraid to run a comb through it these days. Getting thinner every day.'

'That's—'

'Tell you the truth, there's been days lately when I think of taking it all off meself. I picture Picard there, or Sean Connery, and I'm all over the idea. I always talk myself down. I wouldn't look like Sean Connery. I'd look like an egg with a face drawn on it.'

I was almost afraid to say anything. He was doing a bloody good job of talking himself into it without any help from me. But now it seemed that he'd stalled. I connected the final few dots.

'Hey, here's an idea. Why don't you do the charity thing? Perfect excuse. You'd get to find out if it looked all right and no one could laugh at you if it doesn't because you'd be doing it for a good cause. And you really would be doing it for a good cause! Win-win-win.'

He turned to me at once. 'This isn't the stupidest idea you've ever had.'

'Stop. I'll be getting a big head.'

His expression darkened. 'I'd have to get sponsors, though, wouldn't I?'

'That's kind of the point, yes. And you're very late starting. But sure you have a shop, haven't you? Hit the customers up. God knows enough people come into you looking for sponsorship money.'

'That's true.'

I sensed that he was ninety-nine per cent there. Pushing any further could only fuck the whole thing up.

126

'Oh, your man's Irish!' I said, pointing at the telly.

'Colm Meaney,' Jim said absently. He tapped his fingertips together on his belly. Sighed. Tapped some more. 'You know what? I'm gonna do it.'

'The shaving thing?'

I made myself take a breath. Casual, Eugene. Keep it casual. 'Sure, why not? I'll definitely sponsor you. What do I know Colm Meaney from? It's driving me mad.'

'He does those Roddy Doyle ones. *The Snapper* and that.'

'That's it. I knew I knew him from something.'

I yawned for good measure. It was an amazing performance, if I say so myself.

14

Once in a while, McDaid's played host to a musical act. Some unreliable-looking character with an electronic keyboard or guitar, possibly accompanied by a second unreliable-looking character with a guitar or electronic keyboard, would set up at one end of the pub and play bad versions of *Bridge Over Troubled Water* and *Dirty Old Town*. Why they bothered, I had no idea. It never went down well. On one occasion, a particularly poor performer was halfway through butchering *Danny Boy* when a black shoe came sailing through the air and clocked him on the forehead. (It had been launched by Niall Boyle, a famously venomous old coot, for whom the song held special memories.) That was an extreme case, to be fair, but even at the best of times, the clientele leaned towards the view that live music was a distraction from the serious business of drinking and telling lies. There wasn't even a proper stage for these musical acts. That end of the pub was a little wider and more open than anywhere else, that was all. It was here, in any case, that Pat had set up for the Shave or Dye show.

Just as he had predicted, the place was stuffed, and by a much younger than usual crowd. Although seats were available, if you took one you were doomed to spend the evening staring at the small of someone's back. I stood at the side, near the bar, with Frank. There wasn't a single moment when I wasn't in direct physical contact with at least two other people. It was a warm, sticky night and we were all gasping for air. Every couple of minutes a little stream of sweat ran down my back, tickling me, before making its way to the crack of my arse. Comfortable it was not. The dye-jobs were gathered together at the front of the crowd. There were about a dozen of them, men and women. Pink was the most popular colour. There were a few greens. One each of blue, orange and fire-engine red. They were an attraction, for sure, but they were not the stars of the show. That honour went to the five shavees who faced us in a row, perched on bar stools, nervously clutching their drinks. All five were male, which was hardly a surprise.

'I know that fucker on the end there,' Frank said, his lips disturbingly close to my ear. 'He was in the bakery one time complaining about a cake.' He meant his daughter's bakery, which he alone was allowed to criticize.

'Oh yeah?'

'*Bake Off.*' He spat the words. I felt the spittle. 'That's what I blame. Every other prick thinks they're an expert now. "Too dense," he says. Paul fucking Hollywood.'

I looked at the man he was talking about. He was a short fat guy in his thirties. Judging by the goofy expression on his face and the hopeless attempt he was making to converse with someone at the very back of the crowd, the pint he was holding was not his first of the evening.

'WHAT?' he kept shouting, apparently surprised by the limitations of physics. Beside him was a young lad of, I guessed, barely twenty. He seemed desperately unhappy. A few of his pals had pushed their way to the front, right behind the dye-job people. *They* were having the time of their lives. As I watched, one of them squeezed out of the crowd and said something in his ear. Whatever it was, it caused his head to sink even lower and his friends to laugh all the harder. Next to him, in the middle of the row, was Jim. To his credit, he looked unruffled, and not only by comparison with his young neighbour. He was chatting happily to one of the pink hairs and didn't seem to have a care in the world. The guy on his left looked even less bothered. What he looked, in fact, was delighted. He was about Jim's age and I would have bet the house he'd had the same idea – that his hair was on its way out anyway, so he might as well get it over with. Although he had plenty on the sides and back (where he'd grown it a bit longer, in compensation), he was in awful trouble on top. Thin, wispy strands had been scraped back and cemented in place with Brylcreem or some other oily gunk. Here and there, pink scalp shone through under the extra lighting Pat had installed for the occasion. It wasn't a hairdo you'd be sad to see go.

The last of the five was another thirty-something. He had a ponytail, and not the basic model. This one was the result of serious commitment. It was draped proudly over his right shoulder and almost reached down to his belt. Of the five men on stage (as such), he was getting the most attention from the crowd. I caught myself thinking that wasn't fair. So what if the hair he was about to lose was long and full? For all we knew, he'd been in the same boat as Jim and pink-scalp guy – on the verge of lopping the whole lot off anyway. I quickly copped myself on. Regardless of how attached they were or were not to their current hair situation, all of these men were making a major effort for charity, and that was admirable. Jim hadn't just relied on shop customers and acquaintances, either. He'd gone door to door over the past couple of weeks, asking complete strangers to sponsor him. None of them had turned out to be single women who fell madly in love with his kind-hearted nature, but still. I felt proud of him. And hopeful too. He was literally in front of a crowd under a spotlight. It was as good an ad as he was going to get.

Frank poked me in the ribs with his elbow. 'Who's doing the presenting bit, do you know?'

'What do you mean?'

'There's usually some class of a celebrity at this sort of thing, isn't there? Not a real celebrity, now, one of those shitty local ones. A radio DJ or that ginger bollocks with the guitar.'

'Who?'

'The singer. With the guitar! Country and western. Looks about fourteen. Goes on about riding the rails and his drunken ol' daddy living in a trailer and the sweetheart he left in El Paso. He's from fucking Carrickmacross.'

'Can't say I know him.'

'You do. Ginger! With the guitar! Looks–'

He was interrupted, thank God, by the appearance of Pat the barman, microphone in hand. 'There's your answer,' I said. 'Pat's doing it.'

'Shite,' said Frank, disappointed.

Pat tapped his microphone and asked for a bit of order. To my surprise – amazement, really – he made a pretty decent MC. He ran through the thank-you-all-for-comings and the very-good-reason-we're-heres without stutter or hesitation and, better yet, at speed. When he was done, the dye-jobs got to parade themselves and talk a bit about their new lives as fake weirdos. There were a few laughs, but most of it boiled down to, 'My hair used to be a normal colour and now it's a funny colour'. And then, before anyone had time to start looking at their phone, we were on to the main event.

'Now,' Pat said, staring ominously down the row of seated men. 'Would anyone like to see these lads getting their heads shaved?'

There was a lot of hooting and hollering, which Pat encouraged by wafting his arms towards the ceiling. He went left to right, starting with the fat drunk guy.

'Good evening,' he said. 'Tell us your name.'

The drunk cheered and raised his pint in response. Even though it was half empty, he still managed to spill a good bit of it on to his own lap. Laughter all round.

'That's your name?' Pat deadpanned, and got a big laugh of his own.

'Dan!' the man said, sounding very excited about it. 'Dan McGuire.'

Another cheer. Another raising of his glass. No spills this time.

'And how are you feeling? Nervous?'

'Me? Naw. Sure it's only hair.'

This won him some applause which, in turn, prompted another pint raise and cheer combo.

Personally, I thought that was getting old. Everyone else seemed to love it.

'Will you suit the bald look, do you reckon?' Pat asked.

Dan put his lips right on the microphone. 'There's not a damn thing you could do to make me any less sexy.'

That got the biggest reaction yet from the audience. He ruined it immediately by grabbing his crotch. There was a clearly audible 'Ewww' from a lot of the women present. Pat grimaced and moved along to the sad youth.

'Hello, hello! First of all, are you sure you're old enough to be in here?'

The lad smiled weakly. 'Ha.'

'What's your name?'

'Greg.'

'No surname, no?'

'McMahon.'

'And how old are you, Greg, seriously?'

A deep sigh. 'Nineteen.'

Pat glanced towards the crowd, eyebrow raised, like an old pro. 'Would I be right in saying you're not really looking forward to this?'

Greg looked at him with real anxiety on his face. 'Not particularly. No.'

His voice was small and weak. Everyone present seemed to notice at once that he wasn't kidding around, wasn't playing a role. He really wished he hadn't signed up for this. It got as close to quiet as a stuffed-full pub could get. I found myself leaning forward. This was a real test for Pat. He placed a fatherly hand on Greg's shoulder. 'Well,' he breathed into the microphone as he moved away towards Jim, 'it's too late now, so tough shit.'

The whole place went nuts. It felt a bit cruel for a moment, but then even Greg smiled, albeit with a defeated shake of his head. There was so much cheering and clapping that Pat had to give it a moment to subside.

'Jim's next,' Frank roared into my ear, apparently working on the assumption that I'd gone blind.

'*You're* not having second thoughts, are you?' Pat said in a mock-serious tone of voice.

'No,' Jim said. 'I'm not, eh, not having second thoughts. Still, y'know . . . up for it.'

He didn't smile until he'd finished speaking and then did it so suddenly that it looked downright chilling. I winced.

'Give us your name, like a good man,' Pat said.

'Jim. Duffy.'

'And what do you think will be the best thing about being bald, Jim?'

'I've been thinking about this, actually,' he said brightly. 'And the big advantage, I bet, will be that you don't have to care about your hair any more. One less thing to worry about.'

A fucking terrible answer, I thought. It was a chance to say something hilarious or outrageous and he'd taken the question literally. I could almost feel the crowd deciding he was a dry shite. I was angry at him for a moment and had to force myself back to proud.

'Until it grows back,' Pat said, groping for banter. 'You'll be back worrying then.'

'I might stick with it,' Jim said with a shrug. 'Depending on how it looks, of course.'

This was even worse. It was like eavesdropping on two blokes waiting for a bus. Pat cut his losses. He wished Jim good luck and moved on to the fourth guy.

'Christ,' I muttered under my breath. I glanced to my right, into the crowd, and froze. On the far side of the room, squeezed right against the wall, deep in shadow, was a woman who looked an awful lot like Annie. I stared, waiting for the right partings in the crowd, until I made sure. It was her all right. I stared some more. She was talking, every so often, to a middle-aged man in glasses. A friend? A boyfriend? A brother? Her partner in the dance business, what was his name – Philip?

'What are you looking at?' Frank shouted, his lips right against my ear.

'Nothing. Nothing.'

I turned my attention to Pat again. Predictably enough, he was getting great craic out of the fourth lad's hair issues. The whole place was in uproar. I tried, but I couldn't pay attention. My eyes drifted right again. Should I try to talk to her? I wondered. What the hell would I even say? And how would I engineer it? I'd look like a right dick if I just wandered up to her . . . wouldn't I?

'Oh!' Frank cried, laughing. 'Best line of the night there.'

'Yeah!' I agreed, having no idea what had been said.

'Best contestant so far. Miles better than Jim, anyway.'

'They're not contestants, Frank. It's not a competition.'

'Whatever.'

Pat was moving on now. There was huge applause for number four, whose name I'd missed.

'And finally,' he said, 'we have a man who clearly has a lot more to lose than some people I could mention.' More laughs. 'What's your name, my friend?'

'Stephen Mullen,' said the ponytail guy.

'And when was the last time you had a haircut, Stephen?'

'I'd get the odd trim, Pat, every few months. But if you're asking how long I've had hair like this, it's getting on for twenty years.'

This won him a sustained 'Oooh' from the crowd, which

was fair enough. They went back and forth for a while about the shock that Stephen was soon to receive. Nothing particularly funny was said and I sensed growing impatience in the room. Pat must have felt it too. He cut Stephen off, more or less mid-sentence.

'Listen, we could flap our gums about this all night, but there's head-shaving to be done. Will we get going?'

That idea got a huge roar of approval. There was a real hairdresser for each of the volunteers, it turned out, and their entry was loud and messy. It seemed to take several minutes for them to make their way to the front and then arrange themselves behind their guys, clippers and razors at the ready. Pat made some introductions – three women, two men, all from the town – and then we were off. I'd been worried that they might go one at a time and was relieved to see that all five heads were tackled simultaneously.

As soon as the work began, with the tucking in of bright red plastic gowns, the atmosphere in the room changed in a way that I found a wee bit scary. Suddenly, there was a sort of ferocity to the cheers and shouts. It made me think of a revolutionary crowd watching a royal family being hung. I looked around, half-expecting to see people slavering at the mouth. The first hairdresser to finish the clipping stage was the woman doing Jim, as it happened. She can't have been at it for more than thirty seconds. It was a nice change for her not to have to be careful, I supposed. When she was done, she patted his stubbled dome and leaned around to smile at him. He smiled back, worked a hand out from under the gown, and felt around a bit himself, at which point the smile died. I lip-read an unmistakable 'Jesus Christ' and clenched my jaw, afraid that he was horrified. Then he broke into a fit of the giggles. This, curiously, was how they all reacted, once shorn. There were no brave faces, no pantomime panics – giggles all round. Even Greg, the miserable teenager, joined in. The man who cut Stephen's ponytail off tossed it into the crowd, causing half a dozen people to jump aside – or try to at least – as if it were a snake.

'So far, so good,' Pat said. 'But we're not there yet. This is just short hair. We want to see those scalps!'

Someone started a chant, which was immediately taken up. 'SCALPS! SCALPS! SCALPS!' I felt queasy again. If someone was to say they'd changed their mind and didn't want to go through with it, I could see them being chased down the street and beaten. No one did. All five sat perfectly still – giggling no more – as their heads were covered in shaving foam. The hairdressers took a lot more care on this stage, as you might expect, swiping their razors in short, deliberate strokes and rinsing them in pint glasses of water. The room grew a little quieter at first, but normal levels of hooting and roaring were soon restored. A couple of noisy minutes went by. And then, one by one, the hairdressers put down their razors, cleaned away the last of the shaving foam, and removed the gown with a matador's flourish. Each of the five volunteers stood when he was done and – to a man – ran his hands over his skull, eyes wide. Pat produced a hand mirror and handed it to Dan.

'Well? What's the verdict?'

Dan squinted at his new reality. 'It's . . . not great, is it? Ah sure, lookit, it's only hair.'

'That's the spirit,' Pat said and gestured for him to pass the mirror along. 'What about you, Greg?

The teenager stared at his reflection. Having started to

enjoy himself a bit, he went back to looking crushed. 'Fuck me,' he said quietly, not at all trying to be funny, and thrust the mirror at Jim.

I had already formed my own opinion about how Jim looked. It was this: he looked okay. That is, he hadn't suddenly been transformed into an Adonis but he didn't look ridiculous either. He looked like Jim with no hair.

'Oh, wow,' he said when he saw for himself. 'That's, eh . . . Well, it could be worse. Could be a lot worse.'

I took this to mean that he was delighted. That was good. Confidence was good. Maybe there was some woman in the crowd right now, giving him a second once-over and deciding–

'Hello there.'

I turned. It was Annie. 'Oh!' I yelped.

'How are you, Eugene?'

'Grand, grand. I'm grand. Grand. Eh . . . yourself?'

'Never better. Well, I'm a bit bruised. I set out for the bar about five minutes ago. Could have done with a machete.'

'It's packed in here, all right. Did you come in specially for this? Don't think I've seen you in here before.'

We had to raise our voices quite a bit to make ourselves heard. I hoped I wasn't spitting on her as Frank had spat on me. She was so close. Our hips were touching. She smelled of vanilla.

'I'm not a regular, no, but we heard this was on, thought it'd be a laugh. Me and Philip, that is.'

'I'm Frank,' shouted Frank, sticking his head over my shoulder.

'Yeah, this is Frank,' I said, not quite hiding my irritation. 'Annie's the poor woman trying to teach our Jim to dance.'

'Nice to meet you,' said Annie. 'I see he's up there, Eugene. Fair play to him.'

We all glanced to the stage, where Pat was telling the fourth guy that he didn't look any different. Jim was enjoying that greatly.

'He's a good lad,' I said. 'Heart's in the right place even if his hair no longer is.'

Annie chuckled. I found myself banking the moment to be savoured later. 'I think he suits it,' she said. 'Or at least, he doesn't not suit it.'

I nodded with enthusiasm. 'That's exactly what I–'

'He looks like a massive baby, if you ask me,' Frank yelled. 'Sooner he grows it back, the better.'

'The thing is, though, no one did ask you,' I said, even more loudly than I needed to. This won me another laugh from Annie, a nasal snort this time. She looked away, embarrassed.

'Anyway,' she said. 'I'd better get these drinks in. Philip will think I've gone home.'

Several lines popped into my head, all of them delivered in a 1940s movie star sort of tone. *Well, allow me to . . . I must insist that . . . If you will permit me to . . . It would be my pleasure to . . .* None of them made it to my mouth, which was probably for the best.

'Okay,' I said feebly. 'Nice to see you again.'

'You too, Eugene. Frank. Tell Jim I said well done.'

'I will.'

She moved away and squeezed into a space further down the bar. I returned my attention to Pat, who had moved on to Stephen, the last of the five.

'Elegant woman,' Frank said, instantly dragging me back.

'Excuse me?'

'I said, she's very elegant. That woman. The way she carries herself, the way she's dressed. The black and white gear. Stylish.'

This was a staggering development. Frank almost never had anything to say about the opposite sex. Even when he did – once in a blue moon, when horribly drunk – he expressed his admiration using words that somehow managed to be both crude and old-fashioned, like 'chesty'.

'Elegant?' I squawked. 'When did you start finding women elegant?'

'Well, what would you call her?'

'I wouldn't call her anything, Frank.'

'What are you so mad about?'

'I'm not mad.'

'You are, look at you! Your face is all scrunched up.'

'No, it isn't.'

'It is, you're all–'

'Look, they're finishing.'

Pat had said whatever he had to say to number five and was facing the crowd again. 'Ladies and gentlemen, that's the end of our show. Can we hear your appreciation, please, for our hair engineers and, more importantly still, for our brave volunteers?' He paused as a roar went up. 'And if you didn't get a chance to sponsor any of these eejits, don't worry, we have collection buckets all over the place, so don't be afraid to dig deep for a great cause. One very last thing . . .' He stepped to the side and retrieved a Dunnes Stores bag. 'Lads, just a small token of our thanks from the gang here at the pub. Something you might appreciate over the next few weeks at least.'

He walked down the line distributing flat caps, to

universal delight. The five volunteers put them on and, at Pat's insistence, took a bow.

'I know it's a joke,' Frank declared, 'but you should have a word in Jim's ear, tell him it wouldn't be such a terrible idea. Maybe not that specific cap, but something.'

'I certainly will not,' I sniffed. 'I think he looks great.'

'Are you joking? I mean, fair play to him and all–'

'Shut up, Frank.'

I cobbled together a smile to show I was joking. Too late. He had heard 'Shut up, Frank' the way I'd really meant it, which was 'Shut up, Frank.'

We said nothing else to each other until Jim arrived. That took a while. A couple of his old pals, Smokey and Mick, had shown up in support. He chatted to them for a few minutes before pushing his way through to us at the bar.

'Well?' he said, removing his cap. 'What do you think?'

I was less impressed now that he was up close. His head seemed impossibly shiny, like a snooker ball. I wasn't about to say that. 'I like it,' I told him. 'Honestly.'

'It'll grow back,' Frank said. 'That's the main thing.'

Jim ducked down. 'Feel it. So weird. It feels like sliced ham.'

I gave the top of his head a quick stroke and couldn't help but pull a face. 'You're not wrong there,' I said.

'Pat was good, wasn't he?'

'He was. You did very well yourself, fair play to you. So, what's the plan now? Going to do a bit of mingling, maybe?'

'Mingling?'

'Meet your adoring public, like.'

He glanced briefly at Frank, eyebrow aloft. 'All right,

all right, you can just say you don't want to be seen with me. You don't have to make shit up.'

'I didn't–'

'Mingling! I've never mingled in me life.'

All I could do was smile, roll my eyes, and drop it. I didn't trust Frank not to say something incriminating if I pushed it too far. I didn't trust myself, for that matter.

'Your dancing teacher's in here somewhere,' Frank said.

'Is she?'

'Yeah. Very elegant woman.'

'You think so?'

'That's twice he's said that,' I put in, trying to sound amused.

Jim nodded slowly. 'Smitten, are we, Frank? I could put a word in for you next time I see her.'

'Ah, fuck off,' Frank said, but he wasn't irritated. Not a bit of it. He was enjoying this. I regretted having contributed.

'Mind you,' Jim went on, 'I think she might be a bit young for you. She wouldn't be much over fifty. Might as well be a teenager to someone in their late eighties like you.'

Frank jabbed him playfully in the chest with his index finger. 'I'm sixty-seven, ye cheeky bastard. Not even as old as your da.'

'Yeah, but Da isn't *smitten*, is he?'

There was a horrible moment when I almost objected. I took a drink, hiding behind my pint until I was sure the danger had passed.

'Right,' Jim said then. 'I'm going to have a few with the boys. Are you two staying around or–'

'I'm going to hit the road,' I said. This wasn't something

I'd been thinking about. I found out at the same time everyone else did, when I heard the words.

Frank rounded on me. 'What? You're leaving me on me own?'

'I've a brutal headache,' I lied. 'The noise, maybe. The heat.'

'Oh.' He looked like a puppy abandoned on a motorway three days after Christmas.

'You could join us,' Jim said, obviously just being polite.

'Ah, good man,' Frank said. 'There's hope for the Duffy family yet.'

Jim looked to me, pleadingly. His politeness had cost him dearly. I did my best to shrug using only my eyes.

'You kids have fun,' I said. 'I'm off.'

I drained my pint, clapped Jim on the shoulder, and left them to it. Although the crowd had thinned a bit already, it still took me quite a while to push my way to the exit. By the time I made it outside to the blessed air, I was ready to do murder. I didn't walk home, I stomped. Had I really thought that some woman was going to fall for him there and then just because he raised a few quid for charity and wasn't noticeably vain? And what had made me think he would *mingle*, for fuck's sake? Jim wasn't a mingler! He couldn't mingle if his life depended on it. And besides, who mingles in a pub? Madness. The whole escapade had been a complete waste of time.

It wasn't until hours later that I finally admitted to myself what was really bothering me. The admission didn't make me feel any better. I lay there in bed, wide awake, fuming, like a fourteen-year-old. I couldn't even say the words in my head without cringing. But there was no getting away from it. I hadn't left the pub early and marched home in a funk, cursing everything and everyone, because of Jim. I'd done it because of Frank.

He liked Annie. And I liked Annie.

15

After Una left, I was overrun with this weird sensation that almost never left me. I felt like I was driving the kids in something fast and expensive. It had no brakes and the steering only sort of worked. No matter what I did or how lucky I was, sooner or later there was going to be a crash. In the end, I kept the thing on the road for a little over twelve months. My luck ran out in the summer of 1995.

The Leaving Certificate year is tough on any teenager. Eleanor had just seen her mother walk out with no notice and barely a glance over her shoulder. I would have understood entirely if she'd said to hell with school and sat in her room crying for the duration. But no. She never missed a day, worked her arse off, and went into the exams with a level of confidence that wasn't far from frightening. After each one, I'd ask her how it went and she'd say, 'I did very well.' Not *It was fine* or *We'll see* or *Who knows?* She wasn't normally so sure of herself. I started to worry that being abandoned by her mother had made her delusional. When the results arrived and we saw that she'd waltzed into her first-choice university course, I was more relieved about her current mental health than her future prospects. She'd be off to Dublin in September to study Business and Law at UCD. I tried not to let her see how saddened I was by the thought of watching her go and concentrated on joining in with her excitement.

Not long after we got the results, we were all slumped in front of the telly one evening when the phone rang. Jim sprang up to answer it. He was sixteen then and had his first real girlfriend, Claire. It had been going on for a surprisingly long time. Six months or more. Ninety per cent of the calls we received were from her. This one wasn't, he announced with disgust. This one was for Eleanor. Seconds after she got up to take it, I heard her shriek and leapt to my feet. In the hall, I found her slumped against the front door with one hand over her mouth. The other, clamping the phone to her ear, was white-knuckled and trembling. There were tears. When I moved towards her, she waved me away, shaking her head. I tiptoed back to Jim. Eleanor joined us a few minutes later. For all of secondary school and much of primary, she'd had two best friends, Jenny and Orla. The phone call had come from the former. The latter's mother was dead. Got up to make a cup of tea that afternoon, apparently, took two steps, and dropped like a sack of sand off the back of a truck (the cause, the coroner later revealed, was a brain haemorrhage). I knew the woman well, of course. Our daughters were like sisters. Pauline was perhaps the most talkative human being I had ever met. When you bumped into her, you got as far as, 'Hello, P–' and she was off, complaining about the weather, lambasting the current government, insisting you watch some great new programme on the telly. No one ever got a word in, and no one minded.

Pauline wasn't a bore. She was warm and funny and you left her feeling like you'd been at a show. My first ridiculous reaction, as Eleanor croaked through the few details she knew, was that being dead wouldn't suit her. My second wasn't so much a conscious thought as a feeling of non-specific dread. It was like hearing a distant rumble of thunder. Orla's mother was dead. Eleanor's mother wasn't, but she might as well have been. She was undead. A zombie. Comparisons might be drawn. This proved to be one of my sharper predictions.

Meals had been tough since Una left. A large part of the reason was that I had the cooking skills of a child. I was comfortable enough with toast and considered myself to have done exceptionally well if I successfully boiled an egg. Anything that involved more than one ingredient was beyond me. It took me a long time to get even a little bit better and when I did, we were still left with the more serious problem. The emotional one. For most of the day, we could go about our individual business and pretend that nothing much had changed. When we sat down together for a meal, however, there was no getting away from the fact that one of our chairs was vacant. Time and time again, I caught Jim or Eleanor or both of them stealing glances at the empty space with puzzled expressions on their faces, as if they were sure their mother was there but couldn't quite see her at that particular moment. There were silences like the Gobi desert. Although I got very good at filling them with random gibbering (much better than I ever got at cooking), there were occasions when I just wasn't up to the job.

One of these was a Sunday evening a couple of weeks after Pauline passed away. Jim was in bad form because

Claire had spent the day with her family instead of him, and he had banged every door in the house to prove it. Eleanor had been out with pals and hadn't said two words since she arrived home. We sat down to overcooked pasta with a spoonful of pesto stirred through it (one of my staples), none of us, I suppose, particularly relishing the prospect. Jim stabbed angrily at his bows. Eleanor pushed hers around the plate. I couldn't think of a thing to say and the other two looked like they had no intention of trying. Jim coughed at one point and we all jumped as if someone had fired a gun. I'd watched *Casablanca* that afternoon and decided that the best way to get through this was to recap the whole movie, scene by scene. This was a tactic I'd reached for once or twice in the past when things were particularly bad. I never kidded myself that Jim and Eleanor were glad to hear my crappy summaries, but I could tell they liked the result, which was to fill the awful silence. I hadn't got very far into it – we hadn't even met Rick yet – when Eleanor suddenly pushed her chair away from the table and glared at me like she was ready to do murder. Before I could speak, she got up and left the room. The muffled thumps of her stair-stomps seemed impossibly fast, like she had somehow grown extra legs. I braced myself for an epic door slam, and she didn't disappoint. Cups rattled in the kitchen cupboard. The light fixture shuddered. I knew from her earlier teenage years that there was no point in making an immediate approach. That would only lead to screaming (her) and aggravation (me). She would talk to me at some point, but not if I pushed it. I asked Jim if he could shed any light in the meantime. He shrugged and rolled his eyes. Whatever Eleanor's problem was, it had no chance of competing with his own romantic drama. Jim believed he was involved in one of the great love stories of all time. Claire's decision to visit her granny instead of letting him paw at her in an alley somewhere was a tragedy that would one day inspire great poetry. With no other obvious options to pursue, I went back to retelling *Casablanca*.

When we'd finished eating, I asked Jim to clean up and went to knock, ever so gently, on Eleanor's bedroom door. We ran through the 'Go away.'/'Please let me in.'/'Fine then.' formalities, and I entered. She was sitting on the floor with her back to her bedside locker. There were some balled-up tissues by her feet. I hesitated for a moment, not quite sure where I should put myself. In the end, I took a seat on the bed, my knees level with her shoulders.

It didn't take much prompting before she poured it all out. She'd spent the afternoon in a coffee shop with a few of the girls. Orla was there. Everyone had made a huge fuss over her. It was so brave of her to be out and about. She was looking really well, considering. Was her seat all right or did she want to swap? Would she like another chocolate brownie? The bottom line was that Eleanor had wound up feeling – she choked hard on the word – envious. *Her* mother was gone too. Where was *her* sympathy? *Her* fuss? None of her friends ever so much as mentioned it. She might as well have never had a mum in the first place. I listened without interruption. That didn't come naturally. I'd trained myself to do it after reading a parenting article in a Sunday supplement. When she was finished, however, I made a huge tactical blunder. I told her I'd suspected something like this would happen from the moment I heard about Pauline's death. It was supposed to sound calming and wise. The idea I was trying to get across was that, what seemed like a freakish spike in misery to her was, in fact, completely understandable. Natural, even. She didn't hear it that way. All she heard was me congratulating myself on my foresight. She went for my throat. Her attack was long and loud, and quickly stopped making much sense. By the time she stopped, gasping for breath, she had called me an asshole, a loser and, for some reason that escaped me, a coward. She stayed on the floor and barely looked up at me. Even so, I found myself backing away like a frightened kitten. I'd never had this sort of abuse from Eleanor. Jim had called me a useless prick once when I accidentally shrank a jumper he was fond of, but his sister never gave me any lip. I was shocked, and said so. At that point, she got up and repeated the storm-out-and-door-bang combo. This time she went into the bathroom.

Given how it went the first time, I decided not to pursue her and went back downstairs. Jim was watching telly. He gave me a look that indicated he'd heard the way it had gone – how could he not? – but he made no specific enquiries. When Eleanor hadn't joined us after an hour or more, I asked him to go up and check on her. He did so, albeit with a lot of sighing. Thirty seconds later, he was back. She'd told him to fuck off. I fully intended to try again myself, later, when she'd calmed down. She didn't calm down, though. Not for days. Although there was no fresh shouting or abuse or door-slamming, her anger obviously persisted. The pot was no longer boiling over, but it was still boiling.

In the end, I never did get around to talking to her. Before she was willing to give me the time of day again, my attention was dragged to a whole new problem: Claire dumped Jim. When he came home one evening and told me, I clapped him on the shoulder and started into a little speech. It wasn't particularly original. I may even have mentioned the sea and the large number of fish within it. There wasn't much chance he was going to give me a big hug and thank me for making everything all right again, I knew. Still, it was a surprise when he burst into tears and started dry-heaving. I'll give myself credit for one thing, I didn't follow my first instinct, which was to laugh and tell him to wise up. For a minute or more, we just stood there, a foot apart, him sobbing and retching, me frowning and staring. I felt sorry for him, of course I did. He was my child and he was unhappy. Still, I couldn't bring myself to take this seriously. The key word here was 'child'. Eventually, he pulled himself together and moped off up to his room. He stayed there all night.

The following morning he said he was sick and couldn't go to school. I didn't want to get into it with him, so I said that was fine, but I had to go to work, so he was on his own. It was only one day, I told myself. If I indulged him, that'd be an end to the whole thing. It wasn't. He went back to school the next day but remained deeply miserable. It got to the stage where I had to approach Eleanor for help, even though she still wasn't talking to me. That didn't go well. She hissed that it was typical of me to suppose that she wouldn't have already spoken to Jim. Of *course* she had. *Several* times. It had done no good. Then she went back to ignoring me.

Everything returned to normal in due course. Jim became capable of conversation again. Eleanor stopped treating me like something she'd found stuck to her shoe. We had crashed, as I'd always known we would, and while it wasn't fun, we'd all lived to tell the tale.

I wonder what I would have said if someone had told me that this same pair of crises would come back to haunt me, once again joined at the hip, almost a quarter of a century later.

16

A few days after the Shave or Dye event, Jim appeared at breakfast with his scalp glistening anew. I wasn't displeased. I'd come around to the idea that it really did suit him.

'You're keeping it, so,' I observed, pointing above his eyes with a piece of toast.

'I am.'

'Good, it's . . . good. Wait, are you growing a beard too?'

His whole head had been stubbly. His face still was. He started filling the kettle but even over that noise, I heard him sighing.

'No, Da, I am not growing a beard. I know how you feel.'

'Thank Christ,' I said. I'd always been very vocal on this particular subject. In my book, you could be a movie star dressed from head to toe in Armani, and a beard would still make you look like an on-the-run Provo from 1976.

'I'm going to keep it at this length. Bought a wee trimmer yoke.'

I didn't follow him right away. 'Keep what? You want to be stubbly?'

'Yeah.'

'Ah, Jim, that's worse than beardy! This is, what, designer stubble?'

'That's a very 1980's term. No one calls it that any more.'

'It doesn't matter what they call it, you can't go around unshaven all the time. People will think you're hungover every single day!'

He was at the cupboard now, hoking about for cereal. Over his shoulder he said, 'If you must know, with the shaved head, I think it makes me look rugged.'

I squinted at him so hard I gave myself a headache on the spot. 'Fuck me,' I managed to say. '*Rugged*. What weirdo website did you get that on?'

The truth was, I wasn't as bothered as I was letting on. He was taking an interest in his appearance and that was a positive thing. Later, that Saturday night, I turned to say something to him when we were watching a movie and caught myself thinking that his profile looked sort of . . . tough. But not in a bad way. Not thuggish. The word 'rugged' presented itself and my eyes widened. Wherever he'd got it, it wasn't wrong. Toe-curling – but not wrong.

The following day, the Sunday, got off to an entirely normal start. I had a bit of brekkie, wandered out for the papers, contemplated a bath. It was almost noon when Eleanor showed up at the door without warning and turned my whole life inside out.

I was alone in the house at the time. Jim had just astonished me by declaring that he was off out running.

I'd never known him to take a minute's voluntary exercise in his life. There was an app, he said, as if that explained it. Especially for beginners. You start out wheezing when you stand up and next thing you know, you're running five kilometres without stopping. I could see Jim lasting maybe three days with this sort of programme but didn't say so. I wished him all the luck in the world, then watched him through a gap in the curtains as he fiddled with his phone and staggered off up the street. Ten minutes later, when I heard a key turning in the front door, I assumed that he'd snapped out of whatever madness had gripped him. When Eleanor stepped into the room, I jumped a foot and made a noise like a seagull spotting a chip.

'Sorry,' she said. 'Did I frighten you?'

'Eleanor! Jesus Christ.' I got up and we hugged, a little awkwardly. 'You didn't ring or anything.'

'Surprise visit,' she said. There was no smile. Something bad was coming. I knew it like I knew my own name.

'Is everything–'

'Jim around?'

'Went out a few minutes ago. Running.'

Her head retreated. 'After what?'

'Not after anything. Or away from anything. He's just . . . running. For exercise.'

'You're joking me. When did this start?'

'Today.'

'Ah. It won't last.'

Even though that was exactly what I'd thought myself, I felt obliged to defend him. 'You never know. He seems a bit more interested in himself these days. I don't want to spoil it on you but he has . . . a new look.'

'Intriguing. Was this your doing?'

'Nope. His. I seem to be all out of ideas on that front. Eleanor, what's wrong?'

'Charming. Why do you think something's wrong? I can't visit?'

I held her gaze. 'What is it?'

She dropped the act. 'You might need a cup of tea. I'll put the kettle on.'

'No. Just tell me, for God's sake.' I sat down on the sofa. She did likewise. 'It's not Miles, is it? Is–'

'It's not Miles. Or Aidan. Or me. We're all fine.'

'What then?'

She clasped her hands together on her lap. 'Okay, I'm . . . I'm just going to say it.'

'I wish you would.'

'Okay. Well, the thing is . . . I had a message a while back. On Facebook. Weeks ago. From, eh . . . from Mum.'

I blinked at her for several seconds. 'What?'

'I didn't know whether I should tell you or not. I almost did, at the funeral. But I didn't want to upset you.'

'Aha,' I said, ridiculously, remembering her weird mood that day. My voice sounded like it was coming from somewhere else in the room.

'The reason I'm telling you now is that she wants to meet me.'

'Right.'

'A "chat", she called it.'

'Hm.'

She reached out and put her hand on my knee, which, I now realized, was bouncing up and down. Something in her expression told me she hadn't done it to calm me. It was annoying her. 'This must be a bit of a–'

'You know, the thing is, I used to think this was bound to happen, way back when, after she left. I thought, there's no way she can drop out of her children's lives forever. How could she? It might be weeks or months, but she'll have to get in touch. She said she would, didn't she? Then, when it didn't happen, I thought, okay, she's getting her head together or whatever, who knows, it could be a year or two before . . . but she never did, so in the end, I just assumed that was it. She was just . . . gone.'

This was pure babble, but it felt good to be using more than one syllable again. I swallowed hard and concentrated on not bouncing my knee. When Una first disappeared, I had, of course, spent hours, days even, thinking about nothing else. I was completely in the dark. Couldn't have narrowed her location down to a hemisphere. Didn't even know who she'd run off with. But over the years – decades, at this point – I had trained myself not to dwell on it. It felt like I could torture myself with questions or I could finish raising the kids, but not both. I made my choice. I wondered what had become of Una the way I wondered what had become of the little tractor I played with as a boy or that cross-eyed plumber Tommy used to work with. Fleeting thoughts, nothing more.

'I've spoken to her, Daddy.'

'Oh.'

'We messaged back and forth a bit first. Then she suggested a phone call.'

'Right.' The monosyllables were back. I made a conscious effort to produce a whole sentence. It was like lifting a weight. 'How did that go?'

Eleanor exhaled at length. 'I'll tell you everything she told me, if you want to know. If you don't, I won't.'

I hesitated. I couldn't imagine what possible good it would do me to hear what had become of Una. On the other hand, how could I say no?

'Well,' I said, doing my best to sound casual. 'Sure you've come all this way.'

The man Una had run off with in 1994, I learned, was a Dubliner called Denis Brady. He'd been married, but his wife had died (cause unspecified) within twelve months of their wedding. I'd never heard the name and had no idea how Una had met, let alone conducted an affair and planned a whole new life with, a widower who lived two hours away. Eleanor hadn't enquired about those details and seemed irritated by my queries. Brady was some sort of IT manager, apparently. The two of them skipped off to London together. He got a decent enough job and she worked in various offices, doing simple admin work but feeling useful and happy.

Around this early point in Eleanor's report, I started to regret asking to hear all this. It wasn't that I was sorry to learn how happy Una had been after she ditched us – at least, it wasn't just that. I was annoyed by how boring it was. She hadn't gone to lounge around a Monaco penthouse with a shady millionaire. She hadn't gone to rough it on a farm with a handsome Argentinian cowboy. She'd gone to Croydon with a computer guy and had found fulfilment photocopying stuff for estate agents. I was contemplating telling Eleanor that I'd changed my mind when the story took an interesting turn. They didn't last, Una and Denis. She met someone else and walked out on him. I laughed when I heard that, a single crisp 'Heh!' that seemed to echo around the kitchen.

The new man was called Adam Dixon. He was English and worked in banking. Not 'in a bank'. Una had been keen to clarify that, by all accounts. 'In banking.' He was older than she was but had never married. She moved into his apartment in Chiswick the day before the Twin Towers fell. I wasn't surprised to hear that this development marked the end of her career in low-level admin. For almost twenty years, she and Adam had enjoyed 'a lovely life' (Eleanor did the finger-quote thing). There were no details here, but my imagination filled them in. I pictured a lightly wrinkled Una and a leathery old fox – played in my head, for some reason, by Donald Sinden – clinking champagne glasses, flying off to Paris, taking their seats at Centre Court.

Then, in the winter of 2016, they went to visit his brother in Brighton. The brother's pride and joy was a classic Jaguar, which he'd had restored at eye-watering cost. They always took it out for a spin when Adam was in town. On this occasion, the brother seems to have pushed it past the limits of his driving talent. It left the road on a long bend and hit a tree. The brother broke a wrist but was otherwise unharmed. Adam was instantly killed. Una and Adam had never been married – obviously, she was still married to me – but she used the word 'widowed', Eleanor said, wrinkling her nose. I had no issue with that, myself. She'd lived with this banker lad a lot longer than she ever lived with me. In any event, Una suffered more than common-or-garden bereavement in the aftermath of his death. She became deeply depressed. Adam had 'amply provided' for her (finger quotes again), but she lost all enthusiasm for life. Stopped eating properly. Couldn't get out of bed, some days. Her depression persisted for almost two years. At this point in the story, Eleanor paused for so long that I thought she might have finished.

'Is that it?' I asked her. 'Are we all up to date?'

She shook her head and tossed aside the tissue she'd been balling up in her right hand. An old habit. 'No. No, there's more.'

'Go on.'

'During this depression, she noticed that she was getting forgetful. She thought it was another symptom, that was all, like loss of appetite or not sleeping well. But it didn't improve when she started to feel more like herself. It got worse, in fact.'

It was obvious where this was going. But I didn't interrupt.

'There was a deli near her apartment. A little old man ran it. She used to go in there all the time and always had a nice chat with him. One day she went in and realized she had no idea what his name was. It wasn't like it was on the tip of her tongue, she said. It was *gone*. That frightened her and she went to the doctor. They did tests. She has Alzheimer's.'

I didn't know what to say so I went with the obvious. 'How long has she got?'

'Years, but probably not many.'

I folded my arms in front of me on the kitchen table. It had been hard to tell what Eleanor was thinking as she told me all this. Sometimes she'd sounded sympathetic. Sometimes she'd sounded contemptuous. Sometimes she'd sounded like she was mad at *me*. I looked at her intently now, trying to get a clue. She gazed back, face completely blank, like a woman looking out of a bus window.

'How did she sound?' I asked.

Eleanor shrugged. 'I can barely remember what she sounded like before. There's a bit of England in her voice, I did notice that. More than a bit, actually.'

'No, I mean did she sound . . . ill?'

'Nope. It's still early. Still at the "occasionally forgetting stuff" stage. Tends to misplace things, she said. And she's lost her balance once or twice. But you wouldn't know anything was wrong just talking to her.'

'She wants to meet you, she said?'

'Yep.'

'And?'

Another shrug. 'I don't know. That'd be a big step, wouldn't it?'

'Because if you're asking for my permission–'

'I'm not asking for your permission.' She scowled at me, her face reddening with amazing speed.

'Well, don't get testy. You said, when you arrived, that you weren't going to tell me but you changed your mind and I thought maybe you–'

'I changed my mind about *notifying* you. Messages and a call is one thing, but she seems serious about getting into our lives, so I thought you should know. Whatever happens.'

'When you say, our lives . . .'

'What?'

'Well, what about Jim? Or has she forgotten she has two children?' As soon as the words were out, I flinched and felt my stomach roll over. 'Oh! I didn't mean forgotten because of the Al–'

'I know.'

'It was a bad choice of words! I meant–'

161

'I know, Jesus! She did mention Jim, of course she did. Wanted to know all about him. I think she contacted me because she *found* me. My stupid Facebook account's in my maiden name. Jim's not on any social media. You know what he's like.'

'She could have got in touch with me easiest of all,' I sniffed. 'All she had to do was write to the house.' I let Eleanor squirm for a moment before I put her out of her misery. 'That was a joke. I know it's not me she's curious about. Did she even mention my name?'

'She asked about you, yes. I gave her the gist.'

That 'gist' was a kindness. It implied that my life was an incident-packed rollercoaster and no one could hope to describe the whole adventure in all its vast richness. All you could do was take a stab at a big-picture summary. In reality, I guessed she'd said something like, *Retired from the shop, never met anyone new, still lives in the same house*. I imagined Una sneering.

'What did she say about Jim?'

'What do you mean?'

'About the fact that he took over the shop and never, y'know . . . Still lives here. With me.'

Eleanor made a noise with her lips. 'She didn't say much.'

That seemed to kill the conversation stone-dead for a while. We worked on our cups of tea, staring at different walls. I could imagine what Una was thinking. Bad enough that she'd married a useless prick. Now her son was following the same tedious path. Two old bachelors, stuck in a grey little town.

'I'm surprised you haven't thrown it out there yet,' Eleanor said then.

'What?'

'Your theory. About all this.'

'I have a theory, do I?'

'I'd say you do, yeah. I know I do.'

'Go on, then.'

She shook her head, slowly, deliberately. 'I think it's your place more than mine.'

I allowed a dramatic pause. 'Your mother doesn't give a fuck about us, Eleanor. Any of us. She's popped up after all this time because she's going to need full-time care and she has no one else to turn to.'

She nodded, just as slowly, just as deliberately. We heard the front door open. Jim was back.

The three of us went out for lunch, to a hotel. I supposed we'd talk about Una and nothing else, but it wasn't like that at all. Jim had been brought up to speed before we left the house and neither he nor Eleanor seemed keen to stay on the subject after that. We didn't so much as mention her name on the short car journey. That was devoted to Eleanor marvelling – *marvelling* – at Jim's new look. She really couldn't get over it and made such a fuss that I felt guilty about my own tepid reaction. When we arrived at the hotel, Jim headed straight for the Gents. As soon as he'd gone, Eleanor grabbed my arm.

'He's so different,' she gasped.

'Yeah, he used to have hair,' I said. 'Now he doesn't.'

'Can you not see it? He's completely different. It's like he's got a whole new head. His *face* looks different. He's *dressed* better. And he's getting exercise. Jim!'

He was wearing a new shirt, now that she mentioned it. A nice one, for a change. 'Maybe.'

'Definitely. You can't see it because you're too close. He's a new man.'

'Even if that's true, he's a new man without a girlfriend who still lives at home with his father.'

'Nothing to report there, then?'

I wished I'd kept my mouth shut. It wasn't a topic I was keen to discuss. I couldn't shake the feeling that boosting Jim's love life was just one more thing I'd failed at. It wasn't that I'd run out of good ideas – I'd never had any in the first place. Frank had come up with dancing lessons. The head-shaving thing had dropped in my lap and, besides, was by no means a 'good idea'.

'No,' I said. 'Come on, let's get a table. He'll find us.'

The hotel, an old one not far outside town, had recently had its first makeover in forever. Everywhere you looked was chrome and glass. We all hated the new look. They'd finally dragged the place out of the 1970s, we agreed, but only as far as the 1980s. We tried to outdo each other in the bitchiness of our reviews. Jim, fair play to him, won the day with, 'It looks like some-where Olivia Newton-John would have made a video.' A waiter appeared promptly enough, at least, and when he'd left us alone again, we fell into comfortable silence. I knew we'd break it with more talk about Una. It felt like the topic had been quietly baking and now it was time to take it out of the oven. Sure enough, Jim spoke up.

'So, tell us,' he said to Eleanor. 'What were you like on the phone? With herself.'

'What do you mean, what was I like?'

'I mean, were you snippy, were you chatty? What was, y'know, your attitude?'

'I would say I was cautious. Not rude, I don't think, though God knows I had every right to be.'

'I'm pretty sure I would have been rude as fuck,' Jim replied. 'Then again, I'm not sure I would have got on the phone with her in the first place.'

'Are you having a go?' Eleanor snapped.

'Oh my God, *no*, I'm not having a go, I'm saying it must have been weird.'

'It was,' she said in a milder tone. 'Extremely.'

'Why do you think she's popped up after all this time?' I asked Jim. He was taking a sip of water at the time. The glass froze at his lips. His eyes met mine, and his eyebrows slowly rose. He lowered the glass. 'Is it not blindingly obvious to you?'

Eleanor and I exchanged a glance. 'A theory has been aired,' she said carefully.

'She's on her way out,' Jim said with a shrug. 'She's hoping we're dopey enough to forgive everything and be her nurses. Duh.'

I felt a quick flush of shame. What did it say about us that this was our automatic conclusion? Were we bad people? I chased the feeling away. Not a peep out of her for twenty-odd years, not so much as a postcard until she found herself alone and seriously ill? No. Our conclusion was automatic because it was the only one that made sense.

'I think that's more or less right,' Eleanor said. 'But I don't think she's hoping for nurses, plural. I think she has just the one in mind.' She looked at me. I looked back.

'Come on,' Jim snorted. 'Dad's stupid, but he's not that stupid.'

This didn't raise a smile from Eleanor. And it didn't raise

a smile from me. The two of us kept looking at each other. We might have kept it up for minutes if a waiter hadn't appeared at my shoulder, asking who was having the prawns.

17

'Fuck off,' Frank said when I told him the news. It was a phrase that he put to an astonishing variety of uses. In this case, it was an expression of surprise. We were in the pub, a few nights after Eleanor's visit. There was some golf competition on the telly. An Irishman was doing well. Every so often, as I gave Frank the full story, a roar or a groan would go up from our fellow patrons. One of them was timed with exquisitely bad taste: just as I said the words 'Alzheimer's disease' a putt went in and the whole pub cheered in delight.

'I never thought I'd see the day,' Frank sighed when I was finished.

'Me neither.'

'Bloody hell.'

'I know.'

'Fuck me.'

'Yep.'

'Jesus Chr–'

'All right, Frank, you can stop being amazed now. I agree with you. It's an unexpected development.'

I was impatient. His input would likely be horrific, but it would be honest. I wanted to hear it. He mulled it over for a minute, staring into his pint.

'You're dreading all this, I bet,' he said then.

'What makes you say that?'

'Well, we know where it's going to wind up, don't we? Eleanor's already spoken to her and she's going to meet her.'

'She didn't say that. She's thinking about it.'

'Come on. She'll do it. She's curious. And who can blame her? Once she replies to that first message, let alone agrees to a phone call, it's inevitable, whatever she might think of her mother. Back to you, though. Listen, I don't want to be offensive—'

'Christ!'

'What?'

'I've never heard you issue a *warning*. This is going to be good.'

'All right, lookit. My point is, Eleanor's going to meet her, then maybe Jim will start to wonder, and the next thing you know, Una will be here. In Monaghan. At your very door, maybe. Her old door. Even if you don't want to meet her, she's going to hear all about you and you're going to hear all about her. And, well . . . comparisons are going to be made, aren't they?'

'Comparisons?'

'Comparisons. She's been off in London having relationships and jobs and yet more affairs and by all accounts living the high life, while you've been, y'know, not.'

I drank half my pint in three tremendous gulps. 'Wow. Stabbed in the front by my best friend.'

'Ah, Eugene, I–'

'It's all right. This has all occurred to me. Repeatedly. She's the cool one. I get it.'

'I wouldn't say *cool*. She was only in London in the first place because she walked out on her husband and kids. There's nothing cool about it. Dramatic, maybe.'

I nodded glumly. 'Yep.'

'But sure, your life has had plenty of drama too! Repeatedly cheated on, abandoned, left to raise two kids all on–'

He stopped with a strangled gurgle, having copped on that his attempt to find a bright side amounted to pointing out that all my dramas were, at heart, Una's dramas.

I cleared my throat. 'Anyway, what do you make of this: the general opinion seems to be that Una showing up and Una having a serious illness aren't . . . unrelated. She hasn't suddenly taken an interest in us. She's realized she's going to need help.'

Frank chewed on it for a moment. 'Well, not necessarily.'

'Come on. You think it's just a coincidence?'

'No, but it doesn't have to be that she expects you to take care of her. It's bound to make you reflect on things, news like that. Maybe she wants to clear the air before she . . . goes.'

'Clear the air? It's not like we fell out over where to go on holidays, Frank.'

'I know.'

'Jesus.'

'I didn't mean clear the air as in make everything all right again, I meant it more like, whaddayacallit, settle up the accounts.'

'Holy shit! You think *she's* entitled to some sort of pay–'

169

'Why are you being a bollocks, Eugene? Maybe I haven't picked exactly the right words, but you know fine well what I mean.'

He had me there. Of course I knew what he meant. There was every chance that Una didn't expect anything at all from us. Maybe she really was looking for some sort of closure while she could still process it.

'Sorry,' I mumbled. 'Yeah, I know what you mean.'

'And that'd be worse, wouldn't it? If she had the nerve to show up after all this time expecting you to look after her, you could tell her to fuck off. You'd be perfectly entitled. But if she just wants to *talk*. Whole other ball game. How could you say no to that? Despite everything? The simple wish of a dying woman?'

Vintage Frank. Nail on the head. No comfort whatsoever. 'Yep.'

'So, what's the plan?'

'Don't have one.'

He rotated his pint on its beer mat. 'This comparison business.'

'Yeah?'

'I'll tell you one thing you could do to make it a bit more . . . well, to even things out a bit.'

'I'm all ears.'

'You could ask that woman out.'

'What woman?' I had the balls to say.

He laughed and prolonged my agony by taking a drink. 'The one from the charity thing. The one you got all annoyed about when I paid her a compliment. The one you were all moo-eyed over. That one. Ye fucking chancer.'

He had me. 'Annie,' I said.

'Annie. Elegant Annie.'

All of my teenage jealousy had melted away. It was a thrill now to hear him use that word. I enjoyed the feeling for a few seconds. And then it, too, melted away.

'She's an attractive woman, for sure, but good God, I'm not going to ask her out. That's crazy talk.'

'Why not?'

'Be reasonable, Frank.'

'That's not an answer.'

'Well, okay, for a start, the last time I asked a woman out was 1971. You can't go around trying to get a girlfriend at my stage of life. It's ridiculous. Especially when there's such a big age difference.'

'She's not that much younger, is she? I'd say she's getting on for sixty.'

'Ah, no. God, no way. Early fifties would be my guess. You only got that one look at her in a dark pub.'

That gave him pause for a moment, but it didn't give him stop. 'Still. Let's say fifteen years. Sure that's nothing. It's not May to December. It's more like late-August to December.'

I shook my head. 'Won't happen. Can't happen.'

'Why? You're old, you're not dead.'

'Touching words, as ever. What about you? Have you ever thought about–'

'We're not talking about me, we're talking about you.'

'Well, why not? It's been ten years since Bernie–'

'Stop distracting, for fuck's sake. I don't know how I'd react if I met a woman I liked, but it doesn't matter because I haven't. You have.'

I mulled it over for a few seconds. 'That'd be a piss-poor reason for asking someone out, wouldn't it? My estranged wife has shown up and I don't want to look like a lonely oul gobshite who's wasted his life, so would you like to go to the pictures sometime?'

Frank stared at me and shook his head in disbelief. 'For fuck's sake, man. I didn't mean you should ask her *because* Una's back. I was only trying to give you a little push, which you need, on account of your general uselessness.'

'Lovely. That's a lovely thing to–'

'And, for the love of Christ, if you do ask her out, don't suggest the "pictures". You might as well tell her how impressed you are with these new talkies they have now.'

'I won't be telling her anything about anything, because it ain't happening.'

'Grand, so,' he said. 'Pint?'

I nodded and off he went to the bar. This sort of thing happened fairly often with Frank. One minute he'd be trying to convince you of something like his life depended on it, and the next, he'd drop the subject with no hint of a warning. Sometimes it was a tactic. He'd start up again at a later hour or date, armed with fresh arguments. Sometimes it seemed to be genuine boredom. Usually, I was somewhere between not bothered and completely delighted with these sudden cancellations. Not this time. As I watched him fish through his wallet at the bar, I realized I was trying to think of ways to get him back on to the topic as quickly as possible.

18

For a man who definitely wasn't going to ask Annie out, I sure spent a lot of time over the next few days wondering what I'd suggest if I asked Annie out. Idle mental chatter, I told myself. No harm in thinking a few thoughts. In any event, I quickly ruled out any kind of activity. It'd be hard enough trying to make sure I didn't say anything stupid, I wouldn't want to add complications. Also, I couldn't think of any activities. A nice dinner in a decent restaurant, that'd be the chap to go for, if I was going for it, which I wasn't. When I was younger, Monaghan's idea of a decent restaurant was a chip shop that had seats in it. There were options now. I did a search on my phone – just out of curiosity – and saw recommendations for several places I'd never even heard of. The best reviews seemed to be for an Indian called The Golden Tiger. That was a brutal name, I thought. It sounded like a grotty take-away. I pictured threadbare carpet and sticky plastic tablecloths. But the pictures on its website – I looked at its website, for the laugh – showed a large, beautifully decorated room, all cream and beige under tasteful lighting. I tried to imagine myself sitting in there with Annie. On a date. It was impossible. I lowered my sights and tried to imagine myself doing the actual asking. That was impossible too.

One afternoon, feeling oddly deflated by my inability to imagine things I had no intention of doing, I took myself off to the library. I was returning *Churchill: Walking With Destiny* by Andrew Roberts (shockingly uncritical) and *SPQR: A History of Ancient Rome* by Mary Beard (crack cocaine in book form). I intended to pick up William Harbaugh's *Power and Responsibility: The Life and Times of Theodore Roosevelt.* I'd read it twice before. Roosevelt was one of my favourite historical figures and this was the pick of his many biographies. He was some pup, Teddy. He suffered from terrible asthma as a child but seems to have just decided one day that he would kick its hole. The 'sickly child', as he is almost always described, became a cattle-rancher, war hero, and big-game hunter who was an excellent boxer and held a black belt in jujitsu. Which is not to say that his adult life was all roses. His wife and his mother died on the same day in the same house. That might have killed lesser men. It didn't kill Teddy. Neither did the bullet that a mentally ill assassin fired into his chest on the campaign trail in 1912. Not only did he fail to die, he carried on with the business in hand, which was delivering a ninety-minute speech. He didn't so much as talk to a doctor until he was done. He was the first American to win the Nobel Peace Prize and remains to this day the youngest US president. Somewhere along the way, he found the time to write thirty-eight books. There's making the most of life, and then there's Teddy Roosevelt.

The Harbaugh was on loan, it turned out. Not the end of the world. I browsed for twenty minutes or so and finally settled on *Flags of Our Fathers* by James Bradley and Ron Powers, the story of the men who raised the flag on Iwo Jima in that famous photograph. It had been made into a movie by Clint Eastwood, which I'd never seen on the grounds that I wanted to read the book first. Nothing else caught my eye, so I headed to the counter. Peter was on duty today. He was all right, but I much preferred his colleague Siobhán. She was a bit of a history buff too and always made some remark on my choices – had read it and loved it, had read it and hated it, had never heard of it, and so on. Peter might as well have been the robot that would no doubt replace him one of these days. You could be checking out a book called *How to Murder Librarians Called Peter* and he wouldn't bat an eyelid. He was engrossed in something on his computer when I went over. I made a big deal of sighing impatiently and turned to look out the window.

The library was close to the centre of town, on the North Road. It was hardly a tremendous shock to see someone I knew walking past. The fact that it was Annie seemed a bit on the nose. My first thought was that I shouldn't tell Frank. He would start going on about the universe giving me a sign. I'd heard him talking that sort of nonsense on many occasions in the past, when it suited his argument (he never seemed to spot signs that he might be talking out of his arse). Peter looked up from his computer, gave me a nod, and did the necessary with my book. I tucked it under my arm and headed for the door but stopped before I reached it. What if she'd turned around? Remembered she'd left her phone in her car or something? She'd see me and would no doubt stop to say hello. Supposing I lost the run of myself and blurted out an invitation to dinner? I made myself count to twenty before I stepped outside. Annie, I discovered, was not one of life's fast walkers and was still in sight. If I'd been going the other direction, away from town, there would have been no problem. I wasn't. After hesitating for a moment, I decided to risk it. We were going in the same direction on the same street at the same time, that was all. Nothing wrong with that. And when she reached Church Square and turned left, what was I supposed to do? Pretend that I didn't need to do likewise? The only thing that was weird about this, I told myself, was that I wasn't speeding up to greet someone I knew, and even that wasn't so unusual. I'd probably been in that boat hundreds of times in my life. All perfectly normal and above board.

She walked on into the Diamond, the centre of town, and that was where we should have parted ways. I was supposed to be turning left to call into the shop on Glaslough Street. Annie was carrying on straight towards Dublin Street. I didn't actively decide to keep following her, it sort of happened on its own. The truth was, I liked watching her move. If I hadn't already known she was a dancer, I thought, I would have guessed. She *glided*, like she was on castors. Every other time I'd seen her, she was all in black, or black and white. Today she was dressed in various shades of green. Olive green trousers and a sage cardigan over a mint shirt. She looked great. Maybe I should catch up with her for a wee chat after all, I thought. I wouldn't blurt anything out, that was ridiculous. And even if I did, so what? There was a chance, however tiny, that the end result would be the two of us having a nice dinner. Me and this woman, this classy, graceful woman, sitting together in a swish restaurant. On a *date*. I lost the run of myself, I must admit, and only snapped out of it when Annie bumped into someone she knew, a young woman. They'd almost passed each other when they copped on and spun around to say hello. Realizing that Annie no longer had her back to me, I pivoted abruptly to my left and walked nose-first into a street lamp.

The pain was incredible. I staggered backwards, hands to my face, feeling sick and faint. An elderly lady had seen the accident, but she wasn't brimming with sympathy. She shuffled past with her walking stick, clearly trying not to burst her hole laughing. Didn't even ask me if I was all right. Through watery eyes, I checked my fingers. There was no blood. That was a good thing, I supposed, although I couldn't help feeling a bit cheated. How could there be so much pain and no blood? I placed a thumb and forefinger on either side of my throbbing conk and gave it a gentle squeeze, which I immediately regretted. Gasping from the shock, I looked down the street, fully expecting to see Annie staring back at me. No. She was still chatting away, oblivious. I recognized her pal now. She was one of the salsa women whose existence I'd ignored on the grounds that she was too young for Jim. *Much like Annie's too young for you*, an unhelpful voice in my head suggested. I ducked behind the street lamp that had almost knocked me out. This, I told myself, was a good place to draw a line under the whole episode. I could go to the shop, as planned, and have the sit-down that my still-wobbling legs were crying out for. A cup of tea wouldn't go amiss either.

I drew no such line. When I peeked out and saw that Annie was walking once again, I slid around the lamp and followed, keeping my head down in case the young woman recognized me as she passed. Once it was safe to do so, I looked up from my own feet and saw that I'd almost accidentally caught up. Annie had stopped by a jeweller's window and was staring hard at something in there, her hand held over her eyes to block out the light. Eejit that I am, I did the exact same sudden pivot-left manoeuvre that had almost landed me in hospital not two minutes previously. It would have served me right if I'd smacked into something again. I didn't and even managed to scuttle across the street without getting run over. There, I did some more hiding and peeking, this time behind a van. I wondered what she was looking at in there. A bracelet? A ring? A necklace? Whatever it was, I was sure it was gorgeous. She had such great taste. A truck obscured my view then, creeping along in the traffic. When it passed, she was gone. I didn't see her anywhere on the street so I assumed she'd gone into the shop.

Five whole minutes I stood there, peering around the side of the van like a sniper, nose throbbing. What would I have said if someone I knew had tapped me on the shoulder and asked me what I was up to? I didn't know. I didn't care. The spell was only broken when a shouting match erupted on my right. An overweight man with the sort of bright purple face that seems to promise a heart attack within the next half hour had returned to his car to find a traffic warden mid-ticket. He didn't bother with the sweet smiles and humble-apologies approach. Hauling his trousers up by the belt, he went straight for Option B, extremely loud abuse. The traffic warden, a skinny man with a patchy beard, looked like a child trying on his dad's suit. He was soft-spoken and polite. The car owner roared at him, stuck his blunt sausage of a finger in the guy's face and looked for all the world like he was getting ready to throw a punch. Then he took half a step back and spat on the ground between them. The traffic warden mentioned the Gardaí, at which point the driver's face went from purple to something more like black. A crowd started to gather around them.

In any event, it brought me back into my own skin. I blinked and rubbed my eyes like someone emerging from a dream. The voice that had said Annie was too young for me piped up again. *Stalking*, it said. *There's a word for what you're doing, and that word is stalking. Look at yourself, for fuck's sake.* I turned on my heels and headed off in the direction of the shop, scolding myself for my stupid behaviour.

Another thought ran beneath the scolding, though, cold and steady as an underground river. There was one sure way to make sure this sort of foolishness didn't become a regular thing. One, and one only. I'd have to ask the woman out. And I sure as hell wasn't doing that, was I?

Was I?

19

'Ye dirty bastard,' Jim said, shaking his head.

I stood up straight and stepped back from the table. 'Thank you, Son. You're right, it was a delicate wee shot and I pulled it off with great skill, if I say so myself.'

'Dirty bastard,' he repeated, staring forlornly at the cue ball, which was nestled tightly behind the yellow.

'I agree, snookering your opponent is an art form in itself.'

He studied his predicament. There was no obvious path to the last remaining red. 'Three cushions it is,' he said eventually. I was respectfully silent as he calculated angles and got down to make the shot but couldn't contain a snort when he missed his target by two feet.

'Ooh, close,' I grinned.

'Fuck off.'

I was having fun and not just because I was winning. Snooker had been our thing in his teenage years. We'd played at least twice a week in the Imperial Club, as it grandly called itself, despite being housed in a sort of shed down a mossy alley behind a pub. Not a lot was said during those games, especially after Una left. The only sounds were the clack of the balls and the metallic *shhh-bump* of coins going into the meter that turned the lights on over the table. I didn't mind. We'd been doing something together, that was the main thing. It had been years since we'd had a game. And it was Jim's idea. When he'd suggested it earlier that evening, as we polished off our potato waffles and beans, I got a lump in my throat. The Imperial was long gone, of course. We were playing in a new place over a boxing club in a small development on the edge of town. Clean. Modern. I thought it lacked a certain romance, but it also lacked rats and the faint smell of diesel. I was willing to make the trade.

I potted the last red and followed up with an easy pink, then rolled in the yellow and fluked the green (it wobbled in the jaws of a corner pocket for what seemed like several seconds, then hugged the cushion and dropped into the one opposite). Jim swore violently but my break – a pretty long one by my standards – was at an end.

'Shite,' I said as the brown clipped the black I was trying to squeeze it past.

'It's over anyway,' Jim said, nodding at the scoreboard, which showed him forty points adrift. 'One more?'

'Yeah, go on.'

We set about fishing the balls out of the pockets. 'Surprised there's a boxing club here,' I said. 'I'd say rent isn't cheap. Must be a lot of interest in it these days.'

'Must be. People like hitting things.'

'Probably full of women now too.' I let that statement hang there for a second. 'What with Katie Taylor being so big and all.'

'Maybe that's it. New market.'

He didn't look or sound remotely interested. I gave it one last try. 'Very good for you, I'd say. Fitness-wise.'

'No doubt. Sooner or later you're getting punched in the face, though. That's not so good for you.'

It had been a feeble effort and I accepted defeat. 'Yeah. There is that.'

'So,' Jim said, not skipping a beat. 'I had a phone call.'

I stiffened. 'Did you now?'

'From Eleanor. Mother dearest has been in touch again. She's coming to Dublin.'

A red slipped from my hand and rolled away across the carpet. I went after it, slowly, gathering my thoughts, hoping Jim didn't think I'd dropped it in shock, which I had.

'Go on,' I said when I got back to the table.

'Yeah, well, that's it, really. That's the whole story. She's been in touch and she's going to visit.'

'She's not coming over on spec, though, right?'

He placed the blue on its spot. 'Sorry?'

I placed the green and the brown. It seemed important, somehow, that we keep working on getting the game set up. 'I mean, she's coming over because Eleanor has agreed to meet her, correct? She's not just showing up and hoping?'

'Come on, Da. Don't get mad.'

'I'm not getting mad.'

'This is why Eleanor wanted me to talk to you first. She was concerned–'

'I wish she'd make up her mind. When she showed up at the door she was all sniffy about *notifying* me, not asking my *permission*, and now she's Little Miss Diplomacy.' I put the black on its spot with something that could be fairly be described as a thump. A terrible sin in snooker circles. You can damage the slate.

'But you're not mad, though, right?' Jim snarked. 'Lookit, we're all still shocked that she's popped up again after all this time and we shouldn't expect each other to, y'know, to nail down exactly what we think and stick to it all the–'

'Ah! Right. So you're saying you want to meet her too?'

'What? Where did you get that from? I said no such thing.'

'Frank was right. He said this would happen.'

'*Frank?* What's Frank got to do–'

'He said it was all inevitable. Once the first message was answered, that was–'

'So, you don't think Eleanor should have answered the message? Is that what you're saying?'

I passed my hand through the air. 'Forget about it. She wanted you to relay this important information and you've done it, so now I know. Eleanor's meeting your mother in Dublin. Got it. Now, are we going to play again or not?'

Silence. I could see the cogs turning. He was giving serious thought to fucking off. 'Yep,' he said then and grabbed the frame from under the table. 'Your turn to break.'

He set up the pack and rolled the cue ball down the table. I placed it next to the yellow and played my first shot, scattering the reds a lot more widely than I would have liked. Before they'd even stopped moving, Jim was bent over the table, ready to pounce on one hanging over a corner pocket. And off we went again. Clack. Clack. Clack. Nothing being said. Just like the old days.

Our walk home was tense. Once we'd said everything

there was to say about our game, we fell into a grim silence, broken only by occasional sniffs or sighs. As soon as we were through the door, we went our separate ways. Jim plonked himself in front of the telly. I sat at the kitchen table with *Flags of Our Fathers*. After a while, I concluded that I could do with a serious drink. We didn't keep a stock of spirits in the house as a rule, but a vague memory promised I'd find something if I dug deep enough in the cupboard next to the cooker. Sure enough, right at the very back, behind half-rolls of tin foil and battered old baking trays, I found two candidates. One was a small bottle of rum, unopened. The other was a third-empty litre of vodka. I had no idea where either had come from. Unwanted gifts, I assumed. I didn't fancy either, really – whiskey was the only hard drink I had any time for – but the rum struck me as a particularly bad idea. Half an hour later, I had a good buzz on and was wondering if vodka might not be the spirit for me after all. Half an hour after that, I was well and truly polluted. When Jim wandered into the kitchen, he stopped dead, looked from me to the bottle and back. His eyebrows crept up his forehead like two caterpillars ever so slowly racing.

'Not going to offer your son any?' he said. 'Rude.'

He grabbed a glass from the draining board, pulled a chair back and sat down. I poured him one of the measures I'd been pouring for myself. 'Generous' wouldn't begin to cover it.

'Didn't know you were a vodka man,' he said.

'I'm not,' I replied, conscious of how thick my voice sounded. 'I don't even know where it came from.'

'Pub quiz prize,' he said. 'Couple of years ago. Me and Smokey and Hughsie, couple of other lads.'

'Don't remember that at all. And you'd think it'd stick, you winning a quiz.'

He awarded me a small smile and took a drink. 'Look at us, necking vodka neat, like two oul Russians on a fishing boat.'

I groped around for something equally casual to say. The drink had other ideas. 'So, the whole point of the snooker was to do something nice while you were telling me about Eleanor and your mother, is that right?'

He scoffed. 'Oh, we're doing this after all? I thought we were having a moment. Fine. The answer is no, actually. For a start, I really didn't think you'd be all that upset. You already knew she was thinking about it. I mean, she hadn't said she definitely wasn't going to meet her, had she? And anyway, I thought it might be fun, you old bollocks. We used to play all the time.'

I scanned his face for signs of duplicity. There were none. Was it possible that he was telling the truth? That he'd really just fancied a game of snooker with his da? I decided that it was.

'You're full of surprises these days,' I told him. 'This Captain Kirk look–'

'Captain Picard.'

'–getting exercise, salsa dancing, suggesting snooker. Have you taken up drugs?'

'Nothing serious. The odd sprinkle of cocaine.'

We sipped our drinks. 'Listen,' I said, 'I'm sorry I barked at you. I understand that Eleanor would be curious. It's a shock to the system, that's all, now that it's really happening. It's not that I don't think she has any right to see the woman. Same goes for you.'

'Who said I want to see her?'

'You haven't said you definitely won't, have you?'

He stared at the table for a moment, caught by the logic of his own line. 'Fair enough, I suppose.'

'Frank's theory–'

'Here we go.'

'Frank's theory is that it's all inevitable. Dominos toppling. Eleanor will meet her, you'll meet her, and then *I'll* have to meet her.'

'Huh? That's rubbish. Eleanor seems to be meeting her, granted, and I *might* meet her, but you? Why the hell would you want to meet her? What possible good could come from that?'

'Well, I don't want to, do I?'

He tucked his chin in, looking puzzled. 'Then don't.'

'It's not that easy, is it? I can't stop her showing up. It's not like she wouldn't be able to find me.'

'Don't let her in! You–'

'There's more to it than meeting her or not meeting her,' I snapped. We'd both raised our voices, and it had been going pretty well. I paused to let the heat out of the moment. 'I don't want to be judged, Jim. That's what it boils down to. She's going to judge me, and I don't fucking like it. She doesn't have to meet me to do it. She'll get all the ammo she needs from you and your sister.'

'I'm not going to give her any *ammo*. Jesus.'

'I'm not saying you'd do it on purpose. At least, I hope you wouldn't.'

He threw back the rest of his vodka, shuddered, and poured himself some more. 'Now that you mention it, I could tell her about the time you taped over my school play with frigging *Jaws 2*. She'd have a field day with that.'

I appreciated the effort, but he wasn't getting it. 'I'm

not talking about wee everyday mistakes, Jim. I'm talking about my whole life.'

He squinted at me. 'Is this the funeral business all over again?'

'What?'

'Lookit, if anyone's judging anyone, it'll be us judging Mum. All right? Relax.'

Neither of us spoke for a while.

'Come on,' Jim said then. 'We'll watch a bit of telly. I'm sure we can find one of your documentaries. Hitler's dog or some bloody thing.'

He got up, grabbing his glass and the last of the vodka. I stood too. My legs felt like they belonged to someone else.

'Blondi,' I said.

'What?'

'Hitler's dog was called Blondi.'

He held the kitchen door open and ushered me through, sighing.

20

A few days later, Eleanor called. She'd been talking to Jim and wanted to confirm that I didn't object to her meeting her mother. That was the exact phrase she used – 'wanted to confirm'. All business-like. It was a tense conversation with no natural rhythm. There were deathly silences and there were times when we spoke over each other in long strings of babble. The bottom line, I eventually assured her, was that it was her decision. I certainly wouldn't hold it against her if they met. Of course I wouldn't. And then I asked if they had a date in mind. The answer made me screech.

'Tomorrow?'

'Yes. Tomorrow. She's flying in first thing. Has a hotel booked, Jurys in Christchurch'

'How do you know?'

'What do you mean?'

'I mean, did she call again or–'

'She sent me a text. Do you want me to read it out to you?'

Sarcasm. Brilliant. 'No. I don't.'

Eleanor sighed. 'I can hear you rolling your eyes. Listen, these sorts of conversations are awkward enough without doing it on the phone. I'm going to drive up there as soon as we're done. I'll give you the whole story.'

This was exactly what I wanted but hadn't dared suggest. 'Fine. That'd be . . . Thank you. Are you . . . okay?'

'Okay how?'

'Nervous or anything.'

'Of course I'm nervous! Jesus Christ!'

'All right, all right, you don't have to take my head off.'

'I can hear Miles making a mess,' she said. 'He's mad because he'll have a sitter tomorrow. I have to go. I'll see you some time mid-afternoon.'

This was a lie, I was pretty sure. Miles may well have been mad about being babysat, but I hadn't heard a peep. She just wanted to get off the phone.

'Fair enough. Well, take it easy. I hope it goes well. I hope it's not too, y'know . . . I hope it goes well.'

Another loud sigh. 'I'll see you,' she said, and hung up.

Eleanor and Una were due to meet at noon. Giving them a couple of hours to talk and adding a couple more to get to Monaghan, I expected her to show up at around four. The day dragged like few I've ever known. I went for a walk. I cleaned out the shed. I scrubbed the toilets. I hoovered the whole house. I went for another walk. In the early afternoon, a man came to the door wanting to know if I was happy with my current Internet provider. I kept him talking for twenty minutes, even though I had no idea who my current Internet provider was and didn't understand half the things he was saying. After that, I got stuck into the odds-and-ends drawer in the kitchen. I found eight batteries in there and established that four of them worked. Four biros. Six candles. Three rolls of Sellotape. When I'd finished sorting and tidying, I looked hopefully at the clock and saw that ten poxy minutes had passed. I gave up and went into the sitting room, where I sat on the sofa and stared out the window at nothing in particular. Four o'clock came along, eventually. At that point, time seemed to stop entirely. I did a bit of pacing. Sat down again. Moved the telly. Put it back. It was after five-thirty when I finally heard a key scratching its way into the front door.

I jumped to my feet. 'I'm in here.'

I suddenly convinced myself that she'd brought Una with her. My blood ran cold. Then the living room door opened and Eleanor stepped in alone. She looked exhausted.

'There you are.'

'Come in, sit, sit,' I said. 'Cup of tea?'

'No. Thanks. I had a coffee on the way. Stopped in Ardee for a while.'

I nodded and smiled, smiled and nodded. 'Gathering your thoughts?'

'Something like that, yeah.'

She took off her jacket, draped it over the arm of the sofa, and took a seat. I sat beside her, realized I was too close, and scootched away.

'So, did you meet her?'

'I did.'

'And?'

She ran both hands over her lap, smoothing her skirt. 'It went the way you'd expect, pretty much. It was awkward.'

I waited for details. Seconds ticked by. Lots of them. I

wasn't in the mood for more waiting. 'Well, is that all you have to say?'

'What do you want me to say?'

'I don't want you to say anything in particular, Eleanor, but you've driven all this way because the phone's too awkward and now you're sitting here in silence.'

I was being insensitive. She'd been through something huge. I should have been more patient. I drew breath to offer an apology but didn't get the chance.

'Listen,' she said sharply, 'why don't you ask me specific questions and I'll do my best to answer them. Maybe that'll satisfy you.'

Several smart responses popped into my mind. All of them would have made things worse. 'All right,' I said meekly. 'How did she look?'

'How did she *look*?' Eleanor hissed, screwing her face up. It was like I'd asked what Una thought of Van Morrison's last album. 'What, are you wondering if you might still fancy her?'

My best bet, I thought, was not to dignify that with a response. Instead, I counted slowly in my head. I'd got to four when Eleanor piped up again, in a more reasonable tone.

'She looks good, I suppose. For her age. Hair done to perfection. Nice beige trouser suit.'

'Would you know she was . . . sick?'

'No. You'd know she was old.'

'Oi. She's three years younger than I am.'

'Older, then. Good make-up and all, but you can only do so much.'

'How did it start? Did you recognize her, even?'

'If I'd passed her on the street I don't think I would

have, no. She was the only woman of that age sitting in the lobby.'

'And, what – a hug? A handshake?'

'A hug. It wasn't my idea. She did the hugging and I didn't stop her.'

'Then what? Lunch in the hotel?'

'We went out. Walked off down towards the river and found a place straight away.'

At last, she dropped the Q and A format and spoke like a normal person. There were no sensational revelations. Her mother had rehashed the life-story stuff she'd already said on the phone or in Facebook messages, and Eleanor had done the same. Still, there were physical details that you can only get in person, and I found myself lapping them up. Una looked like a woman of means from head to toe, I learned, but wore a cheap digital watch. Her hair was still longish and she'd dyed it dark blonde. She had a habit of tugging an earlobe when lost in thought. There was a short scar on the back of one hand. A burn, it looked like. No glasses – she'd had laser eye surgery, which she seemed to think was the very latest in medical technology. She cleared her throat a lot. She said 'Oh my' a lot. There was no mention of her illness until Eleanor brought it up. Even then, she didn't seem to want to talk about it.

'Did you notice anything?' I asked. 'Symptoms?'

'No. I mean, she couldn't remember names, once or twice, but she was talking about stuff from years ago. Old neighbours, people around town, that kind of thing. So it didn't seem unusual.'

I wanted to ask if she'd said anything suspicious. Anything about needing care in the future. I decided against it. For one thing, even if the worst was true and Una had a plan to that effect, I doubted she'd be stupid enough to give it away right at the start. For another, Eleanor wouldn't need prompting to mention it, if it had happened.

'Must be frightening for her,' I said, 'a thing like that.'

Eleanor tossed her head. 'Here we go.'

I was genuinely confused. 'Here we go where?'

'You. Laying the groundwork.'

'What groundwork?'

'This is the bit where you give in and agree to be her nursemaid.'

'What in the name of God makes you think I'm going to do that?'

She looked away. 'It wouldn't surprise me, that's all.'

'What does that mean?' I knew she was feeling delicate and stressed and all the rest of it, but I couldn't keep the edge out of my tone.

'Never mind. She's very keen to see Jim. Brought it up again and again. I said I'd tell him but I made no promises. She asked about you too. Obviously. Didn't mention a meeting, though.'

'What did you tell her about m– . . . us?'

She shrugged. 'I said you were both in good health and the shop's going well. Told her Jim's on some sort of self-improvement kick. She liked that. Goes to the gym herself.'

'She doesn't want to come here, does she? To meet him.'

'No. She wants him to go to Dublin and meet her. Same deal as me.'

'When?'

'She's here for another few days.'

'So, now, basically? This trip?'

'Yeah.'

'There was no such thing as an apology, I take it?'

'No. It wasn't like that. It wasn't a big heart-to-heart. It wasn't even like a proper conversation. It was like giving evidence in court; *these are the facts, to the best of my recollection.* Anyway, listen. Things got a bit rough towards the end.'

'Oh? What happened?'

A long sigh. 'She said she wanted to meet Aidan and Miles. I told her she could meet Aidan if she wanted to, but she could forget about Miles. She made her arguments, and I listened. I still said no. No way. Absolutely not. I thought the subject was closed. We were kind of winding down anyway – I didn't tell her I was driving here, but I had said I couldn't be out all afternoon. Next thing I know, she's bringing it up again. So I said no again, and this time I was very firm. You know what I'd told Miles about her; that you two had split up a long time ago and weren't in touch anymore. The truth, but not the whole truth. I'd never given him any reason to think she might be showing up one day, asking to meet him. Even if I had, and even if I thought it was a good idea, it certainly wouldn't be happening straight away. She was all for seeing him *now*, before she goes back. And she wouldn't let it go! Kept banging on and on, as if she was being completely reasonable and I was blowing the whole thing out of proportion. The nerve of her.'

'And how did you leave it?'

'It got tense. Way more than it had been. I could see it turning into a full-on screaming match, so I told her I had to go. And I went.'

'Did you make any plans to see her again?'

'No.'

She'd got so worked up her breathing was affected.

I waited for the panting to end. 'With her illness and all, she probably wants everything in her life to happen immediately.'

Eleanor stared at me. Her eyes narrowed. Her jaw clenched. When she spoke, she barely moved her lips. 'Oh. My. God.'

'What?'

'You're taking her side.'

'No, I'm not! I'm–'

'Typical. Absolutely fucking typical. You haven't even laid eyes on her and you're already rolling over.'

'Rolling . . . ? What are you *talking* about?'

'I've been trying to understand this for twenty-odd years and I'm no closer to an answer. Is it magic? Did she cast some sort of spell?'

I was genuinely lost and I didn't think it was my fault. None of this made any sense. 'You're going to have to say what you mean, Eleanor. Because I'm very confused.'

She was so still for a moment that I thought she was about to backtrack. Then she exploded. There's no other word for it.

'Fine, then. Fine. You want me to spell it out? You want it laid out nice and simple? Okay, great. Here it is: you were *spineless*. With her. All those years when we were small. She had an affair, you let it slide. Fair enough. I can see how you might have been clinging to hope. Then she does it again! What kind of doormat thinks, *Oh well, better give her one more last chance, third time lucky?* She must have been laughing her ass off all those years. Couldn't believe her luck, I bet. The easy ride she got. And now she's back, with not so much as an apology, and you can't wait to be Mr Reasonable, Mr Look-at-it-from-her-point-of-view. Next thing you know, she'll be living here, bedridden, with you waiting on her hand and foot.'

It was like being beaten up. There was no pain, yet, just shock. 'You think I was . . . spineless?'

She laughed, or pretended to. 'You think you weren't?'

'I don't understand. Are you saying I should have left your mother before she–'

'Yes!' She applauded, three slow smacks of her hands. 'Congratulations, you worked it out. If you hadn't been such a coward, maybe we'd all have been spared a whole lot of grief.'

Coward. The word immediately brought me back to that teenage fit she'd thrown when her friend's mother died. Whatever this was, it wasn't new. It had been festering for a very long time.

'How would that have helped? If I'd left or kicked her out? You still would have been down a parent.'

'True. But I'd have had a lot more respect for you.'

I dropped my head into my hands. There had to be something I could say. Something that would make this even a tiny bit better. 'I stayed with her for you. And Jim. I thought it was for the best.'

'And easier. Less trouble. Right?'

'No. No, Eleanor. I always–'

'I'm going.' She grabbed her jacket and got up. 'It's been a long, horrible day and I have two more hours driving to do.'

I stood too. She was already moving. 'I'm not going to look after her when she gets bad, Eleanor. I'm not.'

'We'll see.'

196

I followed her into the hall. 'Will you not stay a while? We should talk ab–'

'I want to get back.' She opened the front door and stepped outside. 'Tell Jim she wants to see him.'

She didn't so much as turn around. Said it over her shoulder. I watched her go, then went back to the sofa. Nothing in the room seemed real any more. Everywhere I looked, I saw props from a movie set. Hollow. Weightless. Fake. I stared at my hands and tried to replay the conversation in my head. When that provided no answers, I replayed recent weeks, then months.

My whole life. There had to be an answer somewhere. There had to be a moment when I took the wrong turn and started down the path that would one day lead me here, to promising my daughter that I wouldn't help my wife through her terminal illness.

If the moment existed, I couldn't find it. I closed my eyes and waited for Jim.

21

Monaghan Cemetery, in the townland of Latlorcan, was actually three cemeteries next to each other. The oldest was built in the 1790s, the middle one in the 1920s. The third was opened in 1974. Even though it was getting on for half a century old, everyone called it 'the new grave-yard'. It was set on a hill, and not a gentle one. Anyone middle-aged and up would lose their breath getting to the top of it. On an icy day, you stepped carefully, knowing that one wrong move would send you tobogganing all the way to the bottom on your arse. Tommy and Rose were buried about two-thirds of the way up on the left, in the last plot in their row. The grave was covered in small white gravel and required no real maintenance. I brought a cloth with me when I visited so I could clean the bird shite off the headstone, but that was about the height of it. The day after Eleanor's outburst – that was what I called it in my head, knowing full well that 'outburst' didn't even begin to cover what had happened – I huffed and puffed my way up the hill, cloth in hand. Normally, I swapped back and forth between visiting Tommy and Rose's grave and visiting my parents'. I didn't go very often. Once a month, if that. This was the first time I could remember when I'd broken the pattern. Two in a row for Tommy and Rose, and barely a fortnight gone since the last visit. I'd just woken up that morning, after not much sleep, with a sudden urge to go.

Tommy and Rose's headstone was not ornate. A simple rectangle. Black with gold lettering. His name and the relevant dates. Below that, *HIS BELOVED WIFE*, then her name and dates. That used to strike me as beautifully simple. Now I wasn't so sure. I felt an echo of the way I'd felt in Dublin, at Theresa's funeral. They were born, the gravestone said, they lived for a while, and then they died. That was all they got? Did their gentle and loving natures not deserve a mention? Their selflessness? Their kindness? It was silly, I knew. No handful of words could do justice to a human life. Still, I couldn't shake the feeling that I hadn't even tried. Cleaning the stonework took five minutes. When I was done, I did what I always did, which was to stand at the end of the grave with my hands folded in front of me, looking solemn. A passer-by would have assumed that I was praying. I wasn't. I wasn't doing anything. I didn't think it was right to clean the grave and walk off right away, that was all, and I didn't know how else to arrange myself. In movies and books, I'd noticed, people often visited graves to talk to their departed loved ones, to ask advice, to report the family news. That had always seemed silly to me. For one thing, I didn't see why you'd have to be at the graveside to do it. The dead were no more 'there' than anywhere else. For another, there was no such thing as talking to people who no longer existed. You were talking to yourself. That morning, though, I'd been standing in my customary pose for an unusually long time, not feeling in any particular rush to leave, before it dawned on me that I'd come here for that very reason. I needed someone to talk to and no one living fit the bill. There was Frank, of course, but I felt too delicate for his Frankness. And Jim had been no help whatsoever. He said I was imagining things Eleanor hadn't really said. The fact that he wasn't even there didn't seem to give him pause. So I did the thing I'd always scoffed at, I stood at Tommy and Rose's graveside and I told them what had happened with Eleanor. I hadn't lost my mind. I didn't think they were going to give me any answers. But I did think I might feel better, putting it all out there, getting it off my chest. Needless to say, it didn't work. I'd only been at it for a couple of minutes when I gave up and let my thoughts drift. They went somewhere they hadn't gone in years.

One Saturday morning, about a year after Tommy and Rose had taken me in, I went into town for a wander. I had no friends in Monaghan. My intention was to walk around a bit, stick my head in the record shop, maybe stop for a cup of tea and a bun somewhere. While the first part of this exciting plan was in full swing, I passed a supermarket called Fallon's. This was long before the days of Tesco and Lidl. There were only a few places in Monaghan where people could do their whole weekly shop, and Fallon's was the largest of them. It was owned and run by a scruffy, red-faced man called Gregory Fallon, who was widely disliked. He was one of those people who seem to think that their success – the guy was minted – is a terrible burden. Although he could easily have handed over the everyday management of the place to someone else, he was a permanent fixture in the shop, where he flitted about from aisle to aisle, snarling at employees and brushing past customers without so much as a hello. No one ever saw him smiling. No one ever saw him looking neutral, either. His face only seemed to be capable of one expression, which was somewhere between sour and angry. He always looked like he'd just peeked into a cubicle in a public toilet and decided to wait until he got home.

As I passed Fallon's that Saturday morning, I was struck by an urge to get my hands on some chocolate. I went in and made my way to the sweets, which were housed on a single display near the cash registers. Selecting a chocolate bar in a small Irish town in the 1960s was a much simpler task than it is now. Still, despite the lack of choice, I took my time, examining various candidates. Maybe it was that – the picking up and putting back. Or maybe it was how long I took. Maybe I just looked shifty. I don't know. In any event, I suddenly felt a firm hand gripping my left bicep and turned my head to see Gregory Fallon's beetrooty face inches from mine. His breath stank like he'd been gargling bin juice. He tightened his grip to the point where it was painful and started dragging me away from the sweets. I had absolutely no idea what was happening.

Then he launched into a loud rant about the wickedness of shoplifters and the terrible harm they do to humble small businesses like his own. He wasn't talking to me. It was all for the benefit of the other shoppers. People stopped what they were doing to stare. Fallon stopped too, holding me in place so everyone could get a better look. He was taller than I was and his grip on my left arm caused me to lean awkwardly to the right. The rant went on and on. I didn't panic because I knew I was innocent. If anything,

I felt weirdly thrilled. When he finally shut up, I would show my empty pockets and he would look a complete tit. I'd definitely get my chocolate for free and might even be compensated further. A lifetime's supply didn't seem out of the question. He didn't shut up, though. Still booming about 'the cancer of petty crime', he resumed dragging and didn't stop until we'd gone the whole way through the shop to a small office out the back, where deliveries were made. It wasn't shoppers who stared now, it was van drivers and Fallon's own staff, all of whom looked delighted to have something to think about besides sacks of potatoes and cans of soup. Fallon pushed me into the office, slammed the door and faced me, arms folded. I was afraid now. We were alone. What if he saw that I hadn't taken anything but was too embarrassed to back down? It would be my word against his. And who was going to believe me?

When I showed him my empty pockets, he didn't immediately give up. I could have discarded the loot somewhere along the way, he said. Fine, I told him, let's retrace our steps and check. He looked at me for a long time, still coldly furious. His hands swayed by his sides. I was suddenly convinced he was going to punch me in the face. Tears came to my eyes. Shocked and disgusted with myself, I wiped them away with the back of my hand. That seemed to satisfy him, somehow. He opened the door and told me to get out of his sight. I went back through the shop and noticed several people giving me the eye. Two old women put their heads together as I passed and made clucking sounds of disapproval. I didn't breathe again until I was back outside and heading, as fast as I could move, for home.

Rose was alone in the house when I got back. Tommy was off fishing somewhere. She knew straight away that I was upset. I refused to tell her what had happened and when her questions threatened to bring on fresh tears, I hid myself away in my room. After a while, she called up with a cup of tea and a plate of biscuits. She looked so concerned and tried again to coax it out of me. I hated worrying her. But I couldn't bring myself to tell her what was up. I felt ashamed and that was ridiculous, so I felt ashamed of being ashamed too. It was mid-afternoon when Tommy got back. I knew he would come upstairs to make his own effort and I prepared myself for more stonewalling. Sure enough, he showed up after a few minutes, smiling broadly and wanting to know if I'd bought any records. Within a few sentences, we were on the same ground I'd walked with Rose. Enquiries and denials. Tommy hadn't sat down. He would have towered over me even if I'd been standing too. From my sitting position on the bed, he looked like he was in danger of scraping the ceiling.

He tilted his head and half-closed one eye, giving me the once-over. Something happened, he said slowly, that made you feel embarrassed, made you feel like a little boy? Maybe in front of other people? It could have been a guess, but I don't think it was. I think Tommy was a very wise man, that's all. I almost started crying again and even though I kept it together, Tommy knew he'd hit the bulls-eye. There wasn't much point in holding out, I supposed, so I told him the whole story. He nodded encouragement every so often as I mumbled my way through it, but his expression didn't change. When I got to the end, he coughed gently into his fist and told me we'd be going into town to see Mr Fallon right away. There was no anger in him.

He had the relaxed, competent tone of a doctor issuing a prescription for some minor ailment. Still, I was terrified. He was going to beat the horrible bastard into a paste, I was sure of it. Tommy picked up on my fear. Just to talk, he assured me. Just a chat. He understood that I was nervous, but it was the right thing to do. If I didn't go with him – and he was going either way – then the awful feeling would fester. If I went along, it would be over forever on the same day it happened. He promised. I said I'd get my coat.

We found Fallon as soon as we arrived at the shop – almost literally bumped into him, in fact. He was by the door, barking abuse at an underling who was mopping something up too slowly or too casually. Tommy said his name, going with a formal 'Mr Gregory Fallon', and as he did so, placed a hand on the nape of his neck. Not on his shoulder, not on his back – on the nape of his neck. That hand was so big, the thumb and forefinger almost met under Fallon's chin. Tommy left it in place, as if it was glued there, while he slid around to the man's front. He said a cheerful hello and didn't wait for a response. There had been a misunderstanding earlier, he noted, all smiles. No real harm done. These things happen. Fallon started to speak. Tommy bulldozed on. It seemed to him, though, that a thread had been left dangling. The lad had been accused in public and cleared in private. That didn't seem fair, did it? The thing to do, in his opinion, was for Fallon to announce, here and now, with the same level of volume he'd employed earlier, that he had been mistaken and would like to apologize. Fallon protested – honest mistake this, no need that – but somewhere along the way he seemed to lose confidence in himself. His voice got smaller, like he was moving away from us, and then he clammed up entirely. At the time, I guessed that Tommy had allowed his grip to tighten. Maybe he hadn't been so obvious. Maybe Fallon had painted himself a picture, unaided. In any event, he nodded briskly and said that sounded fine to him. Tommy's hand slid away from his neck and slapped him on the shoulder so hard he took two steps to his right. Good stuff, Tommy said. No time like the present.

Fallon stewed for a moment, then clapped his hands and said he had an announcement to make. Everyone near the door stopped to listen and a few curious heads came poking out of the aisles. He had made an error earlier that day, he said, and he wanted to put it right, because honesty was so important to him. At that point, he turned, caught my eye, and beckoned me forward. I stepped up. This young man was falsely accused of shoplifting, Fallon went on (as if the accusation had happened without human intervention) and the shop owes him an apology, which it is happy to give. He made a sweeping gesture with his arms then, which I took to mean, *show's over, go back to spending money, let's never speak of this again.* Everyone went about their business, looking a bit confused but happy to have witnessed a little drama. Much appreciated, Tommy said, and offered his hand. Fallon took it with bad grace and kept a reasonably straight face when it crushed his. Although it wasn't much, as apologies went – no free chocolate, I'd noticed – I understood that revenge wasn't the point. Tommy didn't care about Fallon. He cared about me. So long as I got to draw a line under the whole affair, my accuser could half-ass his regrets all he liked.

Sleep didn't come easily to me that night. I kept replaying

Tommy's moves in my head, trying to figure out what had made his intervention so perfect. It was nothing to do with his size, I thought. That was just a tool he'd used for this particular job. The real skill was something else. Going back to the shop with him could have been every bit as humiliating as being dragged around the place by Fallon. I could have felt like even more of a child and, worse, a squealer. Instead, I'd walked tall, like I was sticking up for myself in a reasonable, adult manner. Why? Was it something Tommy had said? Some look he'd given me? A wink at just the right moment? What? I had no idea. But I vowed that if I ever had children of my own, I would make damn sure they felt the way I felt at that moment. Loved. Supported. Empowered. They would worship me the way I worshipped Tommy. It was my number one goal in life.

And now look. My daughter had no respect for me. Had been quietly seething for decades. Was inching towards the woman *who abandoned her* as the lesser of two evils. I crept away from the grave, staring at my feet, gagging for a Pringle, wondering what the point of me was.

While I was at the cemetery, Jim was in Dublin, seeing his mother. The day before, Saturday, when he'd finished telling me that Eleanor couldn't possibly have said what she said, he'd rubbed his chin and said he 'might as well get it over with straight away'. We were sitting at the kitchen table with the remains of our fish and chips from the chipper. As was our tradition, we hadn't bothered with plates, eating straight from the greasy paper. There was nothing here for me to feel bad about or sorry about or angry about, he said. He was going to see his mother because he was curious. And he was going in such a rush because otherwise he'd have to take time off work. He only had a few days before she went back to London. What difference did it make whether he went on Sunday or Monday or Tuesday? My mind was still reeling from my conversation with his sister – she'd only been gone an hour – and I had no brain space for this. I let him say his piece and then wandered into the living room, hoping he wouldn't follow me. He did, almost immediately, but only to say he was off to the cinema with the boys. Making an effort not to sound relieved, I said goodbye and spent the evening staring at my book, not taking in a single word.

I'd only been back from the cemetery for twenty minutes or so when he returned from Dublin. I was in the hall when he arrived, standing on a kitchen chair so I could change the light bulb.

'Wait, fuck, wait,' I yelped when the door opened and banged off the chair. I got down and stepped back. 'Right, come on.'

He stuck his head round the door. 'What are you at?'

'Changing the bulb, what does it look like I'm at?'

'I half thought you were hanging yourself, to be honest.'

It was a tasteless remark, I thought. And stupid too. 'You thought I was hanging myself but I'd stopped to let you in before I went through with it?'

'Yeah, fair enough.' He shut the door behind him and squeezed around me. 'Desperate for a cup of tea.'

I followed him into the kitchen, where he was already busy, and sat on the chair I'd just been standing on. 'Well?'

'I'm not sure where to begin.'

'Jesus Christ, Eleanor was the same. Just get on with it.'

'All right, calm down.'

'I am calm.'

He'd taken a pack of digestives from the cupboard. He popped one in his mouth, whole, and started munching. I tried very hard not to roar at him. It wasn't easy. When the biscuit had gone down, he dropped teabags into the pot and waited for the kettle to finish boiling.

'Right,' he said as he poured. 'It didn't go all that great, and I'm pretty sure we'll never see each other again. Let's start with that.'

'Really?'

He brought the tea things over and sat down. 'Oh yeah.'

'Why, what went wrong?'

'Y'know. Stuff just came out.'

'What sort of stuff?'

'"You're supposed to be my mother and you ran off and left me when I was still a child" sort of stuff.'

'Right.'

'I didn't start with that, now. We were doing all right for a while. Just chit-chat. It was like she was an aunt I hadn't seen in ages or something. I was waiting for her to throw herself on my mercy, maybe do a wee bit of begging for forgiveness, that sort of thing. Never happened. So I asked her straight. I said, "Are you not even going to apologize?"'

'And?'

'You know when someone says something and you know they've been practising it? That's what I got. This whole speech about how she could say she was sorry if I really wanted her to, but there wouldn't be much point because she wouldn't mean it. She isn't sorry she left. It was the right thing for her to do, she was so unhappy, and so on.'

'Me, me, me.'

'Correct. I got up and left her to it. In a wee coffee shop this was, near the hotel. I said if she couldn't even say sorry for walking out on her family, whatever her reasons, then I wanted nothing to do with her. Ever. There was a bit of back and forth. It got nasty enough. And that was that.'

We drank our tea in silence for a little while. 'Was she like you remembered?' I asked.

He wobbled his head from side to side. 'Eh. I don't know. The last time I saw her was in 1994. I'd have a hard time even telling you what she used to be like. I think I've blocked it all out, all the wee details. She fucked off – that's what I remember.'

'Did she look sick?'

'She seemed fine to me. And she didn't bring it up, either. I did. I said I was sorry to hear about her illness, she said thanks, and that was the end of it.' He paused. 'She asked about you, by the way. I told her you were on top of the world, never better. Enjoying your retirement.'

'Thanks for lying.'

'I wasn't lying! You're doing grand, aren't you?'

'I wouldn't call it "on top of the world", Jim.'

'Well, there's plenty far worse off. She said she'd be willing to see you, if you wanted that. This was before it all went tits up, obviously. She's flying back Tuesday night. And she'd already given me her address in London, in case we ever felt like visiting. Said to include you in that too. Here, lookit.' He reached into his arse pocket and produced a piece of paper, holding it out for me to read. I hadn't seen her handwriting in so long. Chiswick, W4.

Hope bloomed in my chest. I peered at him.

'And that was it? That was all she said about meeting me? There's no chance of her coming here?'

'Well, I don't know what she's going to do, do I? She certainly seemed to be saying you had to go to her, if you wanted to meet. And, to tell you the truth, I got the impression she was only being polite.'

'Polite!'

'You know what I mean. Like she was willing to meet you if that was what you wanted, but she wasn't going to actually make it happen, and she didn't honestly expect you to either.'

I thought about it. She could still hop on a bus to Monaghan. Even after she went back to London, there was nothing stopping her coming home again any time she felt like it. So long as she was alive, I would never be able to say there was zero chance of her showing up. Still, I felt giddy with relief. The most likely scenario was that she'd stay put in Dublin until Tuesday, then fly back to London, and never darken my door. 'I believe I will decline the invitation,' I said.

'No shit. Me too.'

He half-stood and threw the address on the pile of take-away flyers that we kept on top of the fridge, then settled into his chair again. We sat in silence for a little while, both of us staring at our folded hands.

'Are you sorry you went to see her?' I asked then.

He didn't hesitate. 'Yeah. I am.'

'The stress of it.'

'No, it's not that. She's dying and we ended on a bad note.'

'Jim, you'd already ended on a bad note, remember?'

'That was different. I was a child then, more or less. This was two adults sniping at each other. Leaves a bad taste, is all. When she goes, I'll know the last thing I ever said to her was that she deserved to be alone.'

He looked away, ashamed.

There didn't seem to be much I could say that would help. 'Well. That's the end of it for now, anyway. She reappeared, pissed Eleanor off, pissed you off, ignored me, and now she'll vanish again. Chances are, none of us will ever lay eyes on her–'

'Um.'

'What?'

'I called Eleanor when I got back to the car to tell her how I'd got on. She, eh, she reckons she's going to have her round for dinner after all. Before she goes back. To meet Aidan and Miles.'

I blinked at him. 'Is this a joke?'

'No. That's what she said.'

'For fuck's sake! It's not twenty-four hours since she was telling me your mother had a nerve even mentioning Miles!'

'There's no point shouting at me, Da.'

'I'm not shouting at you! I'm shouting and you're here, that's different! Jesus Christ, what is she thinking? Is she planning to have an actual relationship with her? Because that's where this is going.'

'It was a surprise to me too,' Jim said. 'And I told her so. "Seems a bit quick," I said.'

'That's exactly what she said herself, fucking yesterday! Too much, too soon! This was right before she somehow got into blaming me for the whole shitshow and saying I'll wind up in a nurse's uniform one of these days because I'm so pathetic and weak.'

'Don't get all upset about it, Da. She talks a lot of shite about all this.'

'Oh, so now you believe me? Last night you said I was imagining things.'

211

'I said that because you took me by surprise. Lookit, the truth of it is, Eleanor's always had funny ideas about Mum leaving us. It wasn't the leaving that got to her so much as the timing. It would have been better if you'd split up when we were tiny. Instead of teenagers, like. That sort of thing.'

'Yeah, and it's all *my* fault because I should have kicked her out at the first hint of trouble.'

'That's about the height of it, yeah. Don't get all upset. She'll come round.'

'She'll come round? She'll come *round*? It's been twenty-odd years, Jim! If she's going to come round, she'd want to get a wriggle on.'

He didn't seem to have a good answer for that, which was fair enough, because there was no good answer for it. I watched him thinking. His expression changed as he produced then abandoned various notions.

'Look,' he said, after a long while, 'you're all annoyed and you're not thinking straight. The truth of the thing is, nothing's really changed, has it?'

'I'm looking forward to you explaining that.'

He leaned forward on to the table, clasped his hands together, then showed me his palms. He put me in mind of Tony Blair.

'These weird ideas Eleanor has, it's not like she came up with them yesterday. She's been thinking this way since day one, and you've never noticed anything wrong. The two of you have had a perfectly good relationship, haven't you?'

'That's it? That's your positive spin? She thinks you're pathetic but, not to worry, she's managed to choke it down so far?'

'I wouldn't say *pathetic*.'

'Oh, what would you say?'

That was rhetorical. I was horrified to see him giving it some thought. 'Uh . . . weak?'

'Jesus *Christ*, Jim. Please stop helping.'

We sat there for in silence for a long time. Then Jim said, 'Would you be all right on your own for a while?'

'Why, where are you going?'

'I was planning on heading out for a run.'

'Go on, so.'

He got up and left, giving me a little pat on the shoulder as he passed.

22

The next few days were tough. No matter how much I talked myself down, I couldn't settle while Una was still in the country. I fretted and paced, wishing I knew her exact departure time. Even late in the evening on Tuesday, when she was surely back in London, or at least on the plane, or at very least waiting in Dublin airport, I sat swaying on the sofa, clenching my teeth so hard my jaw hurt. It wasn't until the Wednesday morning, when she was one hundred per cent, definitely, undoubtedly gone, that I finally got some peace. It didn't last. My fear that she'd come visit me in Monaghan had been replaced by the fear that she and Eleanor were now a team. It wasn't even a fear; it was a cold certainty. I could picture them huddled over a pot of tea, rolling their eyes and shaking their heads as they ran through examples of my lifelong uselessness. They would keep in touch. Eleanor would send regular updates on my failures. One day I'd realize that Eleanor had far more contact with her mother than she had with me. Nothing would ever be the same again.

Every passing hour seemed to find me feeling more lost

and hopeless than the one before. Jim came and went – to work, out running, to the pub – while I stayed in the house, wallowing in self-pity. After a while, I started to feel bad about feeling bad. There had to be an end to it, but I couldn't for the life of me imagine what it would take to get me up and about again.

And then I got a text from Frank.

Frank was not a great man for mobile phones. He had one, but he treated it like a wheelchair. It was something he needed, that was all. You could expect him to go along with it; you couldn't expect him to like it. I phoned him for no reason once in a while, purely to annoy him. His spluttering rage, when he twigged that the call had no specific purpose, was always good for a laugh. He only called me when he was gasping for a pint and had lost patience waiting on me to arrange an outing. Texts were a whole other thing. He had somehow arrived at the opinion that text messages were a level above phone calls, even. They were reserved for the direst of emergencies. Frank had only ever sent me two. The first said:

DUCKING BROKE DOWN ON OLD ARMAGH ROAD A FEW MILE OUT OF TOWN COME AND GOT ME

The second said:

WILL BE LATE FOR PUB DUCKING BRUTAL CASE OF THE SHITS GLUED TO THE POT HERE

I think maybe he had confused them for urgent telegrams. You could stick the word STOP in there every so often and do no harm to the meaning. In any event, the third text he ever sent me arrived at noon on the Sunday after Una's visit. I hadn't seen him for a while. When I read his name on the screen, I assumed the message would be pints-related and was already preparing excuses as I picked up the phone. It wasn't pints-related. My third-ever text from Frank said:

IN CAVAN HOSPITAL HAD A DUCKING HEART ATTACH

I almost had a ducking heart attach myself. When the shock passed, I opened his contact details and stabbed his phone number with a trembling finger. No answer. For a second I thought he'd died, but it was more likely that he just wasn't up to talking. I went upstairs, where Jim was entering his second hour in the bath, and shouted the news through the bathroom door. Although his words were indistinct, I heard concerned splashing. Two minutes later, I was on the road. When people describe shocking events they often say stuff like *It didn't seem possible* or *I couldn't believe it was really happening*. I didn't get any of that. Frank was an overweight sixty-seven-year-old who drank like a fish, ate chips with every meal, and counted breathing as exercise. If anything, it was a wonder he hadn't already had a heart attack.

Cavan hospital was about an hour away. It wasn't until I was parking outside it that it occurred to me to wonder about visiting times. I was fine, it turned out, but just about. A surprisingly cheerful woman on reception informed me that the Coronary Care unit was on the ground floor and pointed me down a corridor to Frank's ward. It was a six-bedder. Frank was in the far corner on the left of the large window. I spotted his daughter first – Carol, the baker. That wasn't ideal. I plain old didn't like Carol and it was entirely mutual. When she looked up and saw me coming over, she managed to smile and nod, but not before her true feelings had shimmered across her face. For a fraction of a second, she looked like a woman who'd found a pubic hair in her soup.

'Here he is,' she said.

I bent low and pecked her cheek. 'Carol.'

'Thanks for coming.'

'Of course.'

I turned to the patient. 'Jesus, Frank. What did you do to yourself?'

'I know. I'm sorry.'

'Eejit.'

He looked me over and shook his head ever so slightly. 'Not so much as a fucking grape.' This was a reference to my empty-handedness. Carol sighed and fidgeted. I knew – because Frank had told me – that she wasn't a fan of this kind of back and forth. She thought it was unbecoming in men our age. Wasn't mad about me calling her dad 'Frank' either.

'Take a seat,' she said, gesturing to a spare chair. She said it in the exact same tone you'd use to tell someone to shut the fuck up. I sat. Frank didn't look good, obviously, but he didn't look as bad as I'd expected. I'd been picturing him deathly grey and flat on his back, barely breathing. Instead, he was sitting up – or rather, his bed was holding him up – and he was more or less his normal colour.

'What happened?' I asked him. 'Did you drop to the floor all of a sudden or what?'

He fiddled with the tube going into his nose. 'Didn't drop, no. There was no big moment. I felt like shite for a day or two, then it all came to a head yesterday. No, the day before.'

'The day before that,' Carol said.

'Whatever. Felt like someone was driving back and forward over me chest. I knew what it was and called 999.' He was holding a bottle of water with a straw sticking out of it. With some difficulty, he raised it and took a few sips.

'What are they doing about it?' I asked. 'Do you need surgery or what?'

'Just drugs. Minor, they said. I'd hate to see fucking major.'

I was momentarily stuck for something to say. 'Not a bad wee ward,' I said then, as if there were some wards that had crocodiles in them.

Carol made a tutting sound. 'There's nothing wrong with the ward except that man in the middle bed' – she flicked her head towards him – 'shouldn't be in here.'

I glanced over my shoulder. The man was tiny and very old. Toothless and unshaven, short white hair sticking straight up like the bristles on a toilet brush. He was sound asleep.

'He looks sick to me, Carol,' I said.

'I'm not saying he's not sick, I'm saying he should be in a mental hospital. Never shuts up when he's awake. Talking gibberish to no one. He thought he was on a beach earlier. Roaring about jellyfish.'

This struck me as uncharitable, to say the least. But I didn't want to get into it. I turned to Frank. 'Any idea how long you'll be in?'

He shook his head and took some more water. Carol suddenly stood. 'I'm going to get something to eat,' she announced. 'I'll be back in a while.'

When she'd gone, I shuffled a bit closer to her father. 'I rang you after you texted me,' I said. 'No answer.'

'Carol took the phone off me. She probably saw you calling and ignored it.' He'd never tried to pretend that she liked me.

'Fair enough. I thought maybe you'd died. It was no way for you to go, I was thinking – sending a frigging text.' This was a reasonable effort, I thought. It didn't even raise a smile.

'Don't even joke,' Frank said. 'I thought I was a goner. Honest to God, I did.'

I was embarrassed. 'Of course. Sorry. But you're not in any danger now, are you?'

'No. They say not. A while in here, a few drugs. They were talking about diet, about exercise too.'

'Sure lookit, if our Jim can take up running, you can manage an occasional walk.'

A grim nod. 'I suppose I'll have to.'

That was a surprise. No sneer? No vow to double down on his sitting? 'Cut out the sausages, maybe,' I prompted. 'Have the odd banana.'

'Yeah. Definitely.'

I was at a loss. A normal person might be expected to make lifestyle changes in the aftermath of a heart attack, but this was Frank. The man put butter on crisps. We weren't talking about minor tweaks here.

'You're taking this seriously, then?'

He looked at me like he'd never seen me before. 'Of course I am, Eugene. It was a *heart attack*.'

'I know, I–'

'Time comes when a man has to have a hard talk with himself and admit some things that he'd rather not get to admitting.'

While I agreed with the sentiment – did I ever – I had

no idea why he was suddenly talking like a cowboy. 'Uh, yeah.'

'Time's ticking away here. There's no point pretending that it isn't. The days when we could laugh it off are behind us.'

'You don't have to tell *me*, Frank. I've had some bloody dark thoughts too and they–'

'These aren't dark thoughts, Eugene. They're practical thoughts. What it boils down to is, there's only so much time left so, one, how can you make sure you don't shorten it even further and, two, how are you going to make the most of it?'

I could see that he was in a funny mood and I totally understood why. Still, I couldn't let this slide by.

'So it's going to be all fruit smoothies and skydiving from now on, is it, Frank? Come on.'

'Maybe not,' he sighed. 'But I have good intentions. You have to start somewhere.'

Neither of us spoke for a while after that. The other conversations around us suddenly seemed deafening. My chair dug into my legs. I felt too hot. Frank had the luxury of being able to close his eyes. I had to sit there, telling myself I was a bad hospital visitor, then a bad friend, and finally a bad human being in general. It got so awkward, I was actually glad to see Carol coming back. She was holding a packet of crisps and a can of Coke.

'Restaurant's a disgrace,' she said, retaking her seat. 'Wouldn't eat out of it if you paid me.'

'It can't have been worse than the vending machine,' I said foolishly.

'You didn't see it, did you? At least I can be sure no one spat in the crisps.'

This was a fairly typical contribution. Carol lived in a world whose population was evenly split between morons and scumbags. Everywhere she looked, she saw stupidity and malice. There were days when I felt sorry for her; this wasn't one of them.

'Nobody's spitting in the food, Carol,' I said.

She rolled her eyes. 'You eat it, then.'

'Not hungry,' I mumbled, like a child.

And so began the second awkward silence. Not long into it, I noticed that Frank had nodded off.

'How's the bakery going?' I asked Carol.

'Great,' she said. 'You'd know if you ever came in.'

She faked a laugh and I faked one back. Visiting time ended a few minutes later. It felt like six hours. On the drive back to Monaghan, I got on board a stupid and pointless train of thought. I knew it was no good from the outset but, as with so many of my thought trains lately, I seemed to have no ability to stop it once it got rolling. Eleanor and Carol weren't good friends. They weren't even friends. But they had bumped into each other plenty of times over the years. And they both, apparently, thought I was a complete tool. Had they ever put their heads together to complain about me? Or laugh at me? It didn't seem likely. In fact, it seemed extremely unlikely. Still, I couldn't leave the thought alone. I kept poking at it, like a sore tooth. It fit together nicely with my other fear, that Eleanor and her mother were now in cahoots. Different paintings by the same artist.

Back home, I gave Jim the gist. He was glad to hear that Frank was in no danger and was as amused as I was at the thought of him eating an apple, let alone transforming his diet. We agreed that we deserved pizza later, and I went to have a lie-down. I started thinking about a movie I'd seen years ago. It was about a teacher in some posh school in America who gets all the boys to stop being dicks by explaining that they'll be dead one day (this hadn't already occurred to them, apparently). I hated that movie and I hated the general sentiment. Live every day as if it's your last and all that? It wasn't *possible*. You were setting yourself up for disappointment. Life was hard enough without adding that kind of pressure, that was always my attitude.

On the other hand, I thought now, there was a grain of common sense at the heart of the bullshit. No one, when the moment comes, looks around the faces of their gathered loved ones and says, *Oh well, at least I didn't take too many chances*. It was about balance, I supposed, like so many things. You couldn't live with your foot to the floor every single day. Once in a while, though . . .

I lay there on my back with my hands folded together on my tummy – like a laid-out corpse, it amused me to note – and decided once and for all. No more excuses. No more faffing about. I would ask Annie out for dinner.

23

I didn't know where Annie lived. I didn't know her phone number. I didn't know her *second name*. My only option, I decided, was to talk to her at the salsa night. She would be there before everyone else, I presumed, setting up and whatnot. I could show up, say what I had to say and disappear into the night before her students arrived. The class started at eight-thirty. I'd arrive at eight and hope she did too. Even if she didn't show until, say, twenty past, I'd be fine. If anything, a bit of time pressure might help me get to the point.

When Thursday came around, I got the willies in a big way. This was predictable. So predictable, in fact, that I'd written myself a pep talk on the back of an electricity bill. It was in between the books on my bedside locker. When my anxiety hit its peak, at about five p.m., I went upstairs and pulled out the note. It said:

Eugene, you big bollocks. Don't chicken out. This is what you want to do. You don't have to think about it any more. You've done all the thinking. It's time to do the doing. You'll be raging with yourself if you don't follow through. You can get Pringles after, as a reward.

It had seemed like a foolproof plan at the time. I'd got quite choked up by my own stirring words and spent a happy few minutes wondering if I would have made a good general. Now I could hardly believe my eyes. *It's time to do the doing?* For fuck's sake. On the plus side, being disgusted by my own nonsense distracted me from by my shattered nerves and got me through until Jim's arrival home. It didn't take him long to notice that something was afoot. It didn't take him any time at all. He took one look at me and asked why was I 'all dressed up'. That one was easy enough to field. I wasn't 'all dressed up', I told him, faking offence, I was wearing a shirt that I didn't wear very often. Later, over chicken nuggets and chips, he asked why I was being 'all jittery and weird'. I denied that I was and moved the conversation on to the subject of Eleanor. There had been no word from her all week. I sure as hell wasn't going to call her, so that meant it was down to Jim. He'd been refusing on the grounds of 'Fuck that'. Pressed for a little more detail, he'd said something about not wanting to be a go-between any more. Which was fair enough, really. We repeated our lines now, to little effect. And then it was time to take the first serious steps. I needed an excuse to get out of the house. Normally, I would have said I was going for a drink with Frank, but that was no good. Frank had only been released from hospital the day before. It would be a while, I assumed, before he was up for it. His medical adventure had given me another option, though.

'You know, this business with Frank has given me a bit

of a wake-up call,' I said, doing my best to look thoughtful. 'Health-wise, I mean.'

'Da, you're only after finishing a plate of chicken nuggets and chips.'

'Well, I'm starting small. A bit of exercise, maybe.'

'You needn't think you're coming running with me. I don't want that on my conscience.'

'*Walking*, Son, I'm going to go for an occasional *walk*. Might start tonight, actually.'

'Good for you.'

And that was that. A little while later, I sneaked away upstairs. There wasn't much getting ready to be done. I was already wearing my good shirt, which only saw service once or twice a year. I'd thought it best to put it on ahead of time and try to pass the choice off as a whim, rather than arouse Jim's suspicions by saying I was going for a walk and then putting on something nice. I'd left my shower until late afternoon to maximize freshness and had deodorized my pits three times. All that was left, really, was to brush my teeth again (fourth time that day) and check that there was nothing stuck to my face or hanging out of my nose. When I'd satisfied myself that I looked no worse and smelled much better than usual, I went back downstairs and bid Jim as casual a goodbye as I could muster. He was barely able to contain a grin as he wished me good luck. I understood. It was the same feeling I'd had when he started running. *Okay, fine. I'll go along with this and pretend you've turned over a new leaf.* He reminded me that he'd be out dancing by the time I came back and I tried to look as if I'd forgotten that was tonight.

I felt a level of nervousness now that wasn't far off

physical illness. All of my insides seemed to be on the move. My stomach was headed for my throat and my heart was trying to escape my body entirely. I told myself that things would improve once I was out on the street, putting one foot in front of the other. That turned out to be 180 degrees wrong. The fresh air hit me like five simultaneous pints, making my head spin and my knees tremble. There was a decent chance, I thought, that I'd wind up ducking down an alley to puke. I kept walking all the same and eventually, with a lot of effort, I managed to get myself back down to the state I was in before I left the house. It was like upgrading to 'severely burned' from 'currently on fire', but I was glad of the improvement. I'd practised what I was going to say, of course. The gist, not word by word. I ran through it all again now as I walked, finding comfort in the fact that I could remember it, at least. It might have been a load of old shite, and it might get me laughed at (or slapped), but it was still in there.

I was so engrossed in my rehearsal that when I arrived at the church hall, I almost marched straight in. Catching myself on, I stopped a few feet from the entrance and gave myself one last pep talk, which amounted to *Fuckfuckfuckfuckfuck*. My mouth felt like it was coated with sand and my extremities were all a-tingle. I clapped my hands together, just to feel the sting, and tried the door handle. Locked. I was too early. I'd considered this possibility, of course. The thing to do was leg it and return in a few minutes. I didn't want Annie coming round the corner and finding me waiting there, all twitchy and nervous, like a wee boy who'd been sent to the principal's office. When I turned to go, however, she was standing five feet away with her portable stereo and her paperwork. And her partner, Philip. Whose existence I'd forgotten about.

'I thought that was you,' she said cheerfully. 'You're giving us another go? Great!'

I waved hello – from the wrist, like Forrest Gump. It wasn't a great start. 'Hi, Annie,' I croaked.

'This is Philip. Philip, this is Eugene.'

Philip skipped forward, hand extended. He was younger than Annie, but not young. Probably around Jim's age, I guessed. He was a barrel of a man, not tubby, but broad-shouldered and solid through the trunk. He had what my mother would have called 'a high colour'.

'Oh, *Eugene*,' he said as we shook. 'Jim's dad, right?'

'I'm not going to lie,' Annie said. 'I told Philip all about your first night here.'

'Yeah, that was . . . yeah,' I said, brilliantly.

'You're wild early,' Annie said, sounding very northern. *Wile urly*. 'Eight-thirty, we start at.'

My eyes darted about. I'd intended, at this point, to say that I wasn't there for the class and move with as much grace as I could muster into my big speech. Philip's presence made that impossible. The plan was in ruins and all we'd done was say hello. Obviously, there was only one sensible way to proceed and that was to give up for now. I'd have to think of some excuse and get the hell out of there, go back to the drawing board. I knew how that would end, though. If I pulled out now, I would never work up the courage to try again. I'd tell myself that it wasn't meant to be or some rubbish. It was now or never. I chose now.

'Not to worry,' I said. 'Sure I can help you set up.'

'There's not a lot to set up,' Philip said, producing a set of keys. 'The place could do with a sweep some nights – you're more than welcome to do that, if you like? I fucking *hate* sweeping. It makes me feel like Freddie Mercury in that video and I *hated* that video. It gave me the screaming heebie-jeebies. Freddie had a Hoover, I know, but you get my point.'

I had no idea what he was talking about, so I made no reply. He unlocked the church hall door and pushed through. Annie followed him. Lights snapped on and I heard the beeps of an alarm being reassured. I stepped in too and closed the door behind me.

Philip was right, there was almost nothing to it. We dragged out a little table for the stereo, fiddled with the lighting and pushed some chairs out of the way. The floor was fine. I swept it anyway, to give myself something to do. There was chit-chat, almost all of it about a fire that had gutted two houses in Killygoan. It was widely agreed that it was a 'miracle' no one had been killed. Talk of fires made me think of my father and his pub, of course, as it always did. I drove him from my mind. This was not the time.

It was a big room. If I was able to get Annie alone in a corner of it, it wasn't out of the question that we could have a conversation without being overheard by Philip. But that was both unlikely and risky. I had to get either him or the two of us out of there entirely. How, though? I was pondering this when Annie approached me and asked how come Jim and I hadn't shown up together. It was a reasonable question and I came up with a clever response, which was to stare at the woman with my mouth hanging open, blinking. She stepped closer still, looking concerned. No doubt she thought I was having some sort of medical episode. I might have wound up in the back of an ambulance, protesting, if Philip hadn't saved the day. He sauntered past, wiggling a lighter in the air and said he was nipping out for a cigarette before everyone arrived. This was it. This was my chance. While it was a long way from perfect, it was all I had. When I heard the door close, I looked at Annie and tried to answer her question. Something like a gasp came out. I did my best to produce some saliva and tried again.

'To tell you the truth, Jim doesn't know I'm here,' I said. 'I'm not even staying for the dancing, actually.'

'Oh?'

'I wanted to talk to you and I didn't know how else to find you.'

Her eyes did something I couldn't decipher. 'That sounds serious, Eugene. Is everything all right?'

One last deep breath. One last look around the inside of the plane. And jump.

'Jim's mother walked out on us all a long time ago, Annie. When he was a teenager. And his sister. Maybe I should have done the walking, long before that. She wasn't a good person, my wife. But that's neither here nor . . . The point is, I put all my energy into getting them through the end of their school days and out into the world and what have you, and I never, y'know, moved on. Romantically-wise. The years went by and I never once . . . I mean, no one ever . . . Christ, I had a whole speech ready and it's gone out the window. Lookit, what I'm trying to get at here, and I'm making a balls of it, I know I am, what I'm trying to get at here is I think you're great. I like talking to you and I think you're, um, beautiful. Do you think there's any chance you might consider coming out with me for dinner some time?'

Thinking this moment through, which I'd done dozens of times, I'd imagined all sorts of terrible outcomes. She would smack me in the face. She would recoil in horror. She would laugh. It had never occurred to me that she might burst into tears. I was stunned. She turned away from me, hand over her mouth. Terrible seconds ticked by.

'Is it really that bad an idea?' I asked. I wasn't sure if I was joking or not.

She shook her head. 'It's nothing like that.'

'Why are you crying?'

Finally, she turned to face me. She was recovering her composure. 'People will be arriving in a few minutes, Eugene. I can't talk about this now. I shouldn't talk about it at all, in fact. You should . . . you should talk to Jim. I'm sorry.'

We stared at each other. And while we were staring, the door opened. Seamus and Lilian Doherty, the old couple from the sweet shop, walked in.

'We're a bit early,' Lilian boomed. 'But sure, what harm?'

She noticed me then and rolled her eyes, not even trying to hide it. Seamus stared right through me. When he finally recognized me, he tossed his head in contempt and adjusted course away from me. Philip followed them in. When he got close enough, he saw at once what the other pair had missed – that Annie was upset. He started towards her, looking concerned. She stopped him with a gesture and a tiny shake of her head. Then *he* gave me a dirty look. I had the set. Annie stepped closer and held me by the elbows.

230

'I'm sorry,' she said again. 'Talk to Jim,' she said again. All I could do was leave. So I left.

I knew what it was. Too many pieces fit for it to be anything else. Still, I sat at the kitchen table, pondering all the other things it *might* be. Maybe she was gay. Maybe she was joining a nunnery. My theories got wilder as the night wore on. By the time Jim arrived home, I was toying with the idea that she might be reluctant to start a relationship because she only had weeks to live.

'Well,' he said, placing his keys on the table much more gently than usual. 'Are you all right?'

I'd prepared a small joke. 'It took two tries, but I've got the message now. I'm definitely never going to salsa night again.' He didn't smile. Neither did I.

'I'm sorry this happened, Da,' he said. 'It's my fault. I should have told you long before now. We're an item, Annie and me.'

'Yeah. That's what I guessed.'

He took a seat. 'I didn't tell you in the first place because I didn't think it would last and I didn't want you getting all excited. I know you worry about me on the girlfriend front.'

'Yep.'

'And then, when it had been going well for a while . . . I dunno. I suppose it was a couple of things. We liked it being a secret. She hasn't told anyone either. It was exciting, y'know? Then there was the age business. I was afraid you might think she was too old for me and we'd have a big fight and the whole loveliness of it would be ruined.'

'How old is she?' I braced myself for sixty-odd.

'She's fifty-three. And I'm still in my thirties, just about, so . . .'

'It's not that big a gap.'

'Kids and that, though.'

'*Kids*? You're talking about kids?'

'Well, that's not going to happen, is my point. But yeah, it's serious, Da. Got serious very quickly.'

I was happy for him. I really was. Still, my happiness was a candle, my embarrassment was the sun. 'So, this explains all the nights out.'

'Yeah.'

'The boys didn't get social again, after all.'

'No.'

'Is the running real?'

'That's real. Annie's idea, though, I have to admit. She's a runner. This was her too.' He patted his scalp and then his chin.

'Wait a minute. The hair was *my* idea.'

'The charity part was your idea. But she'd already told me I should lop it all off, since it was going anyway.'

I sighed, long and low. 'I thought you were awful easily talked into it. I met her that night. In the pub. There for you, I suppose.'

'She told me. Dragged poor Philip along so she wouldn't be on her own. He thought she'd lost her mind. She's always right about stuff like hair and clothes. Great taste.'

'This is why you're suddenly dressing better.'

'She has suggested the odd shirt, yeah.'

He seemed to be finished with the explanations. I racked my brain trying to come up with something else to ask or say. Anything at all that would postpone the inevitable. I couldn't come up with a single thought. The inevitable arrived, as it tends to do.

'So, I suppose we should talk about tonight,' Jim said.

I stared at the table. 'I suppose so.'

'Annie's very upset. She's upset at the thought of you being upset. She likes you a lot.' That hurt. I winced. He noticed.

'Da, she doesn't want you to feel bad or embarrassed or–'

'How the fuck am I not going to feel embarrassed?' I snapped. 'How would *you* feel?'

He closed his eyes tight for a moment, as if he was in terrible pain. 'All right, listen: you're not wrong. There's no getting around it. If anything, it would be strange if you weren't embarrassed. She wants you to know that you don't have to be any extra embarrassed on her account, that's all. On top of the normal amount, like. Same goes for me.'

'Pity. I'm getting pity now.'

'Come on. It's not pity. We're trying to say the right things here.'

My anger subsided. Or at least it stopped pointing outwards. 'I'm sorry,' I said. 'I'm glad you found someone.'

'Thank you.'

'It's been a while.'

'It has.'

'I thought you weren't even interested in women.'

'I remember. I remember you asking. It's not that I wasn't interested . . .'

'What then?'

'Ah, never mind.'

'No, what?'

He shrugged. 'Now's not the time.'

If I had antennae, they would have twitched. Something in his tone made me think – let me *know* – that this had something to do with me. 'Not the time for what, Jim?'

'All right, lookit. I had . . . bad, uh . . . bad teenage experiences.'

I was lost and waited for him to explain. Apparently, he didn't intend to. 'What bad teenage experiences?'

'I really don't think you–'

'Jim.'

He exhaled and pushed his chair back on two legs. 'All right. Do you remember Claire Brady?'

'The wee girl you were going out with?'

His eyes narrowed. The chair fell forward again. 'See, that' – he waggled a finger – 'that, right there . . .'

'What? Did I say some–'

'You said "wee girl". Like it was all nothing more than a cute, a cute . . .' Words failed him for a moment. 'I really loved her. I *loved* her. And she dumped me for some other guy. Just like my mother had dumped my father for some other guy.' Anger had twisted his features. He'd made fists. It was so sudden.

'Jim, you were only–'

'Sixteen. I was sixteen. So fucking what?'

'I don't know what to say, Jim. This is all news to me.'

'I know it is. I was ready for the nuthouse and you barely noticed. When you did notice, you told me to buck up or made some crappy joke.'

It took a moment for this to land on me. 'Jesus Christ! So, you're saying, what? You've been mad at me all this time too?'

'I wouldn't say "all this time". It wasn't a constant thing. But I was mad at you, yeah. Mad as hell.'

'And this is the night you choose to tell me? After what just happened?'

His anger had faded away as quickly as it had flared up. He shrugged one shoulder. 'I didn't choose it. You asked.'

I had the distinct impression that if I dwelled on this information, I'd go immediately insane. It was too much, on top of everything else. I had to keep moving forward, like a shark. 'That's why you've avoided women all these years? Because you had a bad break-up twenty-odd years ago?'

'Well, first of all, I haven't avoided women as much as you think I have. I haven't been a monk. What I've avoided is relationships. Not on purpose, not really. I mean, looking back, this is what I think it was about.'

'Just because–'

'No. Not just because. There's the other thing.'

'Which is?'

'Come on. Relationship-wise, I didn't exactly have brilliant role models.'

I had to run over this over in my head a couple of times before I could accept that I'd heard him right. 'You're including me in that? Not brilliant role models, plural? *She* walked out on *me*, if you recall.'

'I'm not saying it was your fault, am I?'

'I don't know, Jim. I honestly don't know what you're saying.'

'I'm saying that, between the two of you, you're my model for what a marriage looks like. Fault doesn't come into it. They're very, whaddayacallit, formative, those years.

And what I took in was that relationships either end in heartbreak or disaster. I'd seen the heartbreak bit and didn't want to end up–'

He stopped himself, looking panicked. I finished the thought for him. 'You didn't want to end up like me.'

'I didn't want to end up in your situation.'

'I know you think that's different. It's not.'

We sat in silence for a while. It felt like we'd gone down a hellish side road. My only choice was to put us back to the hellish main road. 'So it's not a secret any more, then? You and Annie?'

He shook his head. 'It was never a secret, exactly. We didn't tell anyone, that's all. Or go about together much.'

'Sounds like a secret to me.'

'Well that's over now.'

'Chances are I'm going to bump into her, then. If you're serious.'

'I suppose so. And we are.'

It occurred to me that a psychologist would have a field day with the age difference, what with the missing mother and all. I wondered if Jim had thought about that. He probably had.

No good could come from asking him. I stood up. 'I'm going to bed. Good night.'

'Da. We're fine. You and me. You and Eleanor too. Don't go running away with this whole thing, now. You're in strange form these days and I don't want–'

'Hm.'

'Okay?'

'Yep.'

'All right. Good night.'

I left him and started up the stairs, wondering which

thought would do the most to keep me awake – that both my children, apparently, had been harbouring grudges and found me pathetic or that one of these days I'd have to meet the future daughter-in-law that I'd just asked out myself.

24

I'd never been one for big lie-ins. Back when I was working, I might have an extra twenty minutes in bed on a day off, but it would be no more than that. It was some sort of guilt, I assumed, maybe something I'd picked up from Tommy, who thought laziness was the worst of all sins. I also assumed it would change when I retired. With work taken out of the equation, I thought, I would let go of my (or maybe Tommy's) principles. I pictured myself nipping downstairs to make tea and then sitting up in bed with a history book for an hour or two. It didn't happen. I continued to get out of bed more or less as soon as I woke up, which was always early. Jim found it annoying, at first. He'd plod downstairs in his shorts, yawning and scratching, and find me sitting there fully dressed. Dirty looks and cupboard-door bangs would follow. I think maybe he was worried that if I wasn't sleeping in, then I wasn't really retired. Time took care of that concern, and the early morning tension evaporated.

The morning after my second visit to salsa night, Jim tapped on my bedroom door and stuck his head in. He was off to work and wanted to make sure I was all right. How come I was still in bed, he wanted to know. I told him I fancied a lie-in. He blinked at me for a moment, waiting to see if I would retract this obvious bullshit. When I didn't, he said goodbye and left. The truth was, I didn't feel capable of rising. I hadn't slept much, but that wasn't the reason. Getting out of bed just felt like a bad idea. Everything was terrible. Matters wouldn't improve if I got up, and they (probably) wouldn't get worse if I stayed put. All of my troubles, when I stopped to think about it, had started with getting out of bed. I lay there for hours, curled up on my side, staring at the wall. Thinking.

It was about self-image, I decided. Not Annie – the other stuff. I'd always quietly congratulated myself on the brilliant job I'd done as a single parent. Right from the moment Una left, I'd been a rock for my children, in my head. They'd had terrible luck with their mother, I imagined people saying, but they really won the lottery with their dad. Now I knew that between them they thought I was a snivelling pushover, a pathetic cuckold, an insensitive oaf, and a cautionary tale. I wasn't who I thought I was, and it didn't seem fixable. My thoughts got so dark and muddled that the Annie situation started to feel like something I could tackle. I couldn't turn back time and not stand there mumbling about her beauty, but I could at least minimize the damage. Jim could invite her round to the house. Or maybe the three of us could go for coffee. Something like that. It would be awful, obviously, but it'd get it over with. Ripping the plaster off quickly and what have you. What was the alternative? Creeping around town in the shadows, terrified of accidentally bumping into her?

I was so taken with the idea that I decided to act immediately. Fifteen minutes later, I was dressed and on the street. The plan was to find Jim at work, where I hadn't set foot in ages, and get the ball rolling. Alas, my courage fell away with every step I took. It was too soon. I wasn't thinking straight. This was no time for rash moves. I should have stuck with the original plan and stayed in bed forever. When I reached the shop door, I didn't even slow down. Marched right past it. Straight away, I fell victim to the very thing I'd been trying to avoid in the first place – the terrible fear that I would bump into Annie unprepared, panic, and say something stupid, thus doing the near impossible and making the whole situation worse. I decided I needed a drink and scurried to McDaid's. The first thing I saw when I walked in was Frank, sitting alone at the table we called ours, even though we only managed to snag it about once every five visits. This was heartening. It was great to see him out and about, for one thing. For another, I had a lot to talk over with him. Then it hit me: he was drinking . . . without me? My breath hitched. I approached.

'Frank?'

I half-expected him to hold his hands up and say this wasn't what it looked like. Instead, he nodded and shifted along the seat to let me join him. He was working on a bottle of Heineken. I had never known him to have anything other than a pint of Guinness. Or rather, several pints of Guinness.

'What the hell is that?' I said, pointing to the offending item.

'Don't start. I feel bad enough.'

'I'm doing my best here, Frank, but it's hard not to be offended. Since when did you go to the pub without me?'

'I'm not "going to the pub". This isn't "going to the pub".'

I looked around, acting confused. 'I don't know, it looks an awful lot like the pub to me.'

'You know what I mean, smarthole. I'm trying something out.'

'Heineken?'

He produced a long sigh, like you would with an annoyingly persistent child. 'I'm supposed to cut down on the pints. I wanted to see what it would be like to have one wee bottle of beer and then go about my business. That's what the doctor said.' He put on an irritatingly cheerful voice, '"You don't have to have a plethora of pints, Mr Clarke. You can have a small bottle of beer, maybe two, and go about your business." A fucking *plethora*. That's what he said.'

'And?'

'I'm only after sitting down. So far, it's shit.'

'It's not the same, no.'

'Not the same. At all.'

'Then again, you're on your own. You should have given me a shout.'

'No. Not when I'm only trying it out.'

'You're . . . practising?'

'I'm practising.'

'Do you want me to go?'

I was joking, but he seemed to mull it over for real. 'No,' he said finally. 'You're here now.'

'Well, can I have a pint or do I have to–'

'You can have a pint, yes, for fuck's sake.'

Clearly, Frank was in bad form. I went to the bar. 'How are you feeling, anyway?' I asked on my return.

'All right.'

'Yeah?'

'Yeah.'

'Good.'

I tucked into my pint. He stared at his beer. It seemed neither one of us could think of a single thing to say. I wasn't about to bother him with my many woes and had literally no other thoughts I could air. I'd never once felt awkward sitting in a pub with Frank, and I didn't care for it one bit. We started chatting, eventually, about this and that. Mostly about his health. I heard the word 'salt' more times in five minutes than I had in the previous five years. Your health, he said gravely, as if he'd come with the line himself, is your wealth. Sooner or later, I thought, he's going to ask about the latest on Una or maybe even Annie and that'll be my excuse. It'll be okay to start complaining because he'll be the one who brought it up. But it didn't happen. When he got to the bottom of his beer, he burped and said he wanted to get home for a nap. What could I do? I said that was fine and I'd see him soon. Maybe we'd have a proper night in the pub, even if he was stuck on the bottle or two of Heineken? He nodded sadly and off he went.

I stayed and had a small nervous breakdown.

'Come on, Da. Let's get you home.' Jim was sitting beside me, where Frank had been. I was aware that he'd been there for a while and had been saying lots of stuff, but I had no details. I was blind drunk, almost literally. My peripheral vision was gone and focusing took a lot of effort.

'Why are you here?' I said. My lips seemed to have trebled in size. *Wyooeer?*

Jim looked to the ceiling and exhaled. 'Once again, Pat called me. Pat from the pub. Because you've got yourself into a bit of a state.'

I looked around for more information, which necessitated closing one eye. There were lots of faces turned in my direction. All of them turned away.

'Pub?' I said. 'Still?'

'We're still in the pub, yep. We're going now, though. Isn't that right?'

'Okay.'

'I'll help you up.'

'Okay.'

'Up you get.'

'Okay.'

He was on his feet then and struggling to get me on mine. My legs weren't playing ball. Pat appeared and took the other side. 'Hello,' I said.

Pat nodded grimly. 'Well, Eugene. You'll be grand now. We'll get you out to the car and you'll be home in no time.'

They hoisted me up. I turned to Jim. 'Pat wouldn't serve me.' *Pawunnaserme*. 'Too drunk. I went to the off-licence. Came back. Still wouldn't serve me!'

'Even then?' Jim said. 'Pat, you monster.'

'I don't know what I was thinking,' Pat put in. I could tell they were mocking me but I couldn't work out what I'd said wrong. It turned out that, once upright, I could walk more or less unaided. Jim and Pat stayed by my side, guiding me, like those rails they put down the side of the alley when kids are bowling. Outside, I noticed that the light had changed. 'What time is it?' I asked.

'It's about half six,' Jim said.

I chewed this information over. 'Work!' I yelped. 'Shop?'

'It's all right, Da. Noel's looking after it.'

'Noel's an arsehole.'

'He is, yeah.'

We were at the car within seconds, it seemed. I saw the passenger door open and felt myself sort of falling into the seat. The door closed. On the pavement, Jim and Pat had their heads together. They both looked very serious. Then they shook hands. Jim went around the car and got in beside me.

'I'm all right,' I heard myself saying. 'I'm all right, Jim.' He patted my leg and drove off. Didn't agree, I noticed.

When we got home, Jim stood over me while I drank two pints of water and then made sure I got into bed without cracking my head on anything. At some point, I got up to vomit. It might have been twenty minutes after I lay down. It might have been three o'clock in the morning. No idea. I made it to the bathroom, that was the main thing.

Next morning, I woke up with a horrible feeling of dread. It was there the second I opened my eyes, making me instantly curl up and pull the duvet to the top of my head. *Something terrible has happened. What?* The basic concept came to me at the same time as the physical pain, which was biblical. My head felt like someone was kicking it. Not had been kicking it recently – was kicking it now. There seemed to be some sort of small animal loose in my stomach. Something the size of a guinea pig. On top of that, every muscle was aching, which seemed plain unfair. It wasn't like I'd been working hard or taking exercise. I wondered what time it was. My watch was on the bedside locker but I couldn't see its face and there was no way in hell I was going to reach out and grab it. That much movement all at once could easily prove fatal. I lay there for a while, trying not to breathe too seriously. Eventually, Jim knocked on the door. So it was early, I thought. He hadn't gone to work yet. I tried to tell him to come in. A sort of dusty rasp escaped my throat. No words, though. I tried again. Same result. Jim lost his patience and came in. He was holding a pint of water. If I'd had a tail, I would have started wagging it.

'Ugh, fuck me,' he said, approaching. 'Stinks in here.'

I worked my trembling hands out from under the duvet and took the water in both of them. It was like getting out of prison. 'Thank you,' I said.

'Not feeling all that great today, I would imagine.'

I shook my head. Big mistake. 'I'm not going to lie, I've felt better.'

'I bet. Time you got up, I would say. We have to have a wee conversation.'

'Later. Later. I have to lie here for a while and–'

'Da, it's almost noon.'

'What?'

'Yep. Time you were up and about. Up, anyway.'

'Did you not go to work?'

'No. I didn't. I stayed here to talk to you. Didn't think it'd take you this long to come around but whatever.'

He turned on his heels and left me to it.

I got up, but not quickly. When I got out of the shower and checked my watch, I saw that it was half past twelve. I dressed and went downstairs, gripping the handrail for dear life. Jim was in the kitchen, pulling toast from the toaster. The kettle was on. I sat.

'Can I have some toast too, please?' I said.

'This is yours. I've had lunch.'

'Oh. Thank you.'

'No butter. Too greasy.'

'Fine. Grand.'

'We don't want any more little accidents.'

'What? What little–'

'You threw up.'

'I know, but in the toilet.'

'*Mostly* in the toilet.'

'Oh.'

'Hmm.'

'Sorry.'

'Hmm.'

He put a plate in front of me and went back to making tea. I'd thought I was hungry but now that it was under my nose, even dry toast seemed like a risky proposition. I took an experimental nibble and immediately wished I'd waited for the tea. The tiny morsel was like a flint arrowhead in my mouth. I pushed it around with my tongue, marvelling at the fact that it wasn't getting any softer. When Jim put a mug of milky tea down beside me, I fell on it like a lion on a wounded gazelle.

'A headache tablet wouldn't go amiss, I'm sure,' he said.

'It would not.'

He got a packet of Panadol from the cupboard and tossed it on to the table. I did the lion/gazelle thing again. Jim sat across from me with his own mug of tea. I took another toast nibble.

'So,' Jim said. 'Where do we begin?'

I chewed and swallowed. 'I got drunk, Jim. It's not a big–'

'You were bawling crying, Pat said. In the pub. Do you even remember that?'

I did, but not in any detail. It was like vaguely knowing the gist of a movie you'd seen as a child. 'Sort of.'

'And what do you put that down to?'

'Should I get on a couch for this, Jim?'

'When you get a call from a pub–'

'All right.'

'–saying your father was so footless drunk he–'

'All *right*.' I pushed my plate away. Toast wasn't happening, tea or no. 'I've been . . . things . . . I've had a stressful few weeks, and it all got on top of me a bit.'

'This is about Mum?'

I chose my words as carefully as could be expected of a man in my feeble condition. 'And associated matters. Yes.' I hoped he wouldn't get into it. I hoped he wouldn't tell me, again, that everything was fine with him and Eleanor and that I was imagining problems where they didn't exist. That wasn't his call to make, as far as I was concerned, and I wasn't up to talking about it.

'Then the thing with Annie . . .'

'Doesn't help. Nope.'

A long pause. 'Do you think you need to talk to someone?'

'I was hoping to talk to Frank but–'

'Not fucking *Frank*, Da. Jesus. A professional.'

'So you *do* want me on a couch?'

'I think–'

'No, Jim. No. That's not for me. What would I tell them? *Boohoo, my life's nearly over and I'm realizing I made a balls of the one thing I thought I'd done right?*'

'Is that what you think?'

'Sort of. Yeah. I suppose.'

He drank some tea, staring hard at me over the top of

his mug, letting me hear myself. 'Have you spoken to Eleanor since?'

'No.'

'All right. Here's what we're going to do. It's my birthday on Sunday. Saturday night, we're going out for dinner. You, me, Annie, and Eleanor. We'll have a nice meal, bit of a chat, everything will be fine with Annie, everything will be fine with Eleanor. It'll be great.'

'You think I'll be all back to normal after that?'

'I can't stop you getting old, Da. But it'd be a start, yeah.'

'Listen, it's nice of you to try and–'

'So it's settled.'

'It is not settled!'

'Italian, maybe.'

'Jim!'

'That new place where the video shop used to be is supposed to be lovely. By the roundabout there.' He gave me a hard stare. I understood that there was no point making any objections right now. All I could do was kick into touch.

'I'll think about it, I said. 'Now you should be getting into the shop, Noel has probably–'

'I'm staying here. We'll watch a movie or something. Come on, take your tea and toast, we'll go see what's on.'

He grabbed his own mug and got up to stand by the door, where he waited, like a teacher making sure every child had left class. I did as I was told.

25

My plan regarding Jim's birthday dinner idea was beautifully simple: I was going to pretend he hadn't suggested it and hope that he would forget. It worked perfectly for almost twenty-four hours. Then he came into the kitchen, where I was staring into a cup of tea that had long since gone cold, and said he was phoning Eleanor. Was I happy enough with the Italian place or did I want to suggest somewhere else? I started telling him that I had no intention of attending so it was entirely up to him. He ignored me, just as he had the day before, and strolled away to make the call. It was going to be bloody hard to pretend this wasn't happening, I realized, if he was going to keep bringing it up and then pretending I wasn't objecting. I didn't feel good about being one of two grown men having a pretending competition; I felt much worse about losing. Ten minutes later, he came back. I was still sitting with the cold tea. There was much less of a spring in his step, I noticed.

'Well?' I said.

He put his phone down on the counter and spun it around with one finger. 'Um.'

'What?'

'Eh . . . Eleanor can't come.'

I was relieved. 'Grand. That's the end of that, then. Sure you and Annie can have a nice–'

'Wait. Not can't – won't.'

'Won't?'

'Won't. Nothing to do with the date or anything. She just . . . won't. Doesn't want to.'

I didn't want to ask why. But I had to ask why. 'Why?'

Jim did a slow-motion shrug. 'I would tell you if I knew. She wouldn't say. Said she didn't want to get into it.'

'Well, it's not Annie, is it? She isn't staying away because she has some problem with Annie, who she's never even met, is she?' I delivered this with a lot of sarcasm in my voice, but I really wanted to know. There was a tiny possibility that actually, yes, she had something against salsa instructors. I clung to it for the three seconds it took Jim to choose his next words carefully.

'It's not Annie, Da. No. She says she's very happy for us.'

'Right,' I said, as if glad to be proven correct. 'So it's me.'

With a bluntness that would have made Frank himself proud, Jim said, 'Looks that way, yeah.'

For the want of something to do with my hands, I took a swig of the tea. As it reached my lips, I remembered it was stone-cold. I proceeded anyway. Putting it down again would have felt like yet another defeat, somehow.

'Listen,' Jim went on, 'don't get all annoyed about it. We have all week to work on her.'

'There's no "we", Jim. I don't want to go to this dinner, for fuck's sake.'

'I'll work on her, then.'

'I wish you wouldn't.'

'She probably—'

'How did it go with her mother?'

'She didn't say.'

'Jesus Christ, Jim, how can you not have asked her about this? It's been—'

'I did ask her. She didn't want to talk about that either.'

I knew what had happened. Una had gone there and charmed them all. Presents for Miles. Compliments for Aidan. Although it was early days, Eleanor had begun to see how much she'd missed out on when her mother left. They'd probably had a serious heart-to-heart. Una had explained herself. Marriage to me was a living nightmare. I was so useless. No ambition. No spine. It was too soon in the process for Eleanor to agree out loud, I imagined. Still, she'd seen the sense of all this. It chimed with her own opinion. And, yes, it had been for the best that Una never made any contact after she left. A clean break was painful but better in the long run. No confusion for the kids. No tug of love. Now she was a grown woman, Eleanor was free to make her own judgements. And she had. I was out. Una was in.

Strangely enough, Eleanor's dinner refusal didn't immediately make me any more miserable. The principle, I supposed, was that you couldn't add water to a full glass. I floated through the next couple of days, never exactly sure of the time or the conditions outside or whether I needed to eat. Jim came and went. Cups of tea materialized beside me and later vanished. Sometimes the telly was on. Sometimes the telly was off. I was nothing, less than a ghost. On the Tuesday morning, however, I woke up in a terrible state, like my entire being was a single exposed nerve. I didn't know whether I needed a doctor or a psychiatrist or a priest. Something had to be done, that was clear. The phrase started repeating in my head, like a song lyric I couldn't shake. *Something has to be done. Something has to be done. Something has to be done.* I didn't consciously decide to drive to Dublin. There was no debate. No weighing of pros and cons. I woke up in bits and next thing I knew, I was on the road. Next thing I knew, in fact, I was in Dublin. It was like I'd been teleported there.

Eleanor lived in Glasnevin, on the north side – the Monaghan side – of the city. I had always been glad about that. Driving around Dublin was not one of my favourite pastimes. It was a lanes thing. There were too many and it was too easy to be in the wrong one. As I passed the airport and got my first angry honk on the subject, I struggled to remember my last visit, not counting Theresa's funeral. More than a year ago, I concluded. It was around the time when Eleanor and Aidan were worried that there might be something seriously wrong with Miles. He'd always been a sullen wee boy, but when he got to preschool, he became downright violent. There was a lot of kicking and, later, biting. Not just other kids, either. He had to be hauled off his teacher's leg one day, having sunk his little teeth into her calf. And then there was the incident that everyone referred to as 'the fire', even though it was no such thing, really. Miles got his hands on a cigarette lighter, somehow – neither of his parents smoked and swore they'd never had any such item in the house – and managed to set some other boy's scarf alight. The boy wasn't wearing the scarf at the time and there were questions to be asked about the materials involved (it went up, according to eyewitnesses, with an audible 'woof'). Nevertheless, it was worrying. Eleanor was beside herself and didn't take it well when I pointed out – more than once, I admit – that this wasn't 'a fire'. A fire was something that happened to a whole building, as I knew all too well. At the end of the day, we were talking about a scarf here. It all blew over, anyway. Maybe it was the fuss. Maybe Miles, even at the age of four, sensed that he was pushing his luck. Whatever the reason, he settled down before professionals had to get involved.

The place was called Apple Grove Court, which was a name I had awful trouble remembering. I was sure someone had chosen it by throwing darts at a load of Post-it notes, each one saying Apple or Pine or Oak or Grove or Walk or Way. Once, I referred to it as 'an estate'. Aidan rested a single finger on my forearm and corrected me. It was 'a development', he said. There were eight large detached houses arranged in a keyhole shape. Eleanor's was the first on the left. I hadn't called ahead for fear of spooking her and was worried that she wouldn't be home, but her car was there, at least. Spotless, as usual. I pulled in behind it, feeling vague shame about the state of the Punto, and killed the engine. Worries arrived in droves. What if she opened the door, took one look, and slammed it in my face again? Would I knock again? What if she was looking out a window, spotted me, and pretended to be out? Would I knock anyway? What if patience was the key here and this whim of mine completely and utterly fucked everything up?

I took some deep breaths, or tried to at least, and got out of the car. As I walked up the path, the world suddenly seemed too bright. Too colourful. The red front door looked like it was moving, pulsing almost, like some bodily organ. I wiped my sweaty hands on my thighs and gave the knocker three sharp knocks. They echoed around the estate-slash-development. I waited thirty seconds or more. No answer. When I reached out to try again, the door suddenly opened, just a crack. Eleanor's right eye peered out at me and widened in what could have been plain surprise but might well have been horror. I couldn't tell. Then the door opened properly. I barely had time to register that this was a good sign before I saw her features sort of spasm, and then crumble into dismay. Her hand went to her mouth. My doubts came flooding back. She was going to tell me to turn around and go right back the way I'd come. It was only when she threw herself on me, sobbing the word 'sorry' over and over again, that the rollercoaster finally ended.

'My turn to visit unannounced,' I said to the top of her head. I felt her nod. 'Are you going to ask me inside or what?' She didn't immediately let go. I couldn't remember the last time she had hugged me this hard. As a child with a skinned knee, I suspected.

'Okay,' she said then, pulling back. She dabbed at her eyes. 'Let's go in.'

Miles was on the stairs, playing with some small plastic figures. 'Hiya, Miles!' I said. 'Ooh, dinosaurs!'

'I'll put the kettle on,' Eleanor said in a trembling voice, carrying on down the hall. I took that to mean I was supposed to play with her son, or at least stop and talk to him for a bit. Miles looked every bit as comfortable with that as I felt. I settled down on the stairs below him. My knees cracked.

'What was that?' he asked.

'The noise? My knees. They crack sometimes.'

'Is that because you're so old?'

'I suppose so.'

'How old are you?'

'How old do you think I am?'

He screwed his face up. 'A hundred?'

'Right first time.'

'Wow. A hundred.'

'Yep.'

'That must be cool.'

'You think so?'

'Yeah. Three numbers in your age. The word for that, if you don't know, is digits. I only have one digit.'

I nodded that this was so. 'Have you got a T-Rex?'

He frowned at me, momentarily confused by the change of subject. 'Oh! I do have a T-Rex but I don't play with him much because his eyes are all wrong, painted on all wrong, and he looks stupid.'

'Who's your favourite then?'

He held up a dull-grey lad. 'This one. I don't know what kind of dinosaur it is, though, and I can't find it in any of the books, I have a lot of dinosaur books, so I think maybe it isn't even a real dinosaur? Maybe someone made it up?'

'Maybe. Do you ever–'

'I have to go now.' He jumped to his feet and disappeared up the stairs before I could draw breath to reply. I didn't mind. By our standards, it had been a lengthy and pleasant conversation. I got up – *crack* – and went through to the back of the house. It had long been my theory that one of the most revealing things you could know about a person was whether or not their kitchen had an island in it. An island meant a big kitchen. A big kitchen meant a big house. A big house meant money. It didn't mean obscene wealth, necessarily. But you couldn't cry poverty if you had an island, that was the point. Eleanor was standing at hers, putting buns on a plate and the plate on a tray.

'Will we sit outside?' she said. You would never have known she'd been a mess a few minutes earlier.

'Fine by me.'

She put the tea things on the tray and picked it up delicately.

I stepped across. 'Here, let me–'

'I'm grand.'

'I can–'

'It's fine, Daddy. It's fine.'

She gave me a small smile. I gave her one back. Walking on eggshells, both of us. I skipped ahead of her and slid open the large patio door. We did some more smiling. The patio wasn't enormous but it was big enough for some furniture and a barbecue. We sat. Eleanor poured tea.

'Miles went upstairs. Will he be all right on his own?'

'Yeah. He likes his own company. He won't be shy about letting us know if he needs anything.'

'We had a nice little chat. He seems to be . . .' I hesitated. What I wanted to say was 'more normal than usual'. That seemed ill-advised. 'He seems to be in good form.'

'He is, yeah. He's much less . . .' Now it was her turn to hesitate. 'Uh, he's less of a handful than he used to be. Still quiet, still not great at making friends, but I don't worry about him the way I used to. I mean, it's not that I don't worry about him, it's . . . You know what I mean.'

'I do. You never stop worrying about them, Eleanor. I can assure you of that.'

Although it wasn't a particularly subtle way of getting us on to the real subject, it did the trick. We latched eyes for a second.

'I'm not sure where to begin,' Eleanor said.

I shrugged as if to say that I was willing to give it a shot. 'Jim called you at the weekend?'

'He did.'

'Invited you to dinner?'

'Yes.'

'I got the impression that you'd said no because you didn't want to see me. Nothing to do with him or his new girlfriend.'

She started peeling the paper wrapper from a bun, working as delicately as a surgeon, as if every crumb was precious. 'That's true. I didn't want to see you. But not because I didn't *want* to see you.'

'What then?'

She kept her eyes on the wrapper. I understood that it was all that was keeping her from breaking down again. 'I didn't want to see you because I'm so ashamed.'

'About what?'

'The last time we spoke, specifically, and my whole life, or most of it anyway.'

'I don't–'

'I invited Mum round.'

'I know. Jim told me.'

'I said I wouldn't because it was too soon and then I did. Maybe because of the way it went with you, I don't know. I was upset. And confused. It's been very confusing, all this. Anyway, she was delighted. We made arrangements for dinner here, so I could introduce her to Aidan and Miles. It was all supposed to be very casual.'

'Would I be right in guessing it didn't turn out that way?'

She shook her head. 'Wait, I should go back first.' The wrapper was off now. She stared at it for a moment, then scrunched it between her fingers. There was a long pause.

'Eleanor, are you all right?'

'I was seventeen when she left. If I told anyone about it later, they always said the same thing. They always said, well, it could have been worse, you could have been a little girl. I was a grown-up, more or less, so it was horrible and all, but look on the bright side. You might as well tell them your mother walked out on you when you were thirty-five. No one gets it. It was the tail end of my childhood, yeah, but it was still my fucking childhood. I wasn't ready for it, I didn't have the skills for it. All I had from being older was the ability to take it in. Do you remember what you told us the night she left?'

'Some of it.'

'You told us we should never think she was disappointed in us in some way because she'd been having affairs since we were tiny.'

'Yes. Two anyway, that I knew about.'

Her face lit up. 'Exactly. That you knew about. You assumed there were others.'

'I don't know that I'd say "assumed". I wouldn't have been surprised, put it that way.'

'You stayed with her anyway. She'd had some unknown number of affairs that you knew for a fact was at least two, and you stayed with her anyway. I couldn't get my head around it. I obsessed about it, playing through all the different scenarios. If you'd walked out after the first affair, when I was only a toddler, then so and so. Or if you'd kicked her out after the first affair, then so and so. Same with the second affair. Same with all the years and ages inbetween. No matter how I sliced it, I always came out with the same answer: that would have been better. So I blamed you. I don't mean I hated your guts or thought about it every time I thought about you. I only mean, when I was down, when it was getting to me, I didn't blame her. I hated her so much I couldn't stand to have her face in my mind. I blamed you. It was stupid. I knew it was stupid and I felt terrible about it, but that didn't stop me.'

She went quiet then. Birds chirped. A neighbour's baby wailed. I wondered if it was my turn to say something. To avoid making a decision, I drank some tea. Eleanor did likewise, then resumed her . . . whatever this was. Confession?

'When she got in touch, not long before Aidan's mum died, I ignored her. Had no interest. She kept trying, I kept ignoring. The illness and everything, though . . . I decided it wouldn't hurt to be civil. I didn't want to hear that she'd died and I'd have to feel guilty about freezing her out at the end. That seemed really unfair – the idea that between the two of us, *I'd* be the one with the guilt. So we met, and you know how that went. Not great, not a disaster. But it upset me. Dug it all up again. When I went home to tell you about it, the whole thing was swirling around in me again, the anger, the confusion, the blame, the guilt. I don't know what I was thinking, I don't know what I expected to happen, but I invited her here.'

Someone nearby started up a lawnmower. We frowned

simultaneously, as if they'd deliberately timed it to interfere with the climax of the story.

'And what happened?' I asked.

'Oh, it was a disaster. A complete disaster from start to finish. She seemed, I don't know . . . offended? By the house. Kept making snide remarks that sounded like compliments but weren't; "Someone's doing very well for themselves." No smile, no warmth. I was pissed off and regretting the whole thing before she'd even sat down. Aidan tried his best to tell her about his job and she kept interrupting with these weird put-downs.'

'Like what?'

'Like he'd say something about the office in New York and she'd say, "New York isn't the city it once was." Or he'd say they'd taken on ten graduates and she'd say, "Young people today want everything handed to them." You know? Not having a go at him or even the business, just pouring cold water non-stop.'

'I think I know what that's about.'

'Go on.'

'It doesn't fit the story she wants to tell herself. That she went off and had this fabulous life while the rest of us stayed here eating stale bread.'

'I'm her daughter, for God's sake! She doesn't want her own daughter to do well?' There was an obvious answer to that and it came to her immediately. 'Mind you,' she added bitterly, 'it's not like I usually associate her with parental concern.'

'Bingo.'

'She did some odd bragging too, which she didn't do the first time when we had lunch. There's an apartment in Portugal, apparently? In Cascais. Herself and himself used to go there a few times a year. She's thinking of living there for half the year, don't you know, because it's "so beautiful and spacious".'

'Hm. She might have to rethink that when her health gets worse.'

'That's what I said. She used it as an excuse to talk about the beauty and the space again, how good they'd be for her. She can't even speak Portuguese.'

I shook my head. 'That's a terrible idea. An Alzheimer's patient alone in a foreign country where they don't speak the language?'

'I know. I said all that. "Beauty and space. Space and beauty."'

'Huh. Did you introduce her to Miles?'

She closed her eyes briefly. 'That was the worst part. Well, the worst part before the very end. He was upstairs playing when she arrived. When she was talking to Aidan, I went up to get him. To make a big entrance, you know. I thought she'd be all emotional. He's her only grandchild, for Christ's sake! It was like I was showing her the family cat. No hugs. No little present. She asked him a few really boring questions – did he like school, that sort of crap – and off he went again. He was barely out of the room before she asked me what exactly was wrong with him. Not, *Is there something wrong with him?*, which would have been bad enough, but, "What exactly is wrong with him?" Like, it was so obvious, we didn't have to waste any time debating it, we could get straight to the specifics.'

This stung me hard. I thought of all the times I'd been less than positive about talking to Miles, the most recent being a few minutes ago. My reply was too loud and too shrill. 'Jesus Christ! What did you say?'

'I laughed it off. Or tried to, anyway. Said he was just shy. I was still clinging to the idea that the evening could still work out all right. Anyway, we sat down to eat a while later, the four of us.'

'What did you have?'

'What difference does that make?'

'I'm trying to get the picture here.'

'A beef casserole. Something easy I wouldn't have to keep checking on, was the idea. So, we sit down and it's a bit awkward but we get through it. Small talk, really, with more of the same from herself, pointed little remarks about this and that. A lot of modern women starve themselves to keep thin, good for me for not caring about my weight – that sort of thing.'

'Bloody hell.'

'Ah, I'm making it sound more obvious than it was. She was subtle. But I didn't imagine any of it. Aidan noticed all the same stuff. And then we got on to the subject of Jim.'

'Oh?'

'Their meeting didn't go well. You know that already, I suppose. Maybe she would have had something else to say about him if it had been better. I don't know. Maybe not. Daddy, you're not going to like this. But I have to tell you what she said. To explain.'

'I'm sure I'll cope, Eleanor. Go on.'

'All right. I'll skip to the bottom line. She said she was disappointed in the way he'd turned out. It was a shame that he'd taken over the shop instead of doing something . . . else.'

'Better.'

A regretful nod. 'Yep.'

'She's disappointed because he turned out like me.'

'More or less, yes. And I absolutely . . . lost it. Complete freak-out. Everything I've ever thought about her and never supposed I'd get a chance to say, all through the years. Screaming and roaring. Aidan lifted Miles and ran upstairs with him. I was on my feet with my finger in her face. Called her every name under the sun. And then it was all about you. I had a whole speech in me and I never knew it. About how hard it was for you to be left alone with two kids like that and what a great job you did and how you never once complained and so on. To be brutally honest, at first I thought I was saying it to get to her. I only realized I meant it as I went along.'

My eyes dampened and my throat all but closed over. I reached across the patio table and took her hand. 'Thank you. That's . . . everything to me. Everything.'

She squeezed my hand and blinked away her own tears. 'It's the truth. I'm so disgusted with myself. I've been stewing in this crap all these years. About what you should have done, and when. And the way I spoke to you that last time in Monaghan. I'm so sorry. I'm sorry for all of it.'

'Forget about it.'

'I called you a doormat. And a coward. Said you'd be her nurse and–'

'I remember.'

'I haven't been able to look at myself in the mirror. I half-hoped you'd cut me off and I'd never have to see you again.' She stared off to the bottom of the garden.

'That's gone now, right?'

'I don't know. Do you . . . forgive me?'

I laughed. 'For fuck's sake, Eleanor. Of course I forgive you. There's nothing to forgive.'

'I wouldn't say that.'

'Well, it's true. So you'll come up for dinner, meet Annie?'

She nodded vigorously. 'Yes. I will. Definitely.' Her eyes widened, then darted away. I knew what that meant.

'Right. He told you, then? Jim?'

She tried to look innocent. It was hopeless. Her face quivered with the effort. 'He did, yeah. Are you all right?'

I took a moment. It was an interesting question. I wasn't sure what the answer was. 'I'll survive,' I said. 'So how did it end with your mother?'

'I kicked her out. We hadn't even finished eating. We have one of those notice boards in there in the kitchen you know, with business cards and whatnot pinned to it? I grabbed one for a taxi company and threw it at her, then got her jacket and threw that at her.'

'Wow.'

'Then I basically pushed her down the hall. I felt bad afterwards. Because of her illness. Not at the time, though. At the time, I felt great.'

We were still holding hands, I realized. It was beginning to feel silly. I slid mine away as gently as possible. 'How was she on that score?'

'Didn't notice anything. Mind you, I was too busy being stunned by her personality in general.'

'Do you think she'll be in touch again?'

Eleanor snorted. 'I would very much doubt it.'

The patio door slid open and Miles wandered out with a football under his arm. Eleanor greeted him enthusiastically. I threw in some noises. He raised his free hand and nodded once, slowly, like an old farmer acknowledging a neighbour at the cattle mart. There was even a hint of a smile. I could see how pleased his mother was. Once upon a time, he would have marched right past us like we didn't exist. He started tapping the ball around, concentrating furiously. We settled back in our chairs and watched him in comfortable silence.

'I'm trying to sound all brash and breezy,' Eleanor said after a while. 'But there's no way to feel good about it, is there? Shutting her out when she's facing a terrible decline. And death. I don't want any contact with her. Zero. I don't want to feel like a scumbag either, which I will. I know I will. Forever. She's a terrible mother. And I'm a terrible daughter.'

I didn't reply right away. A vague notion had been scratching away at me for a while and something she'd said had put the tin hat on it.

'Don't worry about it,' I said then.

Eleanor sighed. She thought I was fobbing her off. But I wasn't. I meant that she shouldn't worry because I had a plan.

26

In my entire life, I'd been abroad precisely twice. Both times were family holidays. We rented a caravan in Wales, for some reason, when the kids were small (Tenby: non-stop rain). The summer before Una left, we had a week in Spain (Fuengirola: sunburn all round). But that was it. I had no idea how you went about booking a flight on the Internet and was so sure I'd make a balls of it, I didn't even try. Instead, the day after my trip to Dublin, I called into a travel agent in town and told them my predicament. I wanted to go to London the next day, I said, and come home that night. No staying over. Nothing fancy. Cheap as possible. I was a bit embarrassed to need help and said so. The young woman who served me said it was fine – she knew lots of older people who preferred not to book flights themselves. I was mortally offended for several seconds. But I got over it. I *was* an older person and I *didn't* want to book the flight myself. What was there to be outraged about, really? My flight to Heathrow would depart at nine-fifty in the morning. My flight home left at seven-twenty.

Jim was delighted that I'd been to see Eleanor and that it had gone so well. That night, I told him that I would be away when he got up in the morning and wouldn't be back when he got home. He assumed I was making a return trip to his sister's, for some reason. I assured him I was not but refused to go any further. He was driven half-mad with curiosity. I batted his questions away with promises that all would be revealed in the fullness of time. It was fun for a while. Then he got worried. He stopped asking and started insisting. All jokes aside, where was I going? I stuck to my guns. There was no reason to be alarmed. He'd find out soon enough. He fixed me with a stare. Given recent events, surely I could understand his concern? When I started to protest that things hadn't been all that bad, he looked at me like I was a child covered in chocolate claiming they had no idea what happened to all the chocolate. Life had been so hazy and dream-like lately. Maybe things had indeed been all that bad. I didn't push it. There was no reason to worry, I repeated, and we left it at that.

Next morning, I was up and gone by six. The young woman in the travel agent had asked a few pointed questions and established that I wasn't just nervous about booking the tickets – I was completely clueless about everything. Fair play to her, she gave me a lot of tips that I don't suppose she had to. One of them was about parking. I wanted the Short Term car park, she said. Not Long Term. That sounded like the sort of thing I would have worked out for myself, given the options, but I was grateful nevertheless. This was a one-shot sort of deal. I had to get it done while my blood was up. There would be no trying again in a while if I made a mess of something simple and missed my flight. Finding somewhere to park at the airport proved to be much the same as finding somewhere to park anywhere else – annoying but not exactly complicated. The first real challenge was coming up next, though. It was a few minutes after eight when I entered the terminal building. I had imagined, ridiculously, that it might not be all that busy first thing in the morning. That was desperately incorrect. I stood frozen by the door, over-whelmed. How the hell were you supposed to navigate this? It was complete chaos. Where would you even start? My confusion didn't last. I saw the Aer Lingus desks and joined a queue. It was the wrong queue, it turned out – you couldn't just join any one you fancied – but I was quickly turned around and pointed in the right direction. The way to go about this, I decided, was to follow the ticket-booking model and own up. When it was my turn, I told the Aer Lingus woman there that I'd only flown once before in my entire life, a long time ago, and had basically no idea what I was supposed to be doing. She not only gave me step-by-step instructions from that point to getting on the plane, she wrote them down and even drew a little map. Half an hour later, I had made it through security (although not at first go – turns out I had a surprising amount of metal on me) and was sitting down with a cup of tea and a bun. I knew where the toilets were. I knew where the shops were. I knew where my gate was. All I had to do was wait for what the woman at the desk had called 'the bing-bong'. It occurred to me as I sipped my tea that she might have thought I was simple.

The flight to Spain with Una and the kids all those years ago had been a bit of an ordeal, I remembered. It wasn't

that I was afraid, exactly. It was more like deep discomfort.
I felt like we were doing something wrong. We weren't
supposed to be up there, sitting in wee seats, eating sand-
wiches, *looking down on clouds*. I expected something
similar would happen on the way to London and was
pleased to find that it didn't. This time I was thrilled with
it. I had the window seat and spent the whole journey
staring out, even when there was nothing to see. What
had felt like an insult to the gods first time around felt
like something to be amazed by now. Everyone else on the
plane was used to flying, of course. They behaved no
differently to people on a bus; opening snacks, flipping
through magazines, fiddling with their headphones. I
wondered if I'd have been the same if I'd had a more
adventurous life. No doubt. But it was nice to pretend
otherwise and to pity them a bit.

When we landed, I followed my fellow passengers until
we reached the place where your bags go by and then,
not having any bags, headed for the nearest sign that said
EXIT. I couldn't believe that only a few hours ago I'd been
marvelling at how busy it was in Dublin airport. Heathrow
made it look like a Buddhist monastery. It didn't seem
possible that all these scurrying people knew where they
were going and how to get there. And the diversity! I'd
heard that word used in Ireland, where it meant it was a
good thing if now and again you saw a black lad. Standing
there in Arrivals, I tried not to gawp at the masses of
exotic people rushing by, but it wasn't easy. There was so
much variety, so much colour, so much spectacle. I felt
dizzy and faintly embarrassed by my own dullness. Was
it just an airport thing, I wondered, or was London like
this in general? I couldn't wait to find out.

The travel agent had given me instructions on getting to Chiswick. All I had to do was 'hop on' the Tube, the Piccadilly line going east, then 'hop off' at Acton Town and 'hop on' the District line going south to Chiswick Park. Simple! And not far from Heathrow! It didn't sound simple to me. There was an awful lot of hopping in there. I found the station at the airport quickly enough but buying a ticket proved to be beyond me. There were just so many options. My unblinking eyes flitted all over the machine in panic, hoping it would eventually volunteer to explain itself. After a while, I felt a tapping on my shoulder. I tensed up, certain I was in for a Big City bollocking for being so slow. A short middle-aged man was peering up at me. He was balding, and what little hair he had wafted about in delicate tufts.

'You all right? Need a hand?' A London accent. Not quite the full *Eastenders*, but getting there.

'I'm sorry,' I sputtered. 'I'm a bit . . .'

'Where you off to, chief?'

'Chiswick? Chiswick Park station?'

He moved to stand beside me. 'Single or return?'

'Return, please. To here.'

'Well, yeah. It would be. Got cash?'

'No. I mean, yes, but not sterling. I've a card.'

He pushed buttons. Screens came and went so fast I didn't see what they said. 'Your time to shine,' he said, gesturing to the card reader. I paid. My ticket emerged.

'Thank you so much,' I said, pitifully relieved.

'Welcome, mate.'

He smiled. I felt an urge to shake his hand but that seemed like too much. I smiled back and hoped he'd go with old rather than simple.

I'd never been on the Tube, obviously, but I was sure I knew what to expect from telly and movies. It would be jam-packed and dirty and full of lunatics. There would be drunks. Drug addicts. There was a fifty per cent chance I'd see a stabbing. It was quite possible I would *be* stabbed. Every minute would be torture.

I loved it. It was crowded, granted, and it wasn't exactly spotless and I did see a disturbed old lady talking loudly to a stuffed cat on her lap. None of that mattered to me. I was only on it for forty-five minutes and in that short time I got in as much people-watching as I'd get at home in a month. The young couple, dazed by love, who couldn't take their eyes off each other even though they were both ugly as sin. The stern-looking Japanese man who abandoned his book every few minutes to pull a goofy face, delighting his little daughter. The skinny young woman with enormous headphones who had no idea she was singing along to 'Suspicious Minds', her whispered Elvis impression causing giggles all around. My favourites, though, were Debs and Alan, who lived in Ealing and had one adult son, Nick, an electrician who gambled too much and was crazy if he thought he was going to do better than his current girlfriend, Lucy, who was definitely going to find someone else if he didn't hurry up and marry her. I knew all of this because Debs and Alan never stopped talking and had absolutely no concept of privacy. They got on at Boston Manor and grabbed a metal pole near me, not even bothering to look for seats. I was immediately intrigued because they were one of those couples who've been together for so long, they've started to merge into one person. *Bowl-cut grey hair, brown trousers, green cardigan, white runners* was a description that broadly covered them both. They spoke as if they were in a noisy pub, roaring at each other over a background din that didn't actually exist. There was something endearing about them, I thought. Maybe it was the way they used each other's names, always in enthusiastic agreement.

'You can say that again, Alan.'

'Bang on, Debs.'

'You're not wrong, Debs.'

'Nail on the head, Alan.'

I was sorry when we got to Acton Town and it was time for me to change trains. They disappeared from my thoughts as I navigated the station (asking three separate people for help) but came front and centre again once I'd found my platform. They were still at it, no doubt, loudly and happily agreeing about everything. They'd be at it in an hour's time, when I was confronting my estranged wife for the first time in decades. They'd be at it that night, when I was flying back to Dublin. They'd be at it in five years' time, and in ten, and in twenty. Good for them.

'Too right, Alan.'

'Bingo, Debs.'

I'd studied the map on my phone back home and discovered that Una's apartment block was a walkable distance from the station. There would be no need for a taxi. I'd written the directions down in case something went wrong on the technology front and consulted the bit of folded paper in my wallet as soon as I was off the train. It wasn't complicated: cross the little roundabout outside the station, walk south along Acton Lane, cross Chiswick High Road on to Sutton Lane. The apartment block was on the right, opposite a park. Marston Manor, it was called. As I started to walk, I finally allowed myself to consider the possibility that she wouldn't be home. It wasn't something I'd wanted to contemplate before now, for fear of chickening out. Now that I'd arrived, I realized that there wasn't much *to* contemplate. If she wasn't home, I'd hang around the park or a coffee shop for as long as I could, checking in every so often. If she still hadn't shown by the time I had to head back to the airport, well, there was nothing I could do about that.

The walk from the station was even shorter than it had looked on the map. Twenty minutes, I'd guessed. It was more like five. When I arrived, it felt like every drop of blood in my head made a dash for my feet. I stopped dead and swayed on the spot, genuinely worried I was going to faint. It passed. I was starving, on top of everything else. It was lunchtime and I hadn't eaten a bite since my Dublin airport bun. Marston Manor was a five-storey red-brick building set back from the road. There were well-tended flower beds and a crunchy gravel driveway that looked like it would be highly satisfying to drive on. At first glance, I thought the place might have started life, a long time ago, as a school or maybe even a hospital, but I changed my mind. It was too neat. In all probability, it wasn't even old – it just wanted you to think it was. The front door opened as I was standing there. My breath hitched. The resident who emerged wasn't Una. It was a handsome Sikh man in a dazzlingly silver suit. He looked up and nodded appreciatively at the clear blue sky, as if it were doing him a personal favour, then frowned when he noticed me. I probably looked like I was casing the joint. It was for the best.

His eye contact made me suddenly cross the boundary, doing my best to look innocent. I might have stood there for a long time otherwise.

There was an intercom thingy by the door. I already knew that Una lived in 1c but it was still a relief to see her name printed in capitals on the little strip of card by the button. Her maiden name, that is: CONNOLLY. I was in the right place, at least. A voice in my head told me I had one last chance to bow out. I told it to fuck off and buzzed. She answered so quickly it made me jump.

'Yes?'

My voice failed me for a second. I cleared my throat. 'Una?'

'Who is this?'

'Una.'

'Yes! Who is this?'

'It's Eugene. Duffy.' I knew at once that I would spend the rest of my life cringing about giving her my second name, but there was no time to worry about it now.

'Jesus Christ,' my technical wife said after a thick and heavy pause. 'You're here.'

'I'm here.'

'You're at my front door.'

'I'm at your front door.'

Another pause, this one as long as the Second World War. 'Well. You'd better come in then.'

There was a low humming sound and the front door clicked open. I stepped inside. The hall wasn't as grand as I'd imagined it would be. It was perfectly nice, but the black and white tiles felt cold and uninviting. There was a chandelier overhead that was hanging a bit low on one side. Next to the lift was a giant potted plant that was way too big for the space it was in. Double doors on either side led off to the ground-floor apartments. It was through the set on the right that I caught my first glimpse of herself. She was wearing a pink tracksuit. Dark blonde hair, tied up in a ponytail. A bit of a tan. She looked great. Older, obviously, but great.

'Well, well, well,' she said as she came through the doors.

'Hello, Una,' I said.

She came no further. In fact, she retreated and leaned back against the door, folding her arms. 'I was about to ask how you found me but I gave Jim my address, didn't I?

'Yeah.'

'It was for him, really. And Eleanor. I didn't think you'd use it.'

'Neither did I.'

'But if you did use it, I thought, you'd definitely let me know in advance.'

I shrugged. 'Spur-of-the-moment thing.'

'Are you in town for long?'

'Arrived this morning. Flying back tonight.'

'Not even a whole day?'

'Nah.'

A head tilt. 'Wait, did you come to London just to see me?'

'That's right.'

She stared at me, hard. 'This'll be good. Come on in.'

I approached. She went through the double doors and held one open. As soon as I caught up, she started walking again, her immaculate runners (also pink) swishing on the thick carpet.

'I was about to go to the gym,' she said over her shoulder. 'But I think I'll postpone.'

'Thanks,' I said, aiming for sarcasm but, I suspected, sounding sincere.

The apartment was nice. Very nice. Not that I got a tour. All I saw was the living room and, through an open door, a small kitchen. Almost everything in the former was either blue or grey. Light grey walls, dark grey carpet, navy blue rug, mid-grey sofa, pale blue cushions. There were a lot of small paintings or possibly prints on the walls, all of them abstract. Maybe she'd picked them up in Ikea. Maybe she'd bid on them in Sotheby's. I had no idea.

'Lovely,' I said, looking around.

There was a small sofa and an armchair. Una took the armchair and gestured to the sofa. I sat. 'I redecorated a couple of months back. There was too much Adam everywhere. It was getting me down. My partner, Adam? I lost him not long ago.'

'I heard.' I wasn't sure of the etiquette here so my next contribution came out as a question. 'I'm sorry?'

'Are you?'

'It's what people say, Una.'

'Hmm. So what's up?'

That annoyed me. It was like she was my boss, a busy woman with no time to waste, and I'd dropped into her office unannounced. 'Enough with the small talk, is that it?' I said.

She smiled thinly. 'Eugene. We're not going to get into ancient history. I have nothing to say about it and I don't want to hear anything you might have to say about it. In any case, I don't think you came here for that, did you?'

'No.'

'No. You came here for something specific. So why don't you say whatever it is you have to say and let us get on with our lives.'

'Fine by me. You came to Dublin. You met Eleanor and Jim.'

'Correct.'

'It didn't end well.'

'Correct.'

'With either of them.'

'Correct. They were both extremely rude.'

'Oh my God.'

'Well, it's the truth. You weren't there.'

'I'm not saying they weren't, Una. I'm saying, even if they were, do you not think they're entitled? After you walked out on them and disappeared–'

'Oh, so you do want to bring up ancient history.'

'Stop calling it that! It's our lives you're talking ab–'

'I told you, I have no interest and if this is all you want to–'

'What gives you the right–'

We went on like this for a little while, talking over each other, getting louder and louder. It stopped when Una got up and started for the door, presumably to open it for my exit.

'Oh, sit down,' I said. 'For Christ's sake. I'm going. I'll tell you what I have to tell you, and then I'll go.'

To my surprise, she sat. 'Hurry up.'

I went back to the start, to the words I'd rehearsed. 'You came to Dublin. You met Eleanor and Jim. It didn't go well. They don't want to see you again or hear from you again.'

'And what, you want me to swear I won't make contact? I have no intention–'

'No. That's not it.'

'What then?'

'There's one problem. They're good people. Despite all the heartache you've caused them, they feel guilty. Because of your illness. They're going to wonder about you, as time goes on, and they're going to feel like shit. I don't want that.'

'And what do you expect me to do about it?'

My big moment. I looked her right in the eye. 'I want you to admit that you're lying.'

Her face froze. 'Excuse me?'

'Don't even start, Una. You don't have Alzheimer's. You're fit as a fiddle. They spent hours with you and neither of them noticed any symptoms. Early days, they put it down to. And maybe that would be fair enough, I don't know. But you made a mistake with Eleanor. You couldn't help bragging about this place in Portugal. Space and beauty and whatnot.'

'I don't know what–'

'You've got Alzheimer's but your plan is to live abroad half the time? Alone? Somewhere you don't even speak the language? Come on. You may have fooled them. You haven't fooled me. I know you better.'

'This is outrageous–'

'I know what happened. Curiosity got the better of you and you wanted to see what had become of us. You couldn't say that, though. There was a good chance we wouldn't give you the time of day. You needed some excuse to make contact, something we couldn't easily dismiss.'

She gave me the darkest look I have ever received. I'd been used to her contemptuous stares, back in the old days, but this was something different. It wasn't contempt, it was bottomless loathing.

'Fuck you,' she said. 'What a terrible thing to accuse someone of. Have you no shame?'

'That's not a denial.'

'I don't have to prove anything to you.'

'It'd be so easy to do, though. You must have an appointment letter from a doctor or pills or a prescription or something? No?'

'You want evidence? You come into my home and ask for evidence that I'm dying?'

'Yes, please.'

She stood and pointed at the door. 'Out! Get out!'

I stayed put. 'So there's no evidence. Of course there isn't. Because the whole thing is bullshit. Admit it, Una. Maybe you'll feel better. I mean, I doubt you feel all that bad anyway, but you never know.'

'GET OUT!'

This time I got up. 'All righty, then. I'll tell Jim and Eleanor the good news. Never contact them again, please.'

She cackled. 'Ha! As if! I'm sorry I contacted them this time. I was better off imagining. She's a stuck-up cow and her son is weird. Jim's worse. Jim's just like you.'

'Eleanor's doing pretty well for herself, thank you. Yes, Miles has had some issues socializing but he'll be fine. And you're right, Jim *is* just like me. He's a decent human being, doing his best. Thank you for the compliment.'

She got behind me and shoved me towards the door. 'Out. Out. OUT!'

I felt tipsy, on the verge of laughter. 'Well, this has been lovely, I must say.'

'One day I really will be dying,' she spat, 'and when I'm gone, I hope you all writhe in agony over the way you've treated me.'

That did it. I got the giggles. 'At least you're admitting it,' I said as she threw the door open. 'Feel better now?'

She gave me one last shove and slammed the door. I turned to face it and spoke up to make myself audible. 'No. I didn't think you would. Goodbye, Una.'

I headed to the exit. It was time for lunch.

Jim was still up when I arrived home, shortly after eleven that night. He was parked in front of the telly, watching a space movie.

'Finally,' he said by way of greeting. 'About time.'

'What? I told you I'd be late getting back.'

'Are you going to tell me where you were?' There was no good humour in his voice.

'No.'

His expression upgraded from irritated to angry. 'What?'

'Not yet. I'll tell you at your birthday dinner.'

Now the anger was replaced by pity. His features were getting a little workout. 'Are you sick?'

'Not that I know of.'

'You haven't been off getting tests or anything?'

'You think I've got some terrible medical news but I'm not telling you now because I want to save it for your birthday dinner?'

'So you haven't been off getting–'

'No! I'm fine. It's nothing bad, honestly. I think it'd be nice to tell you and Eleanor together, that's all.'

This was an idea that had come to me on the plane, during my third wee thing of Pringles. It was grandstanding, no doubt. But I felt like I deserved to do a bit of grandstanding.

'Fine then. Whatever.' He returned his attention to the lasers and robots.

'I'm away up,' I said. 'Knackered.'

'Fine.'

He'd turned petulant. I smiled my way up the stairs to bed. Being enigmatic was fun.

27

The video shop by the roundabout – as everyone used to call it to distinguish it from the video shop by the bookies and the video shop by the chemist – had been closed, like all of them, for years. Since then, the premises seemed to have housed a new business every twelve months or so. It had been a shoe shop, a clothes shop, several different cafés – none of them took. Most recently, it had been a Chinese restaurant. That venture was one of the saddest. It lasted a couple of months. Some people said the building was cursed. Other, less stupid people, said it was just a terrible location. No footfall, poor parking, and so on. None of this, it seemed, had put off the new tenants, who'd opened an Italian called Mangiamo within a few weeks of the Chinese going under. Maybe they were working on the theory that two restaurants in a row wouldn't fail.

Two things struck me about Mangiamo when I walked in with Eleanor that Saturday night: it was not fancy, and it was not modern. Not fancy was fine by me. I didn't care for fancy. Not modern was a bit of a disappointment. The place was downright old-fashioned. The walls were covered with tacky pictures of Italian landmarks – the Leaning Tower, the Colosseum – and the tables had candles stuck into old wine bottles. I didn't know a lot about restaurants, but I knew that old wine bottles covered in melted wax went out with the space hopper. Eleanor had timed her run to Monaghan perfectly, arriving just as Jim was leaving to pick up Annie. She'd already spoken to him on the phone and they ganged up on me a bit about The Big Mystery, as they called it. I kept my mouth shut.

Our waiter was a young man, or more correctly, an old boy. I doubted he'd seen his last teenage year. He showed us to our table with a lot of mumbling and sniffing. We were first to arrive and had barely taken our seats when Jim and Annie walked in. There were a lot of firsts in that entrance. It was the first time I'd seen them together as a couple. The first time I'd seen Annie since I'd asked her out. The first time Eleanor had seen her at all. I had a line all ready. Once introductions had been made, I pointed out to Annie that I was getting to go for dinner with her after all. I made sure everyone heard. There was laughter. It was awkward laughter, but how could it not be? I think it helped. She looked wonderful, naturally. Oddly enough, she was all in blue and grey, like Una's apartment. I stole looks at her while we examined the menus, testing to see how I felt. It would be an exaggeration to say I felt nothing – it stung – but it was manageable. A big factor was how happy she and Jim looked together, forever touching and sneaking wee smiles. Although their happiness made me feel a bit ridiculous, given my own intervention, it didn't make me feel jealous. The night of the disaster, when I told Jim I was glad he'd found someone, they were only words. I felt it now. The age difference didn't even bother me. I'd worried they'd look like a joke. But they looked like what they were – a couple in which neither partner was in the first flush of youth and the woman happened to have a few years on the man.

Eleanor was wary of Annie at first, I thought. While she was perfectly polite and all, it wasn't a casual, getting-to-know-you conversation. It was more like a job interview – where-do-you-see-yourself-in-five-years sort of stuff. I half-expected her to ask for references. Although Annie didn't provide any particularly scintillating answers, as far as I could tell, Eleanor must have been impressed. Or maybe she just relaxed. Either way, she'd dropped the tone before we'd even finished our starters. They got on to the subject of Brad Pitt, somehow, and bonded over their admiration for his arms, which, I was led to believe, were very good arms. I wasn't entirely sure when I should say what I had to say. My vague intention had been to wait for a lull in conversation but none arose. In the end, matters were taken out of my hands. Eleanor was staying overnight and was hitting the wine fairly hard. Shortly after we'd ordered our main courses, she produced a tiny 'Oo', as if remembering something she'd forgotten to mention.

'Did you know,' she said to Jim, 'that you'd still be single if it wasn't for your dear old dad?'

Jim looked from me to Annie and back to Eleanor. He had the expression of a man who's not at all sure that the news he's about to get is good.

'I did not,' he said flatly.

'Eleanor,' I warned.

'It's fine,' she insisted, flapping at me. 'It's funny! The thing is, going to salsa lessons was all his idea.'

'I know that,' Jim said. 'I mean, I wouldn't say it was

his "idea". He was putting flyers in the shop one day and we got to–'

'No, no,' Eleanor insisted. 'It was all a ruse. He had a plan. He wanted you to go to salsa lessons because he thought you might meet someone there. And you did!'

Jim and Annie stared at me. Their expressions were unreadable. It was like being sized up by a single four-eyed predator. 'Is that true?' Jim asked.

'Yes,' I said. 'It is.' There was no point in denying it. Jim swallowed so hard I saw his Adam's apple bob. I knew what was about to happen. He was going to lose it. I was getting my head handed to me. There would probably be a storm-out. I made calculations at lightning speed, imagining how this would play out. It wasn't good. Jim would be mad at me and I would be mad at Eleanor. Annie probably wouldn't be all that chuffed either. She would be mad at me and most likely Eleanor, and maybe even (though I wasn't sure how) at Jim. He would feel humiliated. She would feel like she'd been used. There was a chance they'd wind up separating.

'What a lovely thing to do,' Annie said. She reached across the table and briefly rested her hand on my wrist.

'Is it?' Jim said, turning to her. It wasn't sarcasm. He was really asking.

'Of course it is! Eugene, that's the only reason you went yourself, isn't it? So Jim would go?'

'Oh, yeah,' I said. 'God, yeah.'

Annie grabbed Jim's hand now and looked into his eyes like she had something desperately important to tell him. Her voice was low and serious. 'Jim. I'm not supposed to say this because I'm a teacher. I'm supposed to be encouraging. I'm supposed to make sure everyone feels included and energized and encouraged, no matter what their level when they walk through the door. But your father is probably the worst dancer I've ever seen in my life.'

That got big laughs around the table. No two of them were the same. Mine was full of relief. Eleanor's said, *I told you it'd be all right*. Jim's said, *See what a wonderful woman she is?* Emboldened, Annie rolled on. 'I mean, I've seen some no-hopers in my time, but boy. I watched him dancing and I worried about him *walking* anywhere. Still, he put himself out there in front of everyone, didn't he? Didn't care what anyone thought. And he did it for you. I think it's great.'

Jim took a moment to respond, then slowly nodded at her. She raised her eyebrows. He nodded again. She tilted her head ever so slightly in my direction. The penny dropped.

'Uh, thanks, Da,' he said uncertainly. 'Thanks for . . . doing that.'

'You're welcome,' I breathed. My heart rate still hadn't returned to normal. And then Jim hit me with a follow up.

'You're full of secrets these days,' he said. 'So, what about the other one, The Big Mystery? Are you going to tell us where you disappeared to?'

I threw some wine down my throat. This was it. There would be no choosing my moment.

I started trembling. 'Okay. All right then. Annie, what this is about–'

'She knows,' Jim said. 'Get on with it.'

'Right. Right. Well . . . the thing is, I was in London. I went to see your mother.'

Eleanor made a noise like a death rattle. Jim's jaw literally dropped. 'Why?' he said.

'Because I had this theory that I wanted to put to her.'

'What theory?' Eleanor said.

I found I couldn't look at them, or Annie either. I stared at the olive oil. 'I thought she was faking it. The illness. I thought there was nothing wrong with her and she was pretending so you two would agree to see her.'

Everything around me seemed to freeze. I could hear my own heartbeat.

'That's crazy,' Eleanor said then. 'What the hell made you think that?'

'She didn't seem to have any symptoms, you said. That seemed weird but not impossible. What do I know about it? Then you said she was making plans to live abroad, alone. That was the main thing. Plus, I had a feeling. Just . . . a feeling. It seemed like something she would do.'

'I can't believe this,' Jim said. 'It's madness. What did she say?'

'She didn't say sorry, I can tell you that much.'

Brows furrowed. Looks were exchanged.

'Wait,' Eleanor said. 'You were *right*?'

I nodded. 'Yep.'

The terrible stillness that followed my 'Yep' made every other awkward silence of my life, including the one a few seconds previously, sound like a nightclub in full swing. Eleanor ended it by bursting into tears.

'What's *wrong* with her?' she sobbed. 'Who lies to their own children about dying? Why is she such a fucking monster?'

Jim was shaking his head and didn't seem to be able to stop. 'I don't understand. How could that have possibly worked out, long-term? Was she planning on faking it forever? It doesn't make any sense. It doesn't make any *sense*.'

287

'You shouldn't have gone,' Eleanor said, pivoting suddenly in my direction. 'You should have stayed out of it. I preferred it when I thought she had a disease. It was better than this.'

Jim stopped shaking his head. Now he ran both hands over his face, up and down, up and down. He looked like an animal losing its mind in a zoo. Eleanor's sobs were attracting attention. The restaurant wasn't full, by any means, and that made it all the more obvious that heads were turning. I cursed my stupidity. Why hadn't I told them at home, in private? Why had I waited until now? I knew perfectly well why, of course. I'd imagined it as a moment of triumph, and I wanted Annie there, joining in the congratulations. Jesus Christ.

'I went for you,' I said. 'And Jim. You told me, you both told me, you were sorry that it ended badly with your mother and you were worried you'd feel guilty forever because she was–'

'I would have coped!' Eleanor wailed. 'It wouldn't have been the end of the world!'

'And what if you were wrong?' Jim snarled. 'You based this on fuck all.'

'I wasn't wrong.'

'You could have been.'

'This is a nightmare,' Eleanor said. Her crying was under control now but it had already played havoc with her make-up and, somehow, hair. She looked like she'd recently been talked off a roof. 'A fucking nightmare.'

'I thought you'd be happy,' I said quietly. 'I thought I was doing the right thing. And I was so sure of it. You don't plan long-term foreign adventures when you're–'

Our waiter chose that moment to appear with the first

of our mains. If he was aware of the ruckus at our table, he did a good job of hiding it. I suspected he hadn't even noticed. He didn't seem all that committed to his job.

'Lasagne?' he muttered. Jim nodded, still staring at me. 'And a carbonara?' I raised a finger. The waiter deposited the plates. 'Two pizzas coming for the ladies,' he said, managing to make it sound creepy. No one spoke while he was gone. No one spoke when the pizzas arrived either. We all started eating.

After a couple of minutes, Annie spoke up. 'Let's not forget why we're here,' she said. 'Happy birthday to Jim. Life begins, and all that crap.' She raised her glass. We followed suit, miserably. The glasses clinked.

'Happy birthday,' Eleanor and I mumbled as one.

'Thanks,' Jim mumbled back.

More silent eating. This time it only went on for a few seconds. 'Sounds to me like she's a psychopath,' Annie said cheerfully. Everyone gawped at her. 'Your mum,' she said to Jim, as if there might be some doubt.

'Well, she's not dangerous,' he said after a moment. 'At least, I don't think she is.'

'Psychopath doesn't mean axe-murderer,' Annie said. 'I used to think that too. A lot of people do. I read a book about it a while back. It turns out psychopaths are everywhere. Like, one in a hundred or something. It's a mental disorder like any other. You can be a psychopath and never raise a hand in anger, let alone an axe. I mean, I've never met the woman, so maybe I shouldn't start throwing opinions–'

'No, go on,' Eleanor said.

Annie dabbed her mouth with her napkin. 'Well, from what I've read, psychopaths have no regard for right and wrong. They don't think about anyone else's feelings, ever. Only their own. It doesn't really occur to them that other people *have* feelings. They do things impulsively without working out the consequences. So long as it's good for them in some way right now, that's all that counts. And they're charming, at least for a while. They seem pretty decent. Or if they've done something awful in the past, you might think they've really changed. They haven't. They can't.'

There was yet another silence, but this one was different. It wasn't tense. It was thoughtful.

'Jesus,' Eleanor said. 'Is this why she thought faking a terminal illness was a good idea? She took a notion of getting in touch one day and it seemed like the easiest way in? It would also explain why she put a six-inch kitchen knife through any football that came over the garden wall when we were kids. She just did it without a thought. She didn't care who'd be upset.'

A memory leapt up at me.

'I've never told anyone this,' I said. 'When you were about five or six, Eleanor, you were invited to a birthday party. Some little girl from your class. Una would have been expected to stay and chat with the other mums. She didn't fancy it, so she rang on the day and said you'd just been hit by a car and she was waiting on an ambulance. Pretended to cry on the phone and everything. I was standing right beside her. It didn't even make sense – as if you'd think of calling up to cancel with your child lying in bits. Later on, she told people it wasn't a big deal, just a few scrapes and bruises.'

'I've got one,' Jim said. 'Remember how she walked out on us with no notice and then didn't get in touch for almost twenty-five years?'

We all laughed – or started to, at least, before catching ourselves in the act, not sure that it was appropriate.

'The point is,' Annie said, looking at Eleanor, 'I don't think you should waste your energy on hating her. If anything, you should feel sorry for her.'

'I think feeling sorry for her's a long way off,' Jim noted.

'Anyway,' Annie said, cool as a breeze, 'hats off to you, Eugene, for going to see her. Can't have been easy. And you were only trying to help your kids, weren't you?'

'I was,' I said quickly. 'I really was.'

'Did she even know you were coming?' Jim asked.

'No. I just showed up, hoping she'd be in.'

'Wow. Risky.'

'It was.'

'What was her apartment like?' Eleanor asked.

And we were off, talking about the details and the practicalities. It started going the way I'd hoped it would, all curiosity and astonishment. They found the idea of their father wandering around London on his own somewhere between miraculous and hilarious. I answered all of their questions, but my replies gradually became robotic. My mind had drifted elsewhere, to Annie and the effect she was having on us all. If she hadn't been there, the meal would have long since ended in disaster. She wasn't just a blessing for Jim. She was a blessing for all of us. And so subtle in her manoeuvres. Twice that night she had stuck up for me and twice she'd made it seem like no big deal. No one mentioned it. Maybe Jim and Eleanor hadn't even noticed. I had. I'd noticed, and I was grateful. I'd forgotten what it was like to have someone back you up on parenting matters. It was possible, I supposed, that I'd never known in the first place.

Remarkably enough, we eventually got off the subject of Una. Eleanor talked about her holiday plans. Jim talked about a nature documentary he'd seen. Annie talked about taking up baking. I was content to listen. It was all so easy and smooth and normal. We lost track of time and were the last diners to leave the restaurant. Eleanor had sensibly slowed down on her wine intake, but the rest of us had sped up. There was a lot of giggling and a bit of swaying when we made our way outside. As we crossed the threshold, I felt my phone buzz in my jacket pocket. It took me a while to get it out – I seemed to have more thumbs than usual. The message was from Frank. Two texts from him in the same year. A new record.

DUCK THIS ONE BEER BUSYNESS, CHOKING HERE LET GO FOR PINTS THIS WEEK

I knew at once what he would be like. It would be as if he'd never thought any other way. 'Your health is your wealth' would become 'You only live once.' He might even accuse me of having had fancy notions about cutting down. Gobshite. I couldn't wait to talk to him.

Tomorrow, I replied.

28

There was a lot to catch Frank up on. He didn't even know I'd asked Annie out, let alone all the rest of it. I let him run through his reasons for ignoring serious medical advice, which went very much as expected, and then I got into it. He listened well, as always, shaking his head, gasping, frowning sympathetically, slapping his forehead and rolling his eyes, but never interrupting. It took the guts of three pints to say everything I had to say. When I'd finished, Frank was uncharacteristically silent. He'd delivered the Good Listener part of his usual one-two. He seemed to have be having trouble with the Brutally Honest Response bit.

'You're awful quiet,' I said.

He supped his pint for a moment. 'I'm confused,' he said then.

'About what?'

'What set this all off, you reckon, was turning seventy, right?'

'I think so, yeah.'

'You got into a bit of a panic.'

'Right.'

'Did a bit too much thinking.'

'Yeah.'

'Reflecting, like. And then . . . events . . .'

'Events, yes. So what are you confused about?'

'You seem to be in very good form.

'I am.'

'But are you not back where you started?'

'I don't follow.'

'You're still turning seventy, aren't you? I mean, I didn't tune out for a bit of the story where you found a way to stop time, did I?'

'I'm still turning seventy, Frank. Next Wednesday.'

'And?'

I shrugged. 'Reflection over. It's either get older or die, isn't it? I think I'll keep going.'

He wasn't convinced. I could see it in his eyes. I could also see that he wasn't about to argue, so long as I was happy. 'Grand, so,' he said.

We drank in pleasant silence for a while. 'Jim came out with this idea,' I said then. 'Last night, after we left the restaurant.'

'Oh?'

'He was pissed, so I wasn't sure if he was joking or not.'

'What was the idea?'

'He said if I wanted to, he'd have no problem with me going in and helping out in the shop again. Just a few mornings a week. Or afternoons. Whatever suited me. He said we could rename the place. Duffy and Da. That bit was definitely a joke. I think.'

'And what? Are you going to do it?

'I'm not sure. I had another idea of my own.'

'Which was?'

I hesitated. 'Eh, never mind.'

'Go on, for fuck's sake.'

'All right. Look, I never had much of an education. Always regretted it. Never went very far, either. Always regretted that too. Do you think I could get into a history course somewhere? Somewhere not in Ireland, maybe? Edinburgh, say? I've always liked the sound of Edinburgh. Maybe even London. I was only there for a day, granted, but it got to me a bit. All that buzz and colour. There's such a thing as a mature student, isn't there?'

Frank didn't laugh and that meant he hadn't found my idea funny. I could be sure of that. Managing not to laugh was not among his gifts.

'There's mature students, Eugene, yes,' he said solemnly. 'I don't know if there's geriatric students. And I don't think you can go straight from nothing to fancy history courses. Sure you left school when you were six, or whatever. And London? Are you out of your mind? What would you do in the way of accommodation? Unless you've been hiding it very well, you don't have living-in-London kind of money. Plus, knowing your luck, you'd bump into Una twice a day, every day. It's a nice thought, but come on. You're not going to London to study history.'

I sighed and swigged on my pint. 'Yeah. I know. I like thinking about it is all.'

He gave me a look. 'Don't go getting all melancholy now. Don't start reflecting again.'

'Nah. I'm fine.'

'Listen to me. If you'd had a great education and travelled the whole bloody world, you'd be sitting at a bar in New York or Rio de Janeiro or God knows where telling some lad like me that you wished you'd stayed at home and raised a family in a quiet wee town. That's just the way it is. You're grand where you are.'

'Yeah.'

'Do the Duffy and Da idea, that's my advice. Give it a try, anyway.'

'I probably will.'

'Do.'

'Okay. I will.'

We sat back and looked around the pub, waiting for one of our fellow customers to set us off on a new topic. Someone with a shocking haircut maybe, or a stupid hat. Everyone was disappointingly average.

'What about the birthday?' Frank said then. 'What's the plan?'

'No plan.'

He gave it some thought and came up with a brilliant idea.

'Pints?' he said.

I nodded happily. 'Pints.'

Acknowledgments

I'm grateful to all the friends, relatives, and colleagues who offered their services as early readers (or more accurately, were press-ganged into it). But I'd like to single out Corina Bradley, who said exactly the right thing at exactly the right time.

Thanks are also due to Kerri Ward and Conor Nagle at HarperCollins Ireland, and to my agent, Faith O'Grady.

Finally, I owe more than I can say to my wife, Sinéad, and daughters, Ailish and Eimear.